Belonging

TWO NOVELS

BY

Eva Tucker

© 2014 Eva Tucker
ISBN 0-936315-38-5

STARHAVEN, 42 Frognal, London NW3 6AG
books@starhaven.org.uk
www.starhaven.org.uk

Typeset in Dante by John Mallinson

CONTENTS

Berlin Mosaic   1

Becoming English   138

Epilogue   234

THE FAMILY

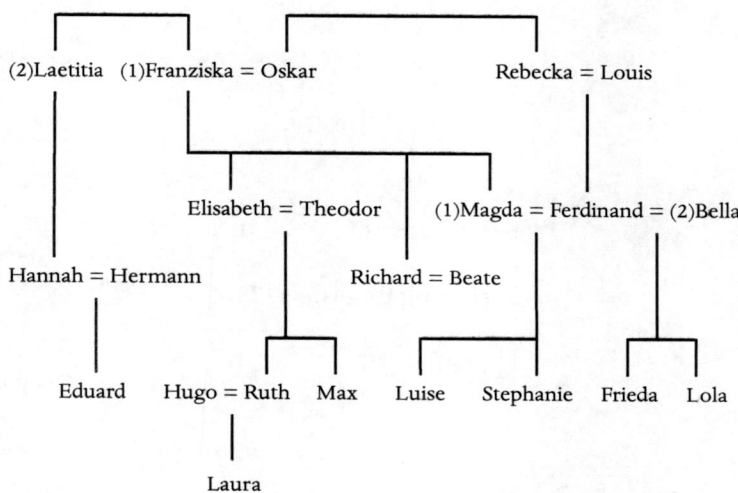

Berlin Mosaic

*to the memory of
Felix and Doris Opfer*

I

1891-1901: UPPER SILESIA

Outside, the fir trees stood motionless in the heavy September heat. Inside, the doctor said, 'She's bleeding away from under my hands!' Somewhere behind a closed door the new-born baby cried. In the bedroom the dying mother whispered 'Promise…'

'Promise?' Laetitia looked at her sister, afraid.

'Promise to marry him!'

'But Franziska…'

'The children – Laetitia, do you promise?' her voice trailed away.

'The children, of course but…'

Franziska raised her head. 'Promise to marry Oskar!' She looked at the Old Testament beside her bed. 'Your hand… on the Bible…'

Laetitia put her hand on the Bible.

'Say it, Laetitia. Say "I promise to marry Oskar…"'

'I promise to marry Oskar.' Laetitia felt her hand pressed.

'Kiss me!'

Laetitia kissed Franziska.

Tiptoeing out of the room, she thought: which one of us is dying?

'Go to her now,' the doctor said to Oskar.

Laetitia walked up and down outside the bedroom twisting a handkerchief in her hands. The letter from Franziska had come to her in Berlin. 'Oh, please come home, I am afraid this time.' One line from Oskar: 'Your family needs you. Come!' Laetitia loved her sister; she was not sure that Oskar did. She had gone home. She had another letter in her pocket; it was from her lover Lorenz, with whom she had been rehearsing for Otto Brahms's new company Die Freie Bühne. Acting and Lorenz were Laetitia's life. She knew his letter by heart: 'The rehearsals are flat without you, Berlin is grey without you, my life is empty without you. I love you. Come back!' Here, half way between Gleiwitz and Ratibor, she was extinguished by her family's needs; the life, the man she loved were reduced to pale shadows. Can you break a promise to a dying sister? She screwed Lorenz's letter into a ball.

Looking down at his feet, hand over the watch chain on his paunch, Oskar came out of his wife's bedroom. He said nothing, but Laetitia knew. She put a hand out towards him; he put both arms round her, drew her to himself.

'Bring the children,' he said.

'The children?'

'Elisabeth and Richard must bid their mother farewell!'

'But she's dead!'

'Laetitia, please…'

Laetitia hurried away.

The baby, a girl, Magda, flourished. Oskar adored her; Elisabeth and Richard adored her. She looked very like Franziska, but as she grew up it became apparent that her sprightly intelligence was more like Laetitia's.

Lorenz's letter stayed crumpled in some forgotten pocket; Laetitia could not bring herself to answer it. For some weeks after Franziska's death, she gazed forlornly out of the drawing room window down the long avenue of fir trees; she ghosted it with Lorenz until his face, preternaturally large, closed in on hers and she almost fainted. If he loves me, she thought, he will find a way. A year must surely pass before Oskar could think of making me his wife. But no.

'What are you waiting for?' Oskar asked her.

Laetitia sensed malice behind the question, as if he knew. He knew. He had intercepted two letters from Lorenz. Laetitia thought: Lorenz cannot truly love me. She said she would marry

Oskar if he promised she could be his wife in name only. He promised. But a few months after they were married, he grew impatient. Laetitia could not endure the thought that she might bear his child. For over three years she avoided conception; then she became pregnant and Hannah, the most beautiful of Oskar's three daughters, was born.

Though she was only four years old at the time, Magda felt responsible for Hannah from the moment she first saw this seraphic baby. Later, Hannah would come to her when she grazed her knee or broke a dolly. Only once did Hannah turn on Magda.

'My Mamma is not your Mamma. Your Mamma is dead.'

'I know!' Magda said with such quiet finality that Hannah never brought it up again.

In effect, neither of them had a mamma. The little girls lowered their eyes when they were with Laetitia. Sometimes Laetitia lost her temper with them. If Oskar happened to hear her, he told her that Franziska had never found it necessary to raise her voice. Elisabeth, growing up, would find something to divert her young sisters.

Oppressed by Laetitia's obvious unhappiness, Oskar offered to take her with him on one of his visits to Berlin, where his sister Rebecka lived. Laetitia could not bear the thought of walking along the city pavements she loved so much as Oskar's wife – what if she happened on one of her old friends? or Lorenz? In a copy of the *Vossische Zeitung* Oskar had left lying about after he came back from Berlin, Laetitia found a photograph of her old lover. Lorenz had the lead in a new play by Gerhard Hauptmann – *Die Weber*. The caption under the photograph announced his marriage to the leading lady, whose photograph appeared next to his. Laetitia flung the paper across the room. Oskar stayed away longer and longer from their home, in rooms near his button factory in Gleiwitz. Laetitia did not care where her husband was, as long as he was not near her.

Once, when Oskar brought the factory manager and his wife to stay for the weekend, Laetitia simply disappeared into her room. Oskar was very angry. Young Elisabeth took over as hostess and did well. The little girls loved the sample cards of buttons the manager gave them. Every kind of button: silver, copper, brass, horn, enamel, glass. When Magda and Hannah showed their button cards to Laetitia, she turned her head away.

The house fell uncannily quiet. Richard went off to school; Elisabeth was sent to Switzerland to be 'finished'; Magda and Hannah lived separate lives with their nanny. Oskar scarcely came home at all, though he had impressed on Laetitia over and over again what a beautiful, what an enviable home she had.

Laetitia wondered who envied her. She made no effort to get to know people and never returned calls. The only times she did not feel her life to be a burden were when she took Elisabeth's mare Cyganka out for a gallop.

'Be kind and gentle with her,' Elisabeth had said with tears in her eyes as she had left for Switzerland.

Laetitia loved the horse too but would not spare her as she tore across the moorlands. When she was on the mare's back, she got an intimation of the oneness she had felt with Lorenz.

After one of those gallops, she came back to the house with everything bathed in autumn sunlight. A wood fire blazed in the sitting room; the dachshund Karlchen lay curled up in front of it. Coffee and yeasty plumcake were brought in; Laetitia felt almost happy. She picked up a notebook with green marbled covers and began to write. 'Thank you Lorenz,' she began. Not that after all these years she was going to get in touch with him – he would not be the same Lorenz anymore than she was the same Laetitia – but she wanted to preserve something of those two young people about whom she had not allowed herself to think since some other self had made her keep her promise to her sister. Now she gave her thoughts free rein. The grey and dutiful present must not be allowed to obliterate that radiant past. There was bitterness and guilt behind the word 'dutiful'. Allowing Oskar into her bed, bearing his child, had removed her from everything towards which she had once lived. When she looked at little Hannah, quicksilvery, elfin child, she could not think 'my daughter'. When her labour pains had begun, it had been the image of Lorenz that had helped her through the elemental process. Did Lorenz have children of his own now?

The dachshund quivered in sleep. Laetitia went on writing. Would there be enough to write about to last her the rest of her life? She sighed. It was a sigh of release, of coming back into herself. 'I could have loved a child of yours, Lorenz, there was such...' She was about to write 'trust', her cheeks glowing in the firelight; but before she could write it, the door had opened and suddenly she felt Oskar's heavy hand on her breast.

'You're looking your old lovely self, my dear!' He took the pencil and notebook from her.

The colour rose higher in Laetitia's cheeks. She stood up and tried to snatch her notebook from him. Breathing hard, Oskar flung it across the room. Before he could pull her towards himself, she had picked up the poker and beat her husband about the head with it until he fell to the ground. Behind them, in the open doorway, their five year old daughter Hannah stood watching.

When Oskar had recovered, he had his second wife committed to a lunatic asylum in Breslau. He put the house up for sale and took a large flat in Berlin behind the Tiergarten. He arranged his affairs in such a way that his connection with the button factory became purely financial. Richard would soon be old enough to take over the practical side of things. In the meantime, the manager could cope.

Elisabeth, recalled from Switzerland, did not understand why her father had decided to uproot them. He had only given her the sketchiest account of what had happened between him and Laetitia. Had he really sent her to a sanatorium simply because she had lost her temper with him? Surely that was not reason enough. Elisabeth had always felt there was something out of kilter between her father and stepmother, who also happened to be her aunt. But she could not close her heart to anyone who was fond of animals, and it had been obvious from the moment Laetitia had come to live with them that the only beings she truly loved were the horse and the dog. Oskar said nothing about what had caused those lurid bruises on his face and why one side of it was covered with a thick plaster.

'Don't worry, it's getting better, healing up nicely,' was all he said.

Richard had not been called away from school. 'It'll do for him to join us in Berlin,' Oskar said.

'But he'll want to…' Elisabeth thought her brother would want to say goodbye to the house; but that was not the kind of thing she could mention to their father, who seemed all too ready to leave it.

At first Elisabeth, who was kept busy seeing that arrangements for the move went ahead smoothly, did not feel that there was anything strange about Hannah standing stock still in Laetitia's sitting room watching the furniture being moved out and carpets rolled up. But when the little girl refused to move from the room even when it was quite empty, as her nanny failed to persuade her and, picking her up, set her off screaming – which set Karlchen off yapping – Elisabeth knew there was something very wrong.

Oskar came rushing in and added to the ghastly din by shouting, 'Can't you control the child! And get that dratted dog out of the way!'

The nanny curtsied inanely. Hannah turned her head away from her father and went on screaming.

'What happened in this room?' Elisabeth asked her father; then, without waiting for him to answer, she went on, 'Papa, I'd like to come and talk to you later.'

Suddenly she was not in the least in awe of him. For the first time Elisabeth acknowledged to herself that, though she loved her father, the love had always been mingled with fear. Now fear ebbed away. She saw him as a rather helpless bumbler, pathetic with those bruises on his face.

Oskar looked at his eldest daughter in surprise. He was used to giving her orders, to having the women obey him.

'Very well, yes, come along later,' he said and held his hands over his ears while Hannah continued to scream.

'You may go,' Elisabeth said to the nanny with new authority in her voice.

As soon as they were left by themselves, Hannah rushed over to Elisabeth and buried her head in her skirt wailing, 'Mamma, Mamma, Mamma…'

'There, there, Mamma will soon be back,' Elisabeth said, not caring that it was a lie. Sometimes words were healers in themselves; they needed saying at certain moments even if nothing followed from them.

Hannah detached herself from Elisabeth's skirt and, going quite stiff, began to scream again.

'Don't want Mamma, horrible, horrible Mamma, hit Papa, don't want...' Hannah began to sob and hiccough '...don't want... don't want...'

It dawned on Elisabeth then what had happened to her father's face. She took Hannah's hand in hers. 'Come, let's take Karlchen for a little walk, shall we? Papa's face will soon be quite better.' At least that was true.

Elisabeth took out a lace-edged handkerchief that had belonged to her mother and wiped Hannah's eyes. Hannah took the hanky from her. 'Do it myself!'

Elisabeth kissed her on the forehead.

'I like you better than Mamma,' Hannah whispered.

Elisabeth stroked her head.

They walked out into the fir tree avenue. 'Let's see if we can find any bilberries in the wood, shall we?'

'Oh yes,' Hannah said. 'I'll get my basket!' and she ran back into the house for it.

Very soon after this, they moved to Berlin. It nearly broke Elisabeth's heart to leave her mare Cyganka behind, but at least she had got her father's permission to bring the dachshund to their new home.

II

1901-1914: BERLIN

They celebrated the new year in the Berlin flat, throwing molten lead figures over their shoulders to see what shapes they would make. Elisabeth thought hers was a heart.

She was being courted by a distant cousin seventeen years older than herself. Theodor was a doctor with a flourishing practice in the Friedrichstrasse. In order for it to flourish further, he needed a wife with money. Theodor was the first in his family of long established Berlin Jews to enter a profession; his father was a corn merchant. Theodor enjoyed the theatre, art exhibitions, concerts and himself played the piano *con brio*. He wanted more out of life than money, but he was not so naïve as to think he could manage without it. Three charming girls without means had wanted to marry him. They would not do. He had known Elisabeth since she was a girl. Now she was a serene, handsome young woman – rather too serious perhaps for her age. When he looked into her eyes, her whole face was transfigured.

'You used to hide under your mother's skirt when I visited,' Theodor teased her. Then there was a moment's good silence between them as they remembered Franziska.

When they danced together, his hand on her corseted back, his moustache tickled her cheek. There was a whiff of cigar smoke about him, which Elisabeth found reassuring. His being a doctor appealed to her enormously. A doctor need never doubt for a single moment whether his life was usefully spent. Not that Elisabeth spent much time wondering about her own usefulness. She was far too busy seeing that the household was properly organised and that the little girls were well looked after.

Magda was no problem: she was very bright, and Elisabeth realised that her young sister would soon outstrip her intellectually. Magda loved talking to Theodor and bombarded him with questions: how long for a broken arm to mend; how long before you knew you had caught scarlet fever (she was away from school in quarantine); had he ever cut anyone open; why did women get headaches more than men and so on. Theodor patted her on the head and said no, he had never cut anyone open, he was a GP not a surgeon, and if she asked him many more questions he would have a headache. But Elisabeth could see he was enjoying himself.

As for Hannah, the minute she heard Theodor's voice she would come tearing in from somewhere and leap straight into his arms. Theodor enjoyed that too. Hannah was quite a handful. The nanny had not lasted long in Berlin. Elisabeth had not got another one; she looked after Hannah herself. She would set out with her, Karlchen reluctantly on a lead, for the Tiergarten, where walking on the manicured lawns was strictly forbidden. Sometimes they walked along the new Siegesallee, Hannah skipping from one laurel-wreathed marble victor to the next. Occasionally they would hear the drone of the Zeppelin overhead. 'Like Papa's cigar,' Hannah would shriek, and passers-by smiled.

Elisabeth hated the Zeppelin; it sent shudders down her spine as it hung in the sky, a malevolent monster. Its ungainly shape and ugly noise menaced the trees and birds and red squirrels in the Tiergarten. She would breathe a sigh of relief when it had disappeared from view.

Sometimes they would walk the other way down Unter den Linden and then turn into the Friedrichsrasse at the Krantzler corner. Hannah would spell out the words on the hoardings: 'K-o-d-a-k, H-o-t-e-l B-a-u-e-r'. When they had first moved to Berlin, the noise of the cars – there were even motor taxicabs now – and the open-topped buses racing down the Friedrichstrasse had overwhelmed Elisabeth, but she was getting used to them. After all, this was where Theodor had his practice. He had not actually asked her yet, but in her heart she knew she was going to be his wife.

Theodor too knew he would marry Elisabeth. Quite soon he would ask Oskar for his daughter's hand. But he still had not got over the fact that Laetitia was confined in a lunatic asylum. He remembered Laetitia as a vibrant young woman who knew half of Lessing and Schiller by heart. Once when Franziska was still alive, they had gone through Schiller's *Die Räuber* together without the text. Laetitia had been in an absolute glow about her work with the Freie Bühne. After Franziska's death, Theodor had had grave misgivings when he heard that she had married Oskar. Now he tried his best to see to it that she was brought to Berlin so that she could be nearer her family, but Oskar was adamant about leaving her where she was in Breslau.

'I pay a hefty fee for her at the… the… sanatorium… I allow her pocket money… *basta!*'

Because he felt she carried too much responsibility as it was, Theodor had not yet spoken to Elisabeth about her stepmother. He so loved to see Elizabeth's face light up; she had such good, such trusting eyes and when he made her laugh they sparkled. She needed to forget for a while whether Magda was getting enough fresh air or Hannah was turning into too much of a tomboy – time enough for all those sort of concerns when she had children of her own. Now Theodor's eyes sparkled. It would be her birthday quite soon. He would give her a copy of that book which had just come out that everyone was talking about, Thomas Mann's *Buddenbrooks*. 'To my dear Elisabeth from her Theodor', he would inscribe it. What an excellent wife, what a devoted mother she would make! And then it suddenly occurred to him that probably Elisabeth had very little idea of what the physical side of marriage entailed. He would have to teach her everything. A Jewish husband was told to see to it that his wife enjoyed the marriage bed.

Elisabeth could not wait to marry Theodor, whom she loved. Before the wedding she found a housekeeper for her father, who was spending too much time and money on champagne for actresses. Richard was preparing to take Oskar's place in the button factory; Magda and Hannah were at school. Every month Elisabeth visited Laetitia in the Breslau asylum. By this time, Theodor had mentioned to her that he thought the moment had come for some less restrictive arrangement, and Elisabeth had agreed with him. Laetitia did not strike her as mad: she had lost her temper in an unfortunately violent way and had had plenty of time to find it again. On one occasion, she had asked for notebooks and pencils, and Elisabeth had brought them without enquiring what was going to be written in them. In fact, they remained blank. On another occasion, Elisabeth brought the little dog Karlchen, now fat and elderly, but having to take him away again was so heart-rending that she did not bring him again. When she tried talking about Magda and Hannah, Laetitia would turn her head away. Hannah's name particularly brought on a violent twitching of Laetitia's mouth.

Theodor and Elisabeth were married in 1902. Oskar received his new son-in-law with enthusiasm: he was delighted to welcome a doctor into the family and gave Elisabeth an enormous dowry and a diamond necklace that had belonged to Franziska.

Being a doctor's wife suited Elisabeth exactly, once the shock of the bridal night was over. There had been no one to tell her what to expect, but Theodor was gentle and, even though she could not share his erotic passion, she knew it was an expression of his love for her. She looked forward with intense joy to being a mother. A year later when a girl was born, she was happy beyond belief, ignoring the veiled regrets some of her more orthodox Jewish friends expressed that she had not had a boy.

Theodor had no such regrets, nor did Oskar, who dandled little Ruth on his knee and opened up in a way Elisabeth scarcely remembered. Oskar had acquired a red nose and a pot belly, and once or twice he arrived at the Friedriechstrasse dead drunk. Elisabeth would put him to bed and restore him with strong black coffee. These occasions established a closer rapport between father and daughter than had ever existed before. But Oskar obstinately refused to talk about Laetitia, and it went against the grain with Elisabeth that he should be so unforgiving. It was for God to see that people got their just deserts, and she believed in an all-merciful God.

'God has nothing to do with it!' Oskar would say.

Theodor tried to convince him that he was ruining his constitution with the heavy drinking, but he did not overdo the preaching. His father-in-law's business acumen was unimpaired. Oskar had got a huge order for army uniform buttons, and Elisabeth's dowry meant that Theodor's surgery gleamed with the latest equipment and the living rooms of the ten room flat radiated tasteful opulence – layers of Persian rugs, a brocade cover on the grand piano, rosewood, green plush and Meissen figurines in the drawing room. It was all exactly as Theodor had hoped; and the number of his patients, Jewish and Gentile, increased every month.

Theodor was particularly touched that Elisabeth continued her visits to Laetitia even after little Ruth was born. Recently he had come across a book by Willy Hellpach, *Neuroses and Culture*, which blamed the new technological age for the increasing nervous diseases and expressed a longing for 'the village of the past'. Though he was trained to diagnose diseases of the body rather than the mind, Theodor was both impressed and repelled by what he read. He was proud to be living in an age of technological progress. Certainly, technology could have no bearing on what was wrong with Laetitia, though there might be something in this longing for the past. In Laetitia's case, it would be a longing for her urban Berlin past rather than for any bucolic bliss.

Theodor had also come across Sigmund Freud's *Interpretation of Dreams*. Much of it struck him as far-fetched and of limited application, but he might perhaps make a point of casually asking Laetitia if she ever had any dreams she remembered. He had never yet been to visit her in Breslau because he found it too painful that a member of the family was in a lunatic asylum; when he did finally go, it was even more painful than he had anticipated.

Laetitia seemed to have shrunk, her cheeks had caved in, her mouth was a thin line across her face, her hair was scraped back in desolate neatness. When she saw Elisabeth, the smallest flicker lit her eyes, but that was immediately extinguished when Theodor stretched out a friendly hand. She kept her head turned from them both, and not even the picnic basket full of home-made goodies moved her. Theodor and Elisabeth carried on a stilted conversation about baby Ruth, hoping that Laetitia might ask who Ruth was. She had not taken in the news that she was now a grandmother. Elisabeth had brought the most recent photograph – herself and Theodor with Ruth between them in white flounces against a studio background of a boat.

'Been at the seaside, have you?' Laetitia asked without commenting on the baby.

Theodor then asked her how she was feeling and, without waiting for an answer, went on to enquire if she slept well. 'Do you ever have any dreams you remember?'

'Dreams!' she said – it came out a hoarse bark. The word shook her whole body, and she began to sob violently.

'You've upset her,' Elisabeth said. It was the first time she had ever reproached her husband.

'Time to go,' Theodor said.

'Come, Mamma, have a little of this plumcake, your favourite,' Elisabeth coaxed.

'Dream! Dream!' Laetitia shouted and picked up the slice of cake and flung it in Theodor's direction.

A nurse came rushing in. 'What's all this? This isn't like our Laetitia!'

Laetitia took no notice. 'I never want to see them again! Never! Never!' She stamped her foot.

Elisabeth and Theodor left. Elisabeth was crying.

Laetitia calmed down as soon as they had gone and enjoyed the picnic they had left, smacking her lips over liver sausage sandwiches.

On the train back to Berlin, Theodor took Elisabeth's hand in his. 'She's best off where she is after all, my dear. And perhaps you need not go quite so often; your time is better spent with our little Ruth.'

'But I must keep on going – usually she's very pleased to see me. What made you ask her about dreaming? That's what upset her so. You can't just give up on people, can you, especially family? Just think of all you do for your patients, complete strangers!'

Though there were other people in the carriage, Theodor leant over and kissed his wife on the forehead. He loved her more every day. As for that man Sigmund Freud, he didn't know what he was talking about.

Elisabeth did her very best to do justice to her duties as wife, mother and daughter. Most of all she loved being with her baby. They had got their old nanny back from Silesia – she was rather feeling her age and, though Elisabeth was glad to have a familiar face about, she was afraid nanny might let Ruth slip out of her hands – she *would* sling the baby over her shoulder while she was getting her bottle ready. On the occasion when they got home from seeing Laetitia, Ruth was in her cradle just waking up and, when she opened her eyes, she gave Elisabeth a shy little smile. Theodor popped in from the study and blew them both a kiss.

Elisabeth was completely happy. She went to her sewing corner by the dining room bay window which gave on to the courtyard at the back of the house where the caretaker's wife waved at her and she waved back. She opened the expanding sewing table and got out the *broderie anglaise* frock she was working for Ruth. When she took up the pointed silver instrument she used for making holes in the *broderie*, Ruth caught its glint and stretched out her hand towards it.

'Soon, my darling, Mamma will teach you how to do it!'

Elisabeth threaded the fine white cotton into the needle and went round the holes with exquisite tiny stitches. She imagined her daughter's future. Oh, she would teach her everything she knew about housekeeping; she would get her ready to be the best possible wife! Elisabeth tried and failed to imagine a young man who would be quite good enough for their daughter. Then she couldn't help smiling at herself. She was rather getting ahead of things, wasn't she?

Theodor came in again waving a letter. 'I've been invited to a medical congress in London. Wives are asked, too. Would you like to come?'

'If you're sure you'd like me to.'

'Of course!'

The only other country Elisabeth had ever been to was Switzerland and that did not feel so very different from Germany. It would be exciting to cross the Channel. She asked Theodor if there would be other Jewish doctors at the Congress.

'What a question!' He sounded irritated. 'As if it matters! I've been invited as a member of the German contingent; it's going to be quite an international affair. The important thing will be the exchange of ideas. I hope to learn a great deal.' Then he relaxed a little. 'There's to be a grand dinner and dance at the end!' After all, his wife was very young.

For a moment Elisabeth had an odd sense of foreboding about England as if… as if… oh, she didn't know. It was silly. She knew she was rather prone to giving into superstition; Theodor had often teased her about it.

In the event, she loved London. Their hosts, the General Medical Council, put them up at the Carlton Hotel and, while Theodor went to lectures and discussions at Harewood Gate, Elisabeth joined a group of wives. The London wives took them round the major hospitals: St George's, Charing Cross, St Thomas's, Westminster. 'Supported by voluntary contributions', it said on the wall of the Westminster Hospital. Elisabeth was impressed by the women's independence; she felt they had more freedom of movement than women at home. She was also impressed by their stylish figures. And yes, there were some Jewish wives – less slender and quite different from the Jewish women with whom she was friendly in Berlin. They looked foreign to her, probably quite recent immigrants.

On the last night, she wore her wedding dress to the ball. The English gentlemen were even thinner than their wives and held themselves very stiffly. She was relieved to be dancing with Theodor towards the end of the evening. He held her close and told her that there was not another woman in the room as beautiful as she was. He had bought her a cashmere shawl which she looked forward to showing off in Berlin. No one she knew had one like it.

'It was lovely – charming people,' she said as they got out of the cab back in the Friedrichstrasse. She had quite forgotten about the odd misgivings she had had before they went.

When Elisabeth's young sisters Magda and Hannah came to visit in the Friedrichstrasse, they would tickle baby Ruth under her chin and Elisabeth would feed them large pieces of sultana cake. She had been rather out of touch with the girls since she had got married. She knew they now went more often to see Oskar's sister, their aunt Rebecka. They would feast on highly coloured *petits fours* arranged on Rosenthal china plates on a dark brown table in Rebecka's dark brown Oranienburgerstrasse flat, opposite the synagogue with its golden dome, where the family worshipped on High Holidays. Magda would look with admiration at Aunt Rebecka's teenage son Ferdinand. His pale face and dreamy eyes fascinated her, though he did not take the least notice of either her or Hannah.

One day a considerable time later when the two girls were stuffing themselves with *petits fours* again and talking about new outfits for Rosh-ha-Shana with their aunt, Ferdinand interrupted them. He said that he thought going to synagogue was an anachronism, that they were Germans and that as soon as he was twenty-one he was going to get baptised. His mother pretended she had not heard; his father Louis, a fur merchant, was seldom about.

Magda looked at her cousin astonished. She had not realised that being Jewish and German did not go together.

Ferdinand had just begun to take notice of her. She struck him as more intelligent than most of the girls that had come his way.

He took her into his confidence and showed her a silver cross he kept hidden in his desk drawer with a copy of the New Testament. Magda was confused; she did not know whether it represented sin or salvation. At home, Papa kept a Hebrew Old Testament on his bedside table. She did not think he opened it often.

'Not a word to my mother,' Ferdinand said, putting a finger to his lips. Then he pressed Magda's hand.

She felt pleased that he was treating her as if she were a real person. I am a real person, she thought.

When Rebecka and Ferdinand came to wish her a happy birthday, he kissed her fraternally on both cheeks. Magda and he looked at each other and both blushed. She thought it suited him not to be quite so pale. She thought also: I've made him blush! It was another boost for her emerging sense of identity.

Rebecka had seen her son kiss Magda and realised his kisses would not stay fraternal.

Elisabeth was there too, with little Ruth. She found a moment to tell her father that she and Theodor had missed him and the girls at synagogue for Rosh-ha-Shana.

'Oh well, yes – rather letting that sort of thing go. We've all got so much on...' Oskar said somewhat lamely.

'But Magda and Hannah must be brought up to know who they are,' Elisabeth said.

'They are young German citizens,' Ferdinand told her. 'Their being Jewish is quite secondary. Besides, when they're of age they may well choose to...'

Elisabeth knew he was going to say 'get baptised', but she would not allow him to voice such an outrageous idea.

'I don't understand you, Ferdinand,' she said gently; she was not going to spoil the birthday party with argument, but she did wish Theodor were with her – he would know exactly what to say. After all, no one could be prouder of being German than Theodor; but she knew it would never occur to him to change his religion. She saw too little of her husband these days; his practice took him out at all hours of the day and night – he never refused a call.

When Ferdinand launched into an explanation of what he meant, Elisabeth turned away from him.

'Your sister doesn't realise the importance of full integration if we are to play a significant part in the development of our country,' he would tell Magda. 'Christianity is a natural progression from Judaism, after all; the birth of Christ was prophesied in the Old Testament. We can't allow ourselves to be stuck in archaic beliefs and practices!'

Magda looked at him astonished. He was only eighteen, but he spoke with such authority!

Just before her next birthday – she was saying goodnight to her father – there was a commotion at the front door, and Ferdinand burst in without waiting for the maid to announce him. Magda had never seen him look quite so pale – 'spectral' was the word that occurred to her.

'What is it, boy, what is it?' Oskar could see that something quite out of the ordinary had occurred.

'It's my father… there's been an accident… canoeing… with a friend… capsized… my father drowned!'

'Oh heavens. Dear God!' Oskar embraced his nephew.

Magda stood there aghast. No one in the family had died since her mother, and that was not something she had been able to experience. Nor was it talked about – she knew the family took great care she was never made to feel that she had been the cause of Franziska's death. Uncle Louis, who had smiled so enchantingly on the rare occasions when they saw him, drowned? It seemed impossible – the sort of thing that happened to other people, people you didn't know. Magda could see that Ferdinand was close to tears.

'Please, Uncle Oskar, please, please come to my mother, she is beside herself…'

'Of course, of course, you should have telephoned, you should not have left her alone!'

'Oh, she's not alone. The young man, my father's friend – they were on the lake together. He's there with her!'

'Young man? what young man?' Oskar asked sternly.

Something he had not put a name to or barely thought began to fall into place. No wonder Louis had hardly ever been seen at family gatherings; Rebecka was always making excuses about how his travels in the fur business kept him away, when he was no doubt enjoying himself with athletic young men! Oskar did not quite think 'serves him right', but he sort of felt it.

After Louis's death, Rebecka and Ferdinand came more often to see Oskar and the girls. Magda was touched to see Ferdinand helping his mother on and off with her coat, opening the door for her, pulling out her chair, all with great affection. She looked forward with keen anticipation and absolute certainty to the time he would be doing all that for her. But for now he only talked about general topics – like Robert Koch's Nobel Prize for his work on tuberculosis, or Max Weber's book *Protestant Ethics and the Spirit of Capitalism*. Magda went bright pink when Ferdinand said 'Protestant'.

'Can't see what one has to do with the other,' Oskar said. He was all for the spirit of capitalism.

'I don't quite follow him myself,' Ferdinand admitted. 'He seems to think that the unequal distribution of wealth is the work of God. But if I understand the New Testament...'

'Christians come out with the rummest ideas if you ask me,' Oskar remarked.

The next thing Ferdinand read was Otto Weininger's *Race and Character*. It astonished him. His leanings towards Christianity had not turned him into an anti-Semite – those sort of views were truly un-Christian. Nor did he feel women to be the incarnation of sin and evil and himself a victim of their nefarious powers. He was very fond of his mother, and his young cousin Magda was becoming increasingly important in his life. To say that all Jews and all women lacked strength of character was ridiculous. He thought he might discuss his thoughts on the subject with Theodor rather than with Oskar.

'If we're to talk in terms of degeneracy at all,' Theodor said, 'and it's not a term I like, then it is he who is degenerate. The way Weiniger talks the human race would die out!'

Ferdinand felt reassured, and for the moment the question of his conversion seemed less urgent.

He was pleased Theodor treated him almost as an equal. They went on to talk about the important work the Society for the Prevention of Sexually Transmitted Diseases was doing.

'Those are the social realities and they give us plenty to work on without dragging in dreams,' Theodor said.

Ferdinand looked puzzled.

'I'm thinking of that man Sigmund Freud. It seems to me he's dabbling in the arcane!'

Ferdinand had not come across Freud.

By this time, Magda had worked on her father sufficiently to get him to agree that she might become a medical student when she left school. At home she felt increasingly impatient with her sister Hannah, who spent a lot of time fooling around with her little niece Ruth in the Friedrichstrasse. Magda made excuses to get out of going there; their housekeeper Frau Schulz would see Hannah there and back again.

Elisabeth, too, found the shrieking that went on when Ruth and Hannah were together got on her nerves. She was expecting another child.

'Your Mamma is very fat,' Hannah said to Ruth.

'There's a baby inside her tummy, that's why,' Ruth told her.

Hannah stared at her. 'The stork brings babies; everyone knows that,' she said, but a seed of doubt had been sown.

When Max was born, the family celebration was extravagant. 'Well, it is good to have a boy for a change!' Oskar said.

The girls looked down their noses, but Elisabeth was radiant.

Elisabeth was the hub of family life. Every Sunday afternoon they would all sit down to coffee and far too much cake: Sandtorte, Streuselkuchen, Mohnkuchen, Käsekuchen, Apfelstrudel and in the autumn lovely yeasty plum cake. That always reminded Elisabeth of Laetitia. She made sure there was some left over to take when she visited her in Breslau.

Oskar would come to the coffee parties but, try as she might, Elisabeth still could not get him to discuss the possibility of getting Laetitia to Berlin. Richard would occasionally manage a weekend away from the factory in Silesia; he would bring sample cards of buttons for Ruth – glass, enamel, horn, brass, copper, silver, every kind of button – and Elisabeth was particularly pleased when her brother came: he was the only person to whom she could talk about their childhood. Magda would come when she discovered that Rebecka and Ferdinand were usually there. Ferdinand would make sure that he sat next to her; Hannah would make sure she sat opposite Ruth and pulled funny faces at her when the conversation got too boring.

Hannah was finding life at home with her father oppressive. Sometimes she caught herself staring at his face to see if he still had those scars. She had to look hard but, yes, they were there – fine white lines on the left temple, and the lobe of his left ear crinkled and withered like a winter leaf. When Oskar saw her looking, he would put his hand over his scars; but nothing was ever said. Hannah knew that Elisabeth continued to visit Laetitia – she could not bring herself to think the words 'my mother' let alone contemplate the idea of going to see her, though she knew that Elisabeth wanted her to do so. Laetitia had never loved her, Hannah believed; and though by now the feeling of never having been loved was beginning to fade, the image of a woman gone berserk with a poker was sharp in her memory. Karlchen, the dachshund, was dead. Tears would start to Hannah's eyes when she thought of that little dog. When I'm married, she reflected, my children will have a real mother – a mother who loves them. A glow would come to her cheeks then; the prospect made her feel deeply happy.

Theodor was happy too. God was being good to him and Elisabeth and the children. Though he never actually put the thought into words, he felt God was making it perfectly plain that it was possible to be a good German as well as a good Jew. If he was not called out on a Saturday morning, he would go to the Oranienburgerstrasse Synagogue. He got annoyed with those prophets of doom who said it would not be long before there was a war; they whipped up the worst kind of nationalism appealing to people's base instincts. Why should England and France unite against Germany when they had so much in common? He was looking forward to the next International Medical Congress, which was to be held in Paris.

The whole family gathered on Oskar's balcony to watch the royal wedding procession of Princess Viktoria Luise's marriage to the Herzog of Braunschweig.

'Look, look, there the Tsar!' Richard was not quite sure whether to be enthusiastic or not. Living in Silesia so close to Poland dampened reaction to things Russian. Not that he identified with the Poles, either. But one thing was certain: neither Russians nor Poles liked Jews.

'There's King George of England,' Oskar said.

Then the Kaiser appeared, and there was endless cheering.

'They all look the same,' Hannah said.

'They're cousins, that's why,' Oskar told her.

He was pleased with the way his youngest daughter was shaping up. She was still high-spirited, of course; but as far as he could tell, she had not a touch of any of her mother's leanings towards the louche. He was not going to let thoughts of Laetitia spoil this splendid occasion, however. He concentrated on the procession again.

Elisabeth, holding Ruth and Max by the hand – both were in sailor suits – turned to her father. 'I think Laetitia might have been able to enjoy all this,' she said.

Oskar scowled at her. 'Cousins,' he said again, 'as like as peas in a pod!'

Magda thought that if you looked closely at peas in a pod they were not really alike. Ferdinand was standing next to her. She felt they had even more in common since his father had died: now they both only had one parent.

'All this makes the idea there might be a war quite preposterous,' Theodor said as they went back into the drawing room.

'Quite unthinkable!' Elisabeth, loyal as always, echoed.

III

1914-1918: BERLIN

In 1914 the preposterous, the unthinkable, happened: war was declared. Elisabeth had the greatest difficulty in conceiving of the charming people they had met in London just a few years before as the enemy. Theodor volunteered immediately for the medical corps and headed a unit. To his disgust, Richard found that he was in a reserved occupation on account of the army buttons. Ferdinand, at the end of his studies, got himself into Theodor's unit, though he had already decided that he would go into research not general practice; that would have to wait until after the war. Rebecka, full of gratitude that her son would not be sent to the front, put herself out for her nieces, who needed a caring eye and a steady hand to guide them. Her brother, she knew perfectly well, was wasting his time and money on wine, women and song in a totally insouciant way.

She took herself to the little baker in the Karlstrasse who made the *petits fours* she enjoyed so much, which were always on the table when her nieces visited. When she got there, the baker told her he doubted whether with the rationing he would be able to go on making them, or the Baumkuchen that turned non-stop on a spit in his shop window.

'No Baumkuchen! Then it won't be Berlin!' she told him, and he put a few extra *petits fours* into her box.

She had noticed other signs of change in the city. The advertisements that carried foreign words had disappeared. No one was supposed to wear *corsets gracieux* anymore on the way to the *palais de danse*. Suits were no longer supposed to be tailor-made in the style of The Prince of Wales. How her dear departed Louis would have hated all the upheaval! though he would, of course, have been ready to die for the Fatherland like everyone else. Then she remembered that he would have been too old to be called up and breathed a sort of posthumous sigh of relief on his behalf. She knew that Richard was longing to be in uniform rather than looking after the production of uniform buttons. What a decent sort of young man her nephew had turned into! Pity he hadn't found himself a nice wife. Not much to look at, is he, Rebecka added reluctantly to herself. She had no idea what they were supposed to be fighting about – just because that Archduke had got himself shot at Sarajevo. Yes, she'd always liked the name 'Ferdinand', but she didn't care two hoots whether the Archduke lived or died. She hoped they hadn't hurt his horse. How long could the war last? Some people said it would all be over in six months.

Back at home she picked up the *Vossische Zeitung*. She hardly read anything in it, but it had been Louis' favourite paper and she hadn't the heart to cancel it. She opened it at the entertainments page. There were plenty of concerts going on, war or no war; the name of Artur Schnabel stood out in heavy print. Perhaps she could get Ferdinand to take her to hear him – take his mind off his work and, even more important, off this stupid idea that he needed to convert. How odd that he, the medical student, was attracted to a religion that worshipped a man who had been tortured to death on a cross, with nails through his hands and feet. One Jew betrayed by other Jews – it was a dreadful story! Did her son really think that turning to Christianity would make him a more acceptable German citizen? What nonsense! Jews were being recruited to fight for the Fatherland without reference to race or religion. And quite apart from that, more and more professions were now open to Jews. Who was it had founded the Jewish Reform Movement? It was a name that had been constantly on Louis' lips and now she'd forgotten it! Rebecka closed her eyes for a moment trying to visualise Louis talking... Yes, yes, it was Arnold Bernstein; that was it. And all the big department stores were owned by Jews – she always shopped at Tietz Bros, who had brought in the idea of these enormous stores from America. She knew the publishers of the *Vossische* were Jews, not Mosse, the other ones, more -steins, yes, Ullstein. Well, none of them had crosses dangling round their necks. She didn't suppose they went to synagogue a great deal either, but that didn't matter. She herself hardly ever went now, but that by no means stopped her being Jewish. Well, least said soonest mended. Perhaps Ferdinand's Christian phase would peter out.

She looked at her watch. He ought to be home. A few minutes later, she heard the key turn in the lock. But it was not only Ferdinand: he had Oskar, Richard and the two girls in tow!

Oskar pressed a bunch of chrysanthemums into her hand. 'These need water, don't they?' she said crisply.

Trying to get round me, she thought; knows perfectly well what I think of the way he carries on. Still, if families can't pull together in wartime, what hope is there? She put the flowers in a multicoloured Japanese vase that had belonged to their mother. Oskar recognised it and patted his sister's cheek. Then he told her that Richard was in Berlin collecting orders for yet more army buttons.

'We've got to make sure they get through in record time!'

'Uniform buttons?' Ferdinand said, and he might as well have said 'pigswill'. With a certain amount of self-importance, he told them he had had to assist at an amputation that morning. 'Poor chap got his leg blown off below the knee and the rest had to come off as well!'

'Where did that happen?' Oskar asked.

'Manoeuvres,' Ferdinand mumbled.

'What a disgrace!' Rebecka was outraged.

Hannah was pacing up and down impatiently. It did not suit her in the least to have coincided with her father. She intended to slip quietly out with no questions asked.

'What's the matter with you?' Oskar asked her. 'Got St Vitus's dance?'

Rebecka was fussing at the sideboard. It was not often she had three men to entertain. She got out liqueur glasses, a bottle of cherry brandy and a box of chocolates she had been saving for a special occasion.

'We only need Elisabeth and Theodor here to make the family complete,' she said.

'They've got their own family now,' said Oskar, who was planning to drop in at the Friedrichstrasse later, in time for one of Elisabeth's delicious cold suppers. No one's Sauerkraut tasted as good as hers.

Richard looked enviously at Ferdinand's uniform. If the production of army buttons was so important for the war effort, why wasn't he allowed to wear a uniform? No girl would look at him now. He knew the family were expecting him to find someone suitable, but it just wasn't happening.

Hannah couldn't wait to get away to stay the night with a her friend Ute – they were at finishing school together, though that was nearly over, thank God. Who wanted to embroider doilies to put between plates or make furniture polish with extract of rose petals now there was a war on? They were about to learn how to make raspberry jam with a proportion of turnips to the fruit. Ute had promised that her boyfriend, with whom she had done 'everything', whatever that might mean, was going to bring along someone for her.

'Coming home, young ladies?' Oskar asked; and Hannah could have killed Magda, who had been chatting quietly with Ferdinand, for her meek, 'Yes Papa!'

'I won't be coming home,' Hannah spoke as casually as she could.

When Oskar heard where she was going, he suggested Richard take her.

'That won't be necessary, Papa.' Hannah surprised herself at the firmness of her voice.

Shrugging his shoulders, Oskar said, 'I shall breathe a sigh of relief when you're both safely married!'

Ferdinand and Magda smiled at each other.

'The war can't go on much longer; our army is so much better disciplined than the French and English!' Ferdinand said.

'Because of our buttons, I suppose!' Hannah burst out.

Oskar couldn't help laughing. 'Of course, my girl, precisely because of our buttons! I shall have to go to Gleiwitz with Richard to lend a hand!'

It was Richard's turn to say, 'That won't be necessary, Papa!'

When Hannah got to her friend's house, she was rather taken aback at the sight of the funny little man, not in the least good looking, who had been brought along for her. But as soon as this Hermann began to talk, something good happened to his face. It wasn't that he said anything out of the ordinary – he chatted about making the most of his leave, doing the rounds for the best beer and avoiding sausages that were full of sawdust – but all the time he was talking, his eyes twinkled and underneath the words there was the promise of... Hannah was not quite sure of what, but it excited her.

The dancing in the beer hall they went to was quite informal. Everyone just got up; none of that business of cards and partners. Hannah had never known such warmth and spontaneity. Hermann's arm round her waist felt as if it belonged there and nowhere else, though she was surprised when suddenly he said *à propos* of nothing, 'After the war I'm going into motor cars, do you think that's a good idea?'

As if her opinion mattered! If she said no, motor cars were not a good idea, then he would go into something else? She nodded as they waltzed to the oom-pah band and said she thought it a good idea, even though by the time she was saying it what it was that was such a good idea had got rather muzzy.

In between dances they ate Frankfurters dipped in mustard, which weren't at all bad, and drank pale beer. Hannah didn't really like beer, but tonight everything was different. Then Hermann abandoned her and asked someone else to dance and someone else after that. Ute's boyfriend danced with Hannah once; he was tall and blond and altogether a picture-book German, but dancing with him was boring compared to Hermann. Two or three other men in uniform asked her to dance, but she couldn't wait for Hermann to come back to her. When he did, he squeezed her hand in a reassuring way and she didn't waste time wondering whether he had squeezed the other girls' hands like that too. The only time his face shut down was when she asked him what he actually did in the army; artillery meant big guns, didn't it?

'I'm on leave – for another whole three days!' he said.

Well, either he was engaged on some very hush-hush mission, which seemed unlikely for a corporal, or it was absolutely terrible in the army. Hannah suspected it was.

'The war can't last much longer,' she said, echoing what she heard everyone round her say.

'Can't it?' Hermann sounded doubtful. 'I hope you're right! But we'll never give in. Germany will win in the end, however long it takes!'

'And however many young men get killed!' Hannah heard herself saying and wished she hadn't.

'Forget it!' Hermann grumbled and swept her off to dance a polka.

The next day, when she got home, Hannah felt out of sorts. Hermann's kisses had felt quite serious when they said goodbye. But were they? She needed to talk to someone; needed someone to be nice to her. Magda was totally wrapped up in her studies and in Ferdinand these days. There was only Frau Schulz, her father's housekeeper, practical, efficient, totally reliable, but not someone to whom she could really warm.

'Is Papa in?' she asked her. Not that she could tell her father about Hermann, but however much she wanted to get away from Oskar, she also felt protected by him.

Frau Schulz nodded, putting a finger to her lips. Hannah gathered what that meant – Papa was sleeping off yet another hangover.

'I thought he was going to the factory, with my brother?'

'Tomorrow perhaps, or the day after.'

'Richard's gone?'

'Yes,' Frau Schulz smiled. 'What a pleasant young man he is. He'll make some lucky girl very happy!'

Hannah had never thought of her brother in that light.

She followed Frau Schulz into the drawing room, where she was taking the beautiful cut glass rummers out of their cabinet and polishing them until they sparkled red, blue, green, lilac, apricot. Some were shallow, some champagne flutes, some more bulbous, others triangular.

'Just lovely, aren't they!' Frau Schulz held a deep purple one up to the light, but Hannah was not paying attention. There was something that had been troubling her for quite a while, and now it burst out of her.

'Frau Schulz, do you mind working for Jews?'

Frau Schulz almost dropped the glass. 'Whatever and on earth put that idea into your head? Why should I mind? I never think about it. Your father's a decent man even though he has a drop too much every now and then. I don't give twopence about what religion people are. We're all in the war together, aren't we? And besides,' she added, putting the purple glass away, 'he's not so very Jewish, is he?'

'Can I help you polish the glasses?'

Hannah was relieved for the moment.

What was troubling her was what Hermann might think if he knew she was Jewish. She polished the rummers as if in a dream, overcome by feelings of insecurity. She wished their little dachshund Karlchen were still about; he'd always known when she was miserable and licked her face with his warm slobbery tongue. She found herself suddenly trembling so much that she had to put the glass down – the scene in Laetitia's sitting room which she had not thought about for years, her mother wielding the poker, striking Oskar again and again, replayed itself and hit her with overwhelming immediacy.

'Whatever's the matter, my dear?' Frau Schulz too set down the glass she was polishing and put her arm around Hannah. 'There, there. Whatever it is, it'll pass; things always do, believe me. Come, let's go into the kitchen, we'll have a bit of my Streuselkuchen!'

'Some things never pass,' Hannah said, but she was glad of Frau Schulz's arm around her as they went into the kitchen.

The family coffee parties went on, though the coffee was very much ersatz. Elisabeth felt ashamed at the meagre fare she was offering the family. They had all lost a good deal of weight on the 250 gramme ration of tough meat per week. Occasionally, Richard magicked a chicken and a few eggs onto their table from friends in a Silesian village. Over the diluted coffee, they would discuss Laetitia yet again; wartime conditions made it much more difficult to visit her in Breslau, but Oskar still turned a deaf ear to any suggestion that the time had come to bring her to Berlin. Once or twice Rebecka expressed her disapproval of the fact that Magda still insisted she was going to qualify as a doctor, even though she and Ferdinand were unofficially engaged. What good would come of so much cleverness in a married woman?

Magda herself never said much at these coffee parties, but one Sunday, when they were talking about the huge number of casualties on both sides, she couldn't help asking what good the war was doing.

'We'll soon have them beaten,' Ferdinand said but did not sound quite as confident as he had a year before.

Hindenburg had just been appointed chief of staff, and there was a good deal of argument in the family as to whether he was the right man to speed things towards victory.

'At least they've arrested that hothead Liebknecht!' Theodor said.

'God damned Communist!' Oskar spluttered.

'I don't understand why wanting peace is considered high

treason,' Elisabeth said to everyone's surprise.

'It is when a Communist wants it!'

'If the war goes on much longer, there won't be any young men left anywhere for the next generation,' Elisabeth put in.

The men were about to contradict her when little Max piped up. 'I'll be left!'

In spite of the seriousness of it all, they couldn't help laughing.

Ferdinand took Magda to hear Tilla Durieux read from Lenz's *Soldaten*. It was a moving occasion which made them long even more for an end to the fighting – for a time when soldiers could simply be men again.

So far they had exchanged no more than the chastest kisses, but on that evening the chaste kisses became passionate. In the Oranienburgerstrasse with Rebecka safely asleep, Ferdinand could hold back no longer. Magda felt herself opening up into a wholeness which she had always known would come to her. And now… now… She and Ferdinand gave themselves up to the elemental forces in their natures. They did what Hannah called 'everything'. They did what men and women who loved each other had always done.

Ferdinand saw no point in delaying their marriage, even though it would have to be a wartime wedding. Much to Rebecka's chagrin, they went to a registry office for the formalities. Ferdinand had not yet got baptised into the Church, but he did not feel he could go through a synagogue wedding. They did without a honeymoon. He took his bride to a Hugo Wolf Liederabend. They sat entranced, forgetting everything except that they loved each other.

Next day, the papers carried news of the Russian Revolution. That had repercussions nearer home. There was unrest among the sailors in Kiel, which escalated into a full blown mutiny. Early in the new year the munitions workers in Berlin went on strike. The war had gone on too long – no one except fanatics like Tirpitz and Dehmel cared about winning any longer; people simply wanted the fighting to end.

'God help us if there's a revolution here!' Oskar said.

'Not while we've got the Kaiser!' Theodor reassured him.

But Theodor felt very uncomfortable with what was happening in Germany. He could not agree with the extreme nationalism of the German Fatherland Party. The very word 'Victory' had become meaningless in face of the millions of dead everywhere. Nor could he stomach the new Independent Social Democratic Party, even though quite a number of Jews had joined it. So when the Kaiser abdicated in November 1918 and the hotel magnate Lorenz Adlon presented him with a bunch of wild flowers – a fine quixotic gesture – Theodor, to his embarrassment, found tears starting to his eyes.

He wiped them away quickly. Ought to be ashamed of himself. His family had survived the war intact. He had got to love Elisabeth more and more during the war years: she had coped with all the difficulties without ever losing her deep sense that in the end all would be well. She is a better person than I am, Theodor thought. And if the Kaiser's abdication averts a revolution, so be it.

IV

1919-1922: BERLIN & UPPER SILESIA

The war was over. There had been a tremendous release of tension when Ebert was made president of the new Weimar Republic. At last a normal life seemed possible again; but the procession of the maimed, blind and shell-shocked was endless. How to give the young men who had survived hope in the face of defeat?

'The old times are gone forever,' Oskar said. He had aged considerably. 'I only hope,' he went on, 'this Ebert will keep the Communists out!'

'Of course he will; he's a Progressive Liberal,' Theodor told him.

'Liberal-quiberal, is Ebert strong enough? Haven't you noticed what's going on here in Berlin?' Oskar was far from convinced.

What was happening was a workers' uprising, orchestrated by the Communists. It was demoralising the city more than the whole war had done.

'The Social Democrats have taken over Zirkus Busch,' Oskar informed his son-in-law.

'I don't believe it!' Theodor had been too busy trying to treat the countless unemployed to keep himself up-to-date.

'Believe it or not, it's true!'

Gustav Noske and his Reichswehr dealt with the Communists, but the general relief in the city was tempered with dismay, because soon after came the news of Liebknecht's and Rosa Luxemburg's murders.

'There's no end to it; I don't believe those two were bad people.' Elisabeth hated violence of any kind.

'Misguided,' Theodor said.

Bloodhound Noske was made Minister of Defence. 'He doesn't make me feel safe.' Elisabeth said.

One day Oskar turned up at the Friedrichstrasse, sat down to Elisabeth's roast chicken, ate with relish, felt suddenly tired, lay down to rest and died.

Elisabeth was shaken. That it should happen just like that, without warning, in her house! She was overwhelmed too by memories of her mother's death, particularly the ceremonial leavetaking Oskar had insisted on when Franziska was already gone. But Theodor was there to help her over the shock; there were Ruth and Max to think about; she could not give way to grief, to the strange sensation of being pushed to the outside edge of generations.

The funeral at the Weissensee Jewish cemetery was quiet and dignified; no one in the family's circle of acquaintance any longer went in for the Orthodox week's wake. Magda, heavily pregnant, did not grieve much for her father; Ferdinand had been the most important man in her life since she was an adolescent. Hannah felt a positive sense of relief: though Oskar had made efforts in recent years to be kind to her, she knew she was a painful reminder of a failed marriage. It was young Ruth who missed her grandpa most. She remembered how he had brought her chocolate drops and marzipan hearts and called her his 'little pigeon'; she still heard him saying to her mother, 'So like Franziska, isn't she?' and was pleased he had thought she looked like the grandmother she had never known.

Elisabeth was touched when she saw how Ruth missed Oskar. She tried to encourage her daughter in domestic activities, but Ruth did not take to baking or counting linen or arranging flowers. When Max saw how upset his sister was, he gave her his silver money box, which was in the shape of a book with a slot in the spine for coins.

Theodor was complaining that all their money did not amount to much more than was in that money box; inflation was galloping away with their capital. Like all patriotic citizens, Theodor had put almost everything into the Deutsche Reichsbank; he had ever darker thoughts about the Communists, who had got themselves organised into an official party. It would suit them if everyone were equally poor! How could you trust atheists? As for Ebert and Scheidemann and the whole Weimar lot, they were turning out more than a touch wishy-washy. Theodor remembered Oskar's doubts: the old boy had not been so far off the mark. More than ever he regretted the passing of the Kaiser. There had not been all these political murders in his day; nor would the Kaiser ever have allowed the primitive bartering that was going on – half a pound of butter for stalls in the theatre! You needed a laundry basket of notes to pay for a glass of beer. True enough, Jews were being more thoroughly integrated under the Weimar Republic; but Theodor felt that if they behaved decently it had always been possible for Jews to make their way. And what absolute balderdash the so-called intellectuals were producing! Baader, the daddy of Dada, Hülsenbeck and his 'art is shit'! What kind of example was that for the young trying to find a direction in the post-war world? No wonder that man Spengler went on about 'the decline of the West'.

Theodor looked with affection at the Adolph von Menzel painting of Berlin rooftops which his father had given him when he had qualified. He wasn't going to barter that for anything. Someone had told him that the great collector Cassirer had actually paid his New York hotel bill with paintings! He unlocked the safe in his study and took out the jewels Elisabeth had brought as part of her dowry; he would hold onto them as long as he could. He had thought that possibly Ferdinand might need support with his research on diabetes, but it turned out that Rebecka was less affected by the inflation than any of them – Louis had been astute enough to stash money away in Switzerland. Theodor locked the diamonds back into the safe.

Magda had become Ferdinand's chief assistant in his research. No one had been able to persuade her to stay at home when she got pregnant. She was determined not to let motherhood interfere with work; hers was going to be a new kind of marriage. Fortunately, they had no financial worries: Rebecka had been more than generous; their flat in the Savignyplatz was furnished in style. They would be able to afford as much help as was necessary when the baby arrived.

As the time for Magda's confinement approached, Ferdinand talked again about their conversion to Protestantism. He wanted their child to grow up in the Christian faith. If it were a boy, he would most certainly not have him circumcised, an outdated, barbaric practice.

'But whatever we do, we'll still be Jewish, won't we?' Magda had an empirical turn of mind.

'Of course not, we will be Protestant Germans!' Ferdinand was shocked.

So they were received into the Church. Though the cross and the New Testament did not mean much to Magda, she realised they were vital to Ferdinand's well-being. He was a deeply religious man. It went entirely against his inner grain when the Minister for Reconstruction, Walter Rathenau, also a converted Jew, publicly declared: 'My people is the German people, my fatherland is Germany, my religion that German faith which is above all religions'. Certainly, Ferdinand felt himself to be German through and through, but there were matters that transcended nationality. His faith in Jesus Christ was absolute. When he finally told Rebecka that they were now Lutherans, Rebecka pretended not to hear; the subject was pushed into the background by the arrival of baby Luise. At least, since it was a girl,

33

the question of circumcision did not arise.

'She need never know her parents were Jewish,' Ferdinand said as he felt her tiny fingers clutch his.

'But she'll have Jewish relations, won't she?' Magda could not help saying.

He was surprised how soon Magda was back in the laboratory with him; Magda was surprised how soon she was pregnant again. Stephanie was born when Luise was only fifteen months.

Stephanie had jet black hair and her eyes, which were violet at birth, turned velvety dark brown. No matter how many pastors baptised her, she was a throwback to Sephardic forebears. The sisters were completely unlike each other. Luise had pearly transparent skin, Stephanie olive; Luise's hair was a fine light brown, Stephanie's shiny and dark. Ferdinand looked at his new daughter in astonishment, but Magda warmed to her in a way she had not warmed to Luise – there was something so earthy about Stephanie. Mother and daughter gazed at each other in a great bonding. Ferdinand was still Jewish enough to have hoped for a boy, but he was a kind man; and when, a couple of years later, Stephanie came toddling in with a bunch of violets on his birthday, he picked her up and hugged her.

'Papa is proud of you!' he said and meant it.

By then, Magda was pregnant for a third time. This time they would surely have a boy.

Magda was totally dismayed. She wanted neither boy nor girl. She could not cope with another baby, even though they had a nanny and a maid. She longed to give herself to her work and had come to dread the love-making with Ferdinand, which she had at first entered into with great passion. She was sexually fully awakened, but the constant threat of pregnancy had frozen her up. She knew Ferdinand was proud of her as his wife and as the mother of his children, but more than that she wanted him to be proud of her as his colleague.

She needed to talk to someone about an idea which had occurred to her, an idea which seemed impossible at first but which after several sleepless nights had become increasingly feasible. If only she could talk to Ferdinand about it; if only he were not quite so devout! Because she dared not be frank, she became short-tempered with him and with the little girls. He put it down to the early weeks of pregnancy and told her to relax – there was no need for her to come to the lab with him; he could manage; he had a student, a young man, to do the donkey work. Magda looked at him with estranged eyes. Didn't he realise what working with him meant to her? So she came to confide in her sister Hannah, who had been living in the Friedrichstrasse with Theodor and Elisabeth since Oskar's death.

Hannah realised that something out of the ordinary was up when they met at the Café Krantzler; but she was not prepared for it when, over a cup of coffee brimming with whipped cream, Magda asked her if she knew anyone who would do an abortion. By this time, Hannah was aware of the fact that doing 'everything' with a man would in all likelihood result in a baby, though her friend Ute had told her there were precautions you could take. Ute had also mentioned that if the worst came to the worst, you could go to someone and have an abortion. But Hannah had never talked about such things with her sister. She could not help thinking abortions were wrong, especially if you were married and had plenty of money.

She urged Magda to discuss it with Ferdinand.

'I cant; he'd be totally shocked!'

'But if you love him?'

'Of course I love him!'

'And he you?'

Magda nodded. She knew Ferdinand loved her, though not in the way she wanted to be loved.

'You see, I'm really good at my work, Hannah, and I want to go on being good at it. We're on to something important in the lab; there are a lot more tests to be done, but we may be on the track of something that will help all diabetics! But medically speaking, there's no reason why I shouldn't have another baby… Ferdinand just wouldn't even begin to understand why I know I can't go through with it…' Magda gripped her sister's arm.

Hannah was not sure she could understand either, but she could see how desperately serious Magda was. So she promised to ask her friend.

Ute, of course, asked her why she wanted to know.

'Don't worry, it's not for me!'

'Who then?'

'Oh someone.' Hannah was not going to give her sister away.

But Ute insisted… 'Your sister! But she's married to a doctor; she's on the way to becoming one herself! If people like them can't find ways and means…'

'Her husband's very religious,' Hannah said.

In the end, after a good deal more persuading, Hannah got an address out of Ute. Then she arranged to meet Magda at the Krantzler again.

'Moabit?' Magda was dismayed when she saw the address: it was one of the sleaziest districts in Berlin.

'You don't have to do it!' Hannah was close to tears.

'I do, I do!' Magda was working herself up into hysterics.

'But what will you tell Ferdinand?'

'That I miscarried – I've tried to induce a miscarriage, but it hasn't worked. And thank you!' Magda bent forward and kissed her sister on both cheeks. 'When it's all over, we'll celebrate. One day I shall make the family feel proud of me!'

So Magda told Ferdinand she was after all taking a day off as he'd suggested. She was going to see an old school friend.

As he was leaving for the laboratory, Ferdinand pecked her on both cheeks. 'Enjoy your day, my dear!'

Magda could not bear to look at him. If he really loved me, she thought, he would know. Behind that there was the uncomfortable thought that if she really loved him she would have been able to talk to him. Was it his piety that stood between them?

When she gave the address to the cab driver, he asked her to repeat it. 'You're sure that's right, Gnä Frau?'

'Quite sure,' Magda said firmly and leant back and shut her eyes.

'Here you are then.' The driver did not call her Gnä Frau as she got out.

Magda peered at the house number, pushed open the heavy door and walked into a courtyard which smelt of soot. When she found the right door, she stood on the threshold for a moment wishing she were someone else. Then she pressed the bell.

The old woman who poked away Magda's embryo son found the telephone number she had been given in case of emergency. It was Theodor and Elisabeth's. Fortunately Hannah answered.

'You'd better come quick, she's bleedin' away from under me 'ands!'

By the time Hannah got to Moabit, Magda was dead.

'It do 'appen every now and then; I'm very sorry, I'm sure.' But the woman did not sound particularly sorry. Perhaps it happened quite often. Then, to Hannah's amazement, she added, 'Don't worry, dearie, she paid me before 'and!'

Hannah was shaking. The last thing she was thinking about was money. 'You'll 'ave ter see ter things quietly, won't yer, ducks...'

Hannah arrived back at the Friedrichstrasse in a total panic. 'Where's Theodor?'

'Whatever...' Elisabeth began.

'I'm here,' Theodor said.

'I have to talk to you...'

'You can talk to both of us!'

So she did, twisting and twisting a handkerchief between her hands, until it tore.

Theodor and Elisabeth could not believe what they were hearing. Theodor got up and paced the length of the drawing room right through the sliding doors into the dining room and back again.

'Outrageous... scandalous... wicked... I can't... but why didn't she come to me if she felt she couldn't talk it over with Ferdinand?'

Elisabeth's lower lip trembled, then her whole body shook. Hannah did not say that it was she who had given Magda the address, but when Elisabeth looked at her she knew. Nothing needed saying.

'It wasn't my fault!' Hannah blurted out, and began to sob.

Elisabeth took her hand. 'No one's blaming you. But I cannot understand... she and Ferdinand have... had... everything... And how will Ferdinand... Luise... Stephanie... how could she... oh, those poor little girls!'

It was Theodor who broke the news to Ferdinand, implying

that as a medical man he might have taken more care. Two young children in quick succession were quite enough without putting a third one on the way. Theodor somehow also implied, or at least Ferdinand read the implication into what was being said, that if he had been content to stay the Jew he was born without any of this Protestant nonsense, things might not have taken such a terrible turn.

Ferdinand failed to see how his conversion could possibly be connected with Magda's ghastly death through a botched abortion. He felt utterly betrayed. He had trusted his wife completely, loved her with all his heart. Obviously, she had not returned that love and trust. But though he felt shattered, his faith in a living God, in the Saviour Jesus Christ and in the Holy Spirit, did not desert him. If only Magda had shared that faith!

Elisabeth could not get over her sister's death. How could God allow such a terrible idea to occur to Magda? Was it because she had never had a mother?

'And everything else is going so well,' Elisabeth sobbed with Theodor's arm round her. 'Only this morning I had a letter from Richard; he's got engaged at last; he wants to bring her... she's a little older than he is... not Jewish but...'

Richard looked at himself in the mirror and smoothed some violet-scented pomade on to his balding head. He smiled at his reflection. Beate had said she would marry him. No one would ever suspect she was five years older than him; she looked so young with her thick fair hair plaited into a knot high on her head. The reason she had taken so long to say 'yes' was that she had been reluctant to tell him that she could not have children. That was sad but somehow it made him love her all the more. He had taken her hand in both of his and kissed it and looked into her clear grey eyes. 'Then I shall always have you all to myself,' he had said. Beate would never, never be in danger of dying his mother's awful childbed death.

He seldom thought about his mother. After all, he could barely remember her, and he resisted Elisabeth's attempts to talk about their childhood. Poor Magda could have no memory of Franziska at all!

Richard concentrated on trimming the hairs growing out of his nostrils. He had never much liked his face; it was too round, like his father's, not in the least romantic. But since Beate had said 'yes', he was more reconciled to the way he looked. He felt a weight lifted off his shoulders since Oskar had died. His father had always made him feel he was not quite up to scratch; in fact, since he had stayed in Gleiwitz while Oskar had swanned around in Berlin, things had gone very well at the factory. Politically, of course, it looked pretty bleak in Upper Silesia since half of it had gone to Poland: refugees from the Polish sector were streaming in, not to mention the street fighting and terrorist attacks. He could not ask Beate to set up house here. If the order he was hoping for materialised, he could afford to go and live in the Berlin flat Oskar had left him. It was temporarily let to an English diplomat and his wife. He would still have to spend more time in Gleiwitz than his father had done in recent years, but at least Beate could live in style.

When the telephone rang, he rushed to answer it – long distance from Berlin. It might be about that order he'd been negotiating. But the voice that came through was Elisabeth's. She sounded agitated.

'First of all,' she quavered, 'I want to say how delighted we all are about your engagement!'

Then why sound so tearful?

'But Richard, there's terrible news!'

'What is it? What's the matter?'

Elisabeth tended to make mountains out of molehills. He hoped Laetitia wasn't playing up: Elisabeth had had to put up with more than her fair share of coping there. Hannah ought really to do some of the visiting, even though Laetitia had been so lamentably lacking as a mother to her. Richard remembered how she had looked the other way whenever any of them came into the room, her neck stiff with resentment. She'd cared more for that yappy little dog and the horse than for any of them.

Elisabeth was saying something about Magda; he concentrated. 'A back street abortion and it went most horribly wrong, oh…' She began to weep into the telephone.

'She died?' Richard could hardly believe what he was hearing.

'Back street abortion' was not a phrase he had ever expected to hear from one sister about another!

Elisabeth, controlling her voice, went on to tell him about arrangements for the cremation. When he had put the receiver down, he sat quite still. All he could think was, 'And that's another thing that can never happen to Beate'.

He got out Beate's last letter, which was from Switzerland, where she was on holiday with an aunt. He put through a call to the hotel in Zermatt – not that he was going to tell her the terrible family news; he just needed to hear her voice. After an age he heard it, distant and crackly.

'I wanted to know how you were. Are you enjoying yourself?'

'Oh it's wonderful here, but you mustn't be so extravagant, Richard! Is all well with you?'

Richard was touched by the concern in her voice. 'Longing to see you again.'

'And so am I!'

There was a long silence. Richard, who was frugal by nature, did not care how much that silence cost; it restored him. He arranged to meet Beate in Berlin on her return journey. He intended taking her to see Theodor and Elisabeth in the Friedrichstrasse; Elisabeth would give any future wife of his a warm welcome, he knew, if she weren't too felled by what had happened to Magda. He was surprised she had said nothing about Ferdinand on the phone; what a sanctimonious ass Ferdinand was with his high falutin' talk about God and the Fatherland, and viruses or germs or microbes or whatever it was he peered at under his microscope! Richard had not forgotten the look of utter contempt on his face at the mention of uniform buttons. Ferdinand could never have afforded to marry so young without Rebecka behind him; she was besotted with her only son. Whatever was going to become of those two little girls now? Ferdinand was certainly not capable of looking after them – hadn't been capable of looking after his wife, had he! It was shameful, shameful!

Richard went down into his office but could not concentrate on the order book and ledgers on his desk. He put on his hat and coat and, though it was the middle of the week, made his way towards the synagogue, where he had not been for some time.

He walked quickly, looking neither left nor right. He wanted no encounters with Korfanty's freebooters, who were out for blood because they thought the whole of Silesia should have gone to Poland. Things were calming down a little since the town had organised a home guard; he had been put on the reserve of the reserve for that – buttons were still considered important enough to exempt him from any kind of active service. After all, without buttons everything would hang open and fall down or have to be tied up with bits of string. If you saw anyone like that, they were bound to be Polish – scruffy disorganised lot; charming women, though... Richard thought with affection about the young woman with skin like velvet with whom he'd had a fling a year or two before. Few people had thought in terms of German or Polish before the war; everyone was simply Silesian. 'But now,' he thought with immense joy, 'I have Beate.' She was indisputably German, though she belonged to that minority of Germans who were Catholic.

He turned out of the Wilhelmstrasse into the Klosterstrasse and began to cough. The air was heavy with fumes from the foundry works and the mines. As he walked past All Saints Catholic Church, he eyed it with curiosity. He had never been inside a Catholic church, though now he was marrying Beate he ought to perhaps – not that she had asked for a church wedding; she said she would be quite content with a civil ceremony. That suited him too.

He got to the synagogue and went in. He sat right at the back and listened to the cantor and the choir practising. He could not fully realise what had occurred; unspeakable things like deaths from abortions happened to other people, not to one's sister. He vacillated between being very angry with and immensely sad for Magda; then he simply sat there trying to let the singing soothe him. When it stopped, he left.

Instead of walking past All Saints Church, he decided to go in. There were a few women clicking rosaries while a priest in lace vestments fiddled about casually at the altar, above which hung a large and not very beautiful crucifix with the tortured limbs of the Saviour stretched across it. Richard did not look at that. How could Beate? There was a good deal he did not yet know about her.

Suddenly he realised he was still wearing his hat. Embarrassed, he snatched it off; but no one had noticed. He wondered who pleased God more: men with covered heads or men with bare heads? A kind of schoolboy titter began to rise inside him, but when it reached the surface it turned into a sob. How could any woman murder the child growing inside her? It went against the very grain of being. Was that what emancipated women used their intelligence for? Richard felt tears trickle down his face and onto his expensive overcoat. When he got control of himself, he left the church quietly.

Back at the office he found a letter confirming the order he had been hoping for. The way to life in Berlin was clear.

He sent flowers for Magda's cremation but did not go. It was the first time in the family that anyone was being cremated rather than buried. He admitted to himself that he minded more about the way his sister had died than the fact that she was dead. They had never been close.

A week later, a day before Beate's return from Zermatt, Richard went to Berlin. He would arrange to show her his father's flat – the diplomat was about to move back to England – and then he would ask her to name the wedding day. When he thought of sharing a bed with her for the rest of his life, he was not so much overcome by erotic longing or raw sexual desire – though all that was there – as by a feeling of total trust, of being able to shed all burdens.

He made his way to a little hotel opposite Mon Bijou Park. He had found several receipts for it among his father's papers and had a pretty good idea why the old boy had needed to stay in a hotel so close to home. He was curious to know what sort of a place it was; Beate would be staying somewhere with her aunt before going back to Breslau where they lived. At some point, he would have to tell her that he had a deranged stepmother in an institution in Breslau.

He took a cab and tried his best to ignore the beggars on crutches, the blind man holding a tray of matches and the yellow band with the three black dots round his arm. A drunk was bawling,

'Jestern warn wa reiche Leite
Heite sint wa Plaite Plaite…'

That man with his broad Berlin accent had never been rich and never would be. But a good many people were much worse off than they ever had been. Richard felt outraged by the reparation demands of the Versailles Treaty – no country could pay those amounts. Yet what good had killing Erzberger done? What alternative had the poor man had to signing the Treaty? That shooting had only undermined confidence in Germany abroad and played into the hands of that loud-mouthed Adolf Hitler in Bavaria. If anyone needed shooting, it was people like him. Still, Rathenau would see them through. A German Jew – like me, Richard thought.

The cab drove past the new Friedrichstrasse station. He would have to go on the underground. It was exciting to be living in the twentieth century: the century of technological advance. If only technology could be harnessed to peaceful uses! Surely, after four years of carnage no one would ever want to start another war? The cab stopped outside the hotel. In Mon Bijou Park, the horse-chestnut leaves were beginning to turn and sycamore seeds were swirling gently to the ground. Richard took a deep breath. The Berlin air did not make him cough.

In the hotel foyer, his eye fell on a heartrending poster of starving children holding out their hands in supplication. He looked at it more closely. In the bottom right hand corner was the artist's signature: Käthe Kollwitz. Whoever she was, her drawing struck home. He put some coins in the collection box standing by the poster.

The next morning when he went to meet Beate's train, Richard was surprised to see her get off by herself. She blushed when he gave her the red roses he had brought to welcome her.

'Where's your aunt?' he asked.

'She couldn't tear herself away from the snowcapped peaks!' And then Beate put her head on one side and asked, 'What's the matter, Richard; what's happened? You look different!'

He looked at her amazed. He had not noticed anything different about himself and tried to evade the question.

'Where are you staying?'

'With you, I hope. Where are you staying?'

Now Richard blushed. 'Oh it's just a little… I don't know whether…'

'Anything that's good enough for you is good enough for me,' she said firmly.

Well, he thought, whatever it had been like in his father's day, the little Mon Bijou hotel seemed perfectly all right now.

He took her there.

'Tomorrow…' he began when they were sipping coffee and crumbling bits of Kranzkuchen.

'Tomorrow you're taking me to meet Elisabeth and Theodor?'

Richard was pleased that she remembered their names. 'Of course, that's all arranged. But tomorrow I also want to show you where we're going to live.'

Beate looked puzzled.

'I've decided to take on my father's old flat behind the Tiergarten. I'd like us to start married life in Berlin!'

'Well, this is a surprise!'

'A pleasant one, I hope?'

'You know I'd be happy with you anywhere, Richard!'

He stroked her cheek. 'All the best Berliners hail from Silesia – you know that, don't you?'

'But you still haven't told me what's made you look so… bereft?'

Arm in arm, they walked out into the park. Richard told Beate exactly what had happened to his sister Magda.

'I wasn't going to burden you with all that. I'm ashamed and angry and – yes, bereft: you put it very well.'

Beate stopped and placed her hand on his shoulder. She looked very serious.

'There is nothing, nothing at all, that we cannot tell each other. And it is wrong of you to feel ashamed, it is simply very, very sad!' She paused for a moment and added, 'And to think that I…' She did not finish the sentence, but Richard knew she was thinking: if only I could have had that baby.

That night Beate made it quite clear she expected him to share her bed. It was an ultimate homecoming for him: nothing, nothing could ever go wrong again.

Next morning at breakfast, with the *Berliner Börsencourier* left unopened by his plate, Richard suggested they should walk down Unter den Linden to the flat. Then his eye fell on the headline on the front page: 'Inflation Catastrophe'. Well, the papers didn't always get things right – he was more interested in the article at the bottom about the new motorway, the Avus.

'We'll get a motor car as soon as we're settled here and go for a spin down the Avus,' he promised. But Beate was not very enthusiastic.

'I'm sure we could manage without a motor, and I don't really like going very fast!' Then she put her hand over the paper and went on, 'You know, we've never really talked about money, have we?'

'And there's no need. Things are going well at the factory. Whatever money you have is yours to keep or spend as you like. Not like…'

He was going to say 'not like Elisabeth whose fortune went to Theodor when they got married'. But that was before the war; things had changed. There might be greater insecurity now but there was also greater freedom. Perhaps the one entailed the other?

Beate moved her hand from the paper and put it over Richard's. 'We will share everything,' she said.

Halfway down Unter den Linden, Beate stopped to buy a pair of shoelaces from a crippled war veteran. Richard shook his head.

'You're too kind. If we gave to all of them, we'd soon be standing there ourselves!'

'They fought for the country; it's not their fault we lost – we can't let them down now!'

They looked over the flat behind the Tiergarten. Richard could still feel his father's presence in it, but he was sure once he and Beate had moved in that would fade. Beate said it was much too grand for them, but Richard could see she loved it.

They went back to the hotel before going on to the Friedrichstrasse, where they were expected for coffee and cake. Surely the topic of Magda's death would be avoided? Richard so much wanted bringing his bride to meet the family to be a happy occasion. He felt irrational anger rise in himself again, but going through the ritual of pomading his hair and sticking his father's pearl pin into his grey and purple cravat helped to calm him. As if to reaffirm their oneness, Beate was wearing a grey and purple silk dress. He helped her into her coat and they set off at a leisurely pace, past the Oranienburgerstrasse Synagogue, its golden dome glinting in the autumn sunshine.

'You'll have to take me to a service there one day,' Beate said shyly.

'I don't go very often myself, though the other day when…'

'… when you heard about your sister, you went? Of course you did!'

Richard pressed her arm. It was so good to have her know what he was going to say almost before he had thought it.

'Yes, that was in Gleiwitz of course. I also went into All Saints Church. I'd never been in a Catholic church before.'

'Oh, it's the same God inside every place of worship; we just make our different ways to Him,' Beate said.

Richard was too happy to ask her how she felt about looking at the tortured figure of Christ.

When they got to the Friedrichstrasse, he pushed open the heavy iron front door and they walked up the stairs, past the bench with the carved lion's head, to the first floor. The door opened almost before they had rung the bell. Elisabeth rushed towards them as the maid was helping them off with their coats.

'Come along in,' she said and kissed Beate on both cheeks as if she had known her all her life.

There were pink and purple asters on the dining room table and the very best dark blue and gold Rosenthal china. Rebecka was there but, to Richard's great relief, Ferdinand was not. Hannah had also arranged to be in – she was still living in the Friedrichstrasse – so that she could have a look at her prospective sister-in-law. Richard's marrying a Gentile was going to make it easier for her with Hermann, who kept urging her to announce their engagement.

Hermann had simply shrugged his shoulders when Hannah had told him she was Jewish. He told her it made no difference to him: he didn't really believe in any kind of God; only a lunatic fringe minded these days about who was and was not Jewish.

In the Weimar Republic that kind of thing hardly mattered; they were all Germans trying to get over the war, though some did take their Germanness to extremes – went around waving swastika flags, shouting anti-Jewish, anti-Marxist slogans – but the government would deal with them. After all, the National Socialist Party had been banned as soon as it was formed.

Theodor was looking pink and benevolent, watch-chain across his stomach, which was beginning to fill out again after the wartime rations. Very soon after they had finished sampling Elisabeth's cakes – she had outdone herself: there was Sandtorte, apple strudel, cheesecake, chocolate cake, hazelnut cake and sablé biscuits – he led the way through the sliding doors into the drawing room, where bottles of Sekt stood ready in ice buckets surrounded by tall stemmed pale green glasses with patterns of grapes engraved on them.

Young Max helped his father open the bottles; his sister Ruth was not about. Theodor raised his glass, but before wishing Richard and Beate every happiness, he was silent for a moment or two. They knew the silence was in memory of Magda. Then, to everyone's great surprise, Theodor sat down at the grand piano and played Mendelssohn's 'Wedding March' *con brio*.

V

1923-1928: BERLIN

After Magda's death, Ferdinand cut himself off from the family. Magda's lack of trust in him had undermined his trust in almost everyone and everything. He missed her every single minute of every single day. Every day he prayed that she might be forgiven and that the Lord would have mercy on him, too. How could he have been so blind, so… so… But no amount of self-recrimination could bring her back. He could hardly bear to look at his daughters. Luise was old enough to ask about Mamma and was told that she would be back soon. Stephanie just cast her great dark eyes round restlessly. Their nanny had left, unable to cope with the upheaval that Magda's death brought with it. Ferdinand did not ask his mother to look after the little girls – Rebecka was suffering from arthritis, which had slowed her down considerably – but Elisabeth never said no when he asked her to have the children. It was she who found him a young housekeeper who was fond of children.

Bella was a hefty country girl. Her family, who lived a few kilometres outside of Berlin, had hit hard times, and Bella knew how to make a little go a long way. The job came as a godsend for her and she enjoyed looking after the girls, especially Luise. The way people stared at dark-haired, sallow-skinned Stephanie, so unlike her fairer sister, rather embarrassed Bella and made her unnecessarily strict with the little girl. Though Ferdinand did not stop missing Magda – he began to realise how valuable she had been in the laboratory – his sexual needs became increasingly urgent. Bella smelt agreeably of lavender water and her large bosom began to figure in his dreams. So one day when she had given Luise and Stephanie their bath and brought him his supper – they did not take their meals together – Ferdinand got her to sit down, poured her a glass of Rheinwein and, without beating about the bush, asked her to marry him. She went bright red when he kissed her chapped hand and said she would have to think about it; she would like to go home and talk to her parents.

In fact, Bella made up her mind to accept Ferdinand the moment he proposed, but she would have to tell her parents that she intended marrying a baptised Jew. She knew that her father, an enthusiastic member of the National Socialist Party, hated Jews; the fact that the party was proscribed by the government only added to his zeal. In spite of all that, Bella was fond of her father. She so much enjoyed being back at home that she left it to the last day of her holiday to break the news.

At first, her parents were delighted – no matter that Ferdinand had been married before, how sad that his wife had died so young; no matter that he already had two children, he would have more. They patted her cheeks. And how splendid to be marrying a doctor! Her life would be better than theirs had ever been. And then Bella said,

'He's a baptised Jew!'

Her father's fist crashed down on the table; his beer spilled on to Bella's dress. 'Pigs, traitors – we want them out of the Fatherland, every, last one of them, stinking pack of…'

'Ferdinand served in the Medical Corps during the war,' Bella interrupted.

'The Kaiser should never have allowed them into the army! Those degenerates had no right to be fighting for our Fatherland, our Germany!'

'But he is German!'

'A daughter of mine has the insolence to tell me that a member of that cursed race belongs to our glorious Aryan nation!'

It was the first time Bella heard the term 'Aryan'. It would not be not the last. 'But father, if you met Ferdinand you would not…'

Her father's face purpled apoplectically. He got up and handcuffed Bella's wrists with his fierce fingers, shaking her hard. 'Meet…' he bellowed. 'Meet… a Jew… If… you… marry… a Jew… never… set… foot… in… this… house… AGAIN!'

'Don't, don't, let her be!' Bella's mother moaned. Bella freed herself from her father's grip.

'He doesn't mean it,' her mother said.

But Bella knew he did.

As soon as she got back to Berlin, she told Ferdinand she would marry him. That night he invited her into his bed, and twins were conceived.

Bella did not enjoy the procreative act, but she knew it was part of the deal. Ferdinand married her the following week, without telling any of the family. As soon as he knew Bella was pregnant, Ferdinand began calling her 'Mother'. He had never called Magda that. When Luise heard him call Bella Mother, she copied him, and from then on she stopped asking about her Mamma. But Stephanie still had that lost look about her and would sometimes sob and sob,

'I want Mam-ma, I want Mam-ma!'

'Mamma is here!' Ferdinand would pick her up and hand her to Bella. Stephanie would turn her head away.

Having solved his immediate problems, Ferdinand spent his spare time reading. He read Nietzsche on nihilism and the logic of decadence. It fitted in perfectly with his mood if not with his Christian faith. He read Robert Musil's *Der Mann Ohne Eigenschaften*, which was being talked about in intellectual circles. Ferdinand was not at all sure he wanted to be classed with intellectuals: they tended to be left wing and had unacceptable sexual mores. (That he had taken both his wives to bed before they were married did not strike him as unacceptable.) But the Musil, too, corresponded to his mood. The thought of being relieved of the burden of personal responsibility appealed to him, though he was rather hazy as to what hovering within a formal system of possible meanings entailed. He was surprised that the thought of a world of qualities without people – of experiences without anyone to experience them – had not occurred to him, because that was exactly how things were for him since Magda had died.

His experience of her hovered about him at an insulated distance. He dared not break through that insulation, dared not allow himself images of the past – the shy girl looking with admiration and astonishment at his cross, the radiant young woman in his bed... no, he would not succumb to those images, because they were immediately followed by the sinking feeling that perhaps his Christian faith was no more than a formal system of possible meanings. He made himself switch to the here and now... What was the possible meaning of the fact that Rathenau had been assassinated? that he was a Jew? that he was responsible for the terms of the Versailles Treaty? for inflation? Was he killed for being an intelligent, able statesman? Had he, the converted Jew, been too strident about his patriotism? Berliners did not think so; the general strike following the assassination paralysed the city. Would Stresemann do any better?

The one thing that really cheered Ferdinand was that he been given laboratory space at the Charité. He only wished his research on diabetes were more conclusive; he so missed Magda's unfailing confidence. His new ultra efficient assistant was no substitute: the man was positively officious.

Exhausted at the end of the day, Ferdinand felt reluctant to go home to his new wife. She too was most efficient, but he had known when he decided to ask her to marry him that she would never be a companion. So he rushed from classical concerts – Furtwängler conducting *Die Meistersinger* – to cabarets – Rosa Valetti was amazing at the Rampe! He resisted the advances of prostitutes – Berlin was turning into the whore of Babylon – and made do with Bella. He knew, too, that she had no idea what it was she wasn't doing for him in bed. It dawned on him that he was only half alive.

Richard, on the other hand, was blissfully married to his Beate. He divided his time between Berlin and Gleiwitz. The old manager was at last retiring, and Richard appointed a man who was popular with the workers. As they shook hands, Herr Müller said he would see to it that they got orders for the uniform buttons of the new Nazi Party. That was where the future of the country lay; the Party would not be banned much longer.

Richard noticed for the first time that Müller wore a tiny swastika in his lapel. He told his new manager that they could not take on any more orders for the time being, but Müller pretended not to hear. Well, it was only right and proper, Richard felt, that in a democracy people should be allowed to hold and voice whatever political views they liked. After the horrors of the war and the economic disaster of the inflation, sanity and moderation would surely prevail. The mark had been precariously pegged to rye by Stresemann, though no one really believed that would do the trick. One could only wait and see.

So Richard put his energies into the opening of a new Berlin head office on the Alexanderplatz and the modernising of his father's flat. Such short-term goals pushed war and violence that much further into the past. But he was put out when Herr Müller turned up at the new office sounding off about Hitler – how perfectly right Adolf was to oppose passive resistance in the Ruhr; who did the French think they were to be marching into German territory?

'We Germans will show them who we are!' he blathered.

'You surely don't want more bloodshed?' Richard asked as mildly as he could, looking pointedly at a livid scar on Müller's forehead, left by a piece of shrapnel.

'We are not going to knuckle under,' the man said, pressing

his thin lips together.

'Did we get all the orders for Weichmann out in time?' Richard became formal and businesslike.

'That Jew!' Müller looked contemptuous.

Richard wondered whether he should remind the manager that he was employed by a Jew or whether to dismiss him on the spot. But he did neither. Sternly he repeated his question.

'Well, did the orders go out in time? Did they or didn't they?' The dictatorial tone of voice had the desired effect.

'Yes sir, they went out on the dot, sir!'

Lickspittle, Richard thought. He hated being sirred and would have liked a manager who could also be a friend like the old one. That was not going to be possible with this man. Damn it, it ought to be possible! As Müller was leaving, Richard tried to be more relaxed.

'Enjoy your time in Berlin!'

'I'm off to buy a copy of Möller Brock's *Das Dritte Reich*!'

'Whatever's that all about?'

'We've been recommended to get it, sir!'

Was there a touch of sarcasm in that 'sir' now? But without enquiring who 'we' were, Richard bade Herr Müller good day and said he would be in Gleiwitz again quite soon.

On the way home from the office, Richard saw *Das Dritte Reich* displayed in a bookshop window and went in to leaf through it. It seemed to be mainly about the mystical qualities of the number three. He could make neither head nor tail of it. Was his manager all there?

'Shall I get rid of him?' Richard asked Beate when they were sitting on their balcony sipping a glass of Riesling. She always managed to see things in proportion; had such a common sense approach to life.

'But I thought he was so efficient?'

'So he is, so he is. But he seems to despise Jews, admire Hitler and has an altogether suspect turn of mind.' Richard mentioned *Das Dritte Reich* with its arcane mumbo-jumbo and added, 'I should have been more careful!'

'Oh, let him read what he likes.' Beate did not take the thing too seriously.

'I'm surprised he reads at all!' Richard said, and they laughed.
The telephone rang.

It was Elisabeth to say she had managed to find somewhere for Laetitia in a house run by two Jewish sisters, trained social workers, rather expensive but well worth it, she thought. Laetitia would be installed there in time for Hannah and Hermann's wedding.

'Are you sure it's the right thing? Will she be able to cope?' Richard was worried.

'She's perfectly alright now,' Elisabeth told him.

Richard was not entirely reassured. He knew his sister never said an unkind word about anyone. He only hoped Laetitia would not disgrace the family at her daughter's wedding.

Elisabeth went to Breslau to collect Laetitia. She had tried to tell her that Hannah, her daughter, was getting married and that it would be lovely to have her at the reception.

Laetitia had little reaction. 'In Berlin?' she asked.

'Yes, you'll be living in Berlin again; we'll be able to see a lot more of you!' Again, the reaction was minimal.

But as they were leaving the mental institution, Laetitia asked, 'So I'm never coming back here again?'

'Never!' Elisabeth said.

In the train, Laetitia hooked her arm through Elisabeth's and asked, 'How long was I in that place?'

Elisabeth looked at Laetitia's thinning grey hair, her parchment yellow skin, her eyes shadowed with cataracts. I should have got you out sooner, she thought

'Well, how long?' Laetitia insisted.

'A longish time,' Elisabeth said softly. 'Are you hungry? I've brought some of your favourite liver pâté sandwiches.'

Laetitia allowed herself to be diverted.

The two sisters who ran the Jewish old age home welcomed her with coffee and cake, and to Elisabeth's relief Laetitia made no objection to being left there. Elisabeth went home to the Friedrichstrasse and told Theodor that they had done the right thing; that it was money well spent.

She kissed him on both cheeks. 'Thank you, Schnucki!'

'I never forget that it's your money – what there's left of it,' Theodor said.

'We should have got her to Berlin sooner.'

'You know we could do nothing while your father was alive.'

'I could have tried harder to persuade him!'

'I haven't forgotten, either,' Theodor went on, 'that it is Hannah who is Laetitia's daughter. Perhaps she will grow into her responsibilities once she's married.'

'You know that Laetitia was no mother to her…'

'Yes, I know – that marriage was a tragedy. Laetitia should never have married Oskar!'

It was the first time Theodor had spoken so openly to Elisabeth. They sat next to each other in the study by a round walnut table that had pull-out trays for playing cards. Theodor put his hand over his wife's. In silence, they felt the blood tingle through their intertwined fingers.

Elisabeth and Theodor gave Hannah and Hermann a splendid send-off in the Friedrichstrasse. Laetitia was there in a brand new grey outfit from Wertheim – there had not been time to have anything made for her. She stared at her daughter, who looked charming in primrose georgette.

'My mother,' Hannah said to various members of Hermann's family. But Laetitia turned away from her daughter now, as she had always done.

Suddenly she asked, looking round the assembled company, 'And Oskar?'

Elisabeth drew her aside and whispered, 'But you know he's dead!' without adding that if he were not, she would still be in the institution in Breslau.

Laetitia blinked behind her thick spectacles, and the lines round her mouth relaxed.

'For goodness sake, take your gloves off!' Rebecka said to her sister-in-law.

Rebecka had come by herself. Ferdinand had not been able to face coming.

Much as Elisabeth tried to draw them out, Hermann's parents, his sister and brother-in-law kept themselves to themselves, the only person talking to them being Oskar's old housekeeper

Frau Schulz, whom Hannah had insisted on inviting. Elisabeth looked round the room. There must surely be other people who were not Jewish. Of course there was Hannah's friend Ute, just married to her Alfons. He rose to make a speech laced with *double-entendres*.

'Whoever is that vulgar man?' Laetitia asked, but fortunately her words were drowned by the general laughter and clapping.

Elisabeth noticed that her Ruth was laughing as loudly as anyone at the jokes.

Afterwards, when it was all over, she said to Theodor, 'I wonder, do you think Hermann's parents mind his marrying into a Jewish family?'

Theodor looked at her frostily. 'Don't you think the boot is rather on the other foot? that it's much more a question of whether we mind Hannah marrying into… into… Well, as I see it, it's *they* who have everything to gain!' He spat out a shred of tobacco from the cigar he was smoking; then he said much more gently, 'You managed everything superbly, my dear, as always!' He blew out a puff of smoke.

Elisabeth loved the smell of that.

Quite soon at one of the coffee parties, Hannah announced that she was pregnant. Hermann beamed; Elisabeth could see they were very happy. She looked at Laetitia wondering if she had taken in the news.

'Pass me one of those waffles, will you?' was all that Laetitia said, stretching her hand towards them.

'Mamma, I'm going to have a baby,' Hannah said again.

'Dear God!' Laetitia said, and her face crumpled.

After that, Hannah did not come to the family gatherings for some time. She and Hermann were determined not to let family concerns ride their marriage, least of all concern about her mad mother, who had never done anything for her.

Elisabeth too would have liked another child, but Theodor was not going to father a rabbit warren. This was the twentieth century, the century of progress; people no longer expected to lose half the babies that were born; one girl and one boy were quite enough. Theodor saw to it that Elisabeth did not get pregnant again.

Elisabeth said very little about Magda's tragic death, but she grieved deeply for her sister. Nor was she at all sure that Bella was coping now that her twins Frieda and Lola had been born, in spite of the fact that Ferdinand insisted Luise and Stephanie call her 'Mamma'. Stephanie particularly was looking pale and listless. Elisabeth said as much to Ferdinand one day when she was visiting and immediately added,

'Of course, I know Bella's got her hands full with the twins.' She hated criticising anyone.

Ferdinand pooh-poohed her anxieties and offered her a glass of eggnog. He knew it was the only liqueur Elisabeth really liked. He poured himself a Schnapps.

'Let's celebrate...' he began.

Elisabeth thought he was going to say something about the arrival of his two new daughters. Very little fuss had been made of the birth of Frieda and Lola. But he went on,

'...the defeat of that lunatic Hitler!'

'Who is Hitler?' Elisabeth asked. – She found out when she got back home to the Friedrichstrasse.

Theodor was listening to their new radio. 'Hitler fails in Munich,' the announcer was saying.

'Of course he failed! After all, we live in one of the most civilised countries in the world!' Theodor said.

'But who exactly is he?' Elisabeth asked again.

'A demented minor politician who blames everything on the Jews – Germany's defeat, the inflation, every kind of criminal act. Well, now he's been well and truly silenced!'

'Do you think Bella is so unkind to Stephanie because she looks more Jewish than Luise?' Elisabeth appeared worried.

'Is Bella unkind to Stephanie?'

Elisabeth nodded unhappily.

'Well, you can keep an eye on things there, can't you, my dear?'

Elisabeth knew Theodor thought all that was her business.

He smiled at her. 'Tomorrow I'm going to take you to see a film with Otto Gebühr. I'm told he looks just like Wilhelm III!'

Elisabeth smiled back at him. Theodor always managed to

make her feel better.

The following year, Hindenburg was elected President. He seemed a reassuring figure to Theodor. Then Ebert died, which was a great blow to the Weimar Republic. After that, one or two scandals involving Jews made headlines – the brothers Bramat were accused of getting loans from the Preussische Bank by bribery; then there was the Sklarek textile fraud, involving Russo-Polish Jews.

Theodor felt deeply ashamed. Jews escaping pogroms in Eastern Europe were giving long-established Germans Jews a bad name. Various people he knew had themselves baptised to dissociate themselves from all that, but it never occurred to him for a single moment to do so. How lucky they were in Germany not to be persecuted! He was disturbed, though, that that ugly little Goebbels had been made Gauleiter of Berlin. His viciously anti-Semitic paper *Der Angriff* was unspeakable and would no doubt be banned. The Weimar government had better pull its socks up. Those irresponsible ultra-nationalists and militarists had to be kept in check.

Slowly, Germany was coming out from under the shadows of the war and hyperinflation. The country was now a member of the League of Nations; it was good to be allowed back into the European community. No one, not even the so-called victors, could ever want another war; everywhere there were grieving mothers, wives, daughters. Theodor thought that a whole race of large-hearted men had been killed, never to be replaced. And when he thought *race*, he did not think in terms of nationality, religion or blood but of the spirit of an extinguished age. There was this ridiculous move by the Socialists and Communists, who wanted to expropriate the aristocracy – the Kaiser still owned a lot of property in Germany – as if that would help the country to recover! What was needed was new productivity – new ideas in every field – if Germany was to take its place in the world. Jews were making an enormous contribution in the field of ideas. Sometimes Theodor wished he had more time to read and go to lectures. Ferdinand had urged him to go with him to a lecture at the new Hirschfield Institute for Sexual Research, but for the moment his day-to-day practice absorbed all Theodor's energy.

Elizabeth, still concerned about little Stephanie, who seemed always to be looking for something she could not find, took her and Luise to see the new traffic lights blinking red-amber-green. Their novelty was attracting such crowds that they were creating the very traffic jams they were intended to prevent. Then she took them to the baker in the Karlstrasse where Rebecka got her *petit fours* and bought them a large iced bun each, one white, one chocolate. For some reason they were called 'Amerikaner'. Elisabeth was pleased to see Stephanie enjoy hers.

The next day at school someone pulled Stephanie by the sleeve. Stephanie was so pleased anyone wanted to talk to her that she smiled. She looked lovely when she smiled. 'Your mother is not your real mother,' the friendly little girl said. 'She's just your stepmother. I know, because my mother said so. My mother knows someone who knows your father, and they used to know your real mother. Your real mother's dead!'

Stephanie listened dumbfounded. She did not want it to be true, but she knew it was. At the same time, she was relieved that Bella was after all not her mamma.

On the way home, she told Luise what had happened.

'Don't be stupid, it isn't true; of course Mamma Bella is our real Mamma!' As she said it, something stirred in Luise's memory, but she ignored it.

'How can you be sure?'

'How do you know that girl knows anything about us?'

They walked twice round the block before going home.

'You're late, girls!' Bella told them off.

Bella felt vaguely guilty about allowing them to walk to and from school by themselves, though it was not far and there were no big roads to cross. It did make life a lot simpler; the twins kept her very busy – four daughters were more than she had bargained for; nor was she at all sure how pleased Ferdinand was to have two more girls. Still, she always worried if Luise and Stephanie were more than five minutes late.

'Yes, you're very late!' she said again and heard herself sounding quite angry. She did not intend to; it was just the way her worrying came out.

Stephanie stared at her long and hard. 'You're not our real Mamma!'

Bella froze. Then she gripped Stephanie round the wrists and shook her hard. 'Of... course... I... am... your... real... Mamma... What... a... cruel... wicked girl... you... are... to say... such... a thing... I... I...'

Before Bella had thought of the next thing to say, Stephanie was sick. Afterwards, when she had been put to bed, Luise was allowed to bring her a glass of warm milk. 'I told you it was rubbish!' Luise said to her.

Stephanie was too frightened to say anything to her father when he came in to say goodnight

Bella knew she would have to talk to Ferdinand, but when? She too was afraid of him; besides, she saw less and less of her husband, who spent more and more time away from the Savignyplatz. When he did come home, he withdrew as soon as he could from the children. Luise reminded him too heartbreakingly of Magda. And Stephanie... Stephanie made him feel very uncomfortable. He took very little notice of the twins and thought he made up for his neglect by continuing to call Bella 'Mother'. He isolated himself in his study and poured out his emotions in religious poems, in words that the scientist in him scarcely recognised. Nor did he recognise that his outpourings about the Crucifixion – Jesus was a Jew – were a filter for his unassuaged grief for Magda. When all that got too much, he went out again and found distraction in nightclubs, where he was entranced by the black singer Josephine Baker.

For the first time in his life he paid for a prostitute, hoping that the amount she was charging meant she was clear of disease. The prostitute had all the sexual expertise Bella lacked, and he visited her again, and again. Then in a fit of remorse, he went to the Gedächtniskirche and prayed, staring at the images of Christ nailed to the Cross, feeling the nails pierce his own hands and feet. But when he left the Church and walked along the Kurfürstendamm, the agony of religious passion threatened to turn itself into raw sexual desire.

He took cold baths; he did strenuous exercises. And he went

to see his mother.

Rebecka offered him coffee, but he asked for tea. 'Tea? You're not ill, are you?'

'No no, thank God!'

'You think too much about God and not enough about your family,' Rebecka said. 'Now what's all this I hear about Stephanie?'

Ferdinand looked at her, puzzled. Then it all came out – Bella, too nervous to talk to Ferdinand, had been to see Rebecka.

'Most unfortunate!' he mumbled. 'I can't think who it can have been whom we knew…'

'There is too much pretence in your life, Ferdinand,' Rebecka said sternly. But then she went across to him and kissed him on the forehead to show that, of course, she loved him as much as ever. 'Pretending that woman is Luise and Stephanie's mother…' she went on and then bit her lip. She had not intended to call Bella *that woman*. 'And pretending to be Christian, what good…'

Ferdinand got up and walked up and down the dark brown room, which had not changed since he was a boy.

'You don't understand, Mother. That is not a pretence. Believing is what's kept me going through the tragedy of…'

Rebecka was so embarrassed she stuffed a pink *petit four* into her mouth. When she had swallowed it, she asked, 'Are you sure Bella is happy pretending to be something she isn't?'

Ferdinand sat down again. He helped himself to a green *petit four*; he wanted to please his mother. 'In due course, I shall talk to the girls, but not until…'

'Until what?'

Ferdinand said nothing.

Rebecka put on her *pince nez* and got out a photograph album. Nearly all pictures in it were of baby Ferdinand between his doting parents.

'I hardly remember Father, apart from the way he smiled,' Ferdinand said.

'Oh yes, his smile,' Rebecka said and looked at her son sadly.

'Do you ever hear from that athlete friend of his?'

'Not any more.'

After a little pause, she shut the album. 'I haven't seen much of the twins; why don't you all come and see me soon?'

'We will, we will,' Ferdinand said.

But Rebecka knew he was hardly listening.

She picked up the *Berliner Tageblatt* – she had at last given up the *Vossische Zeitung* – and asked, 'Who is this man Hitler the papers are full of? And his fat friend Göring? An odd pair, those two, aren't they? It says Göring's war wounds are so bad he has to take morphine all the time. Poor man! But it's Hitler who's got a bee in his bonnet about Jews, isn't it? More than a bee, by the sound of it – a whole hornet's nest!'

'Just rabble-rousers, Mother; we can forget about them.'

'I only hope you're right.'

'Of course I'm right!'

Ferdinand was impressed that his mother was keeping up with the news. When he got home to the Savignyplatz, he made himself get out his first marriage certificate and Magda's death certificate. It was all too terrible. Whatever he eventually told Luise and Stephanie, he would make absolutely certain that they would never know the cause of her death. And he would try to spend more time with all of his daughters.

VI

1928-1932: BERLIN

Elisabeth had been worried about Ruth for some time. She did not admit to herself in so many words that she was disappointed in her daughter, but that was what it amounted to. Where she had hoped for a kindred spirit about the house, there was a rebellious young woman with a streak of deviousness. Even when on High Holidays mother and daughter sat next to each other in the synagogue, it was clear to Elisabeth that Ruth's thoughts were elsewhere. But where?

Ruth had left school with great relief and a silver cup for outstanding achievement in gym. She was down for that finishing establishment Hannah had been to, but Ruth had other ideas; the silver cup had given her confidence. She contrived to play truant from the cookery and flower-arranging classes to train at the physical education college, which was delighted to have someone as talented as her. When it all came out, the parents had to give in.

Almost as soon as the course started, there was a medical inspection. Ruth looked into the doctor's eyes and fell instantly in love with him. After only a few weeks he asked her to marry him and she said yes. She felt sure the parents would approve: he was a doctor; he was Jewish. But when she introduced him at home, it turned out they expected a great deal more. Who was he? *who* underlined. What were his prospects? Where was his practice? He was no one; his prospects were dim; he did not have a practice; he had next to no capital behind him. To Ruth's utter dismay, he was dismissed after a cup of coffee and the smallest piece of cake Ruth had ever seen her mother offer anyone.

'He is not the man for you,' Theodor said when Ruth sobbed that she loved him.

Her brother Max tried to intercede on her behalf but was told to get on with his studies.

Ruth met her doctor once more. 'Your father is quite right – I have nothing to offer you,' he said, his hands hanging limply by his side.

Was this love? Ruth could not believe her ears.

To cheer her up, Elisabeth took Ruth shopping at Wertheim, where they got lost going up and down in some of the eighty-three lifts. Ruth tried on dozens of dresses and took them off again without looking at herself. They spent several hours wandering from department to department, Ruth lagging behind her mother. Elisabeth gave up. She told Ruth to go shopping by herself, gave her a generous wad of notes and told her not to fret, there would be someone else. She was right, though if she had known who that someone else was going to be, she might not have been quite so sanguine about it.

Ruth used some of her mother's money to have her hair shingled. She bought a long black cigarette holder and smoked flamboyantly in the street. She bought the latest thing in shiny short skirts and low cut blouses. She bought rouge, lipstick and *Quelques Fleurs* perfume.

She liked her new image but was not yet quite sure what to do with it. When Elisabeth saw her, she burst out with 'Jesus Maria!', an expression she had picked up from the Catholic maids during her Silesian childhood. Theodor asked Ruth sternly if she had been seeing a lot of Hannah and Hermann – Hannah, too, had had her hair cut; but Ruth had not been seeing her.

She was enjoying the job she had got teaching gym at a Jewish school. It would make her less dependent on the parents. But her salary did not amount to much, and she had got used to buying perfume and make-up and Russian cigarettes. Theodor's contribution continued to be most acceptable, but he would not settle an allowance on her even long after she was twenty-one. She always had to go to his study at the beginning of each month to ask for money.

One crisp winter's afternoon she went skating on the Havel. A tall fair-haired man in a brightly striped jersey was describing perfect figures of eight. As she found him circling round her, she was overcome by sensations she had not felt since the doctor had looked into her eyes. They skated closer and closer towards each other; she found herself grasped round the waist. They were dancing on the ice. His eyes were bright blue and his name was Hugo. As they swung round together, Ruth knew nothing was going to stop her from being with this man. This time it was the real thing.

Hugo took her to the Romanisches Café in the August-Viktoriaplatz, where he introduced her to his friends – writers, painters, actors. He had written articles about them for various left wing papers. There was such a din in the café that Ruth could hardly hear what people were saying. Putting his mouth to her ear and pointing across the room, Hugo said, 'Guess whether that one's a boy or a girl!'

Later, a friend called Rudi invited them back to his studio full of extraordinary paintings – all crags and triangles. Later still, Rudi disappeared and in this room furnished with nothing but a huge soft couch, Ruth lost her virginity to Hugo. She had had some inkling of what was involved, but the real thing was incredibly more magical than she had ever been able to imagine. She gloried in their nakedness. Oh, this was love all right!

Later again, she found out that Hugo was a Communist and a frequent contributor to *Die Rote Fahne*. Well, of course all men, all women, were equal! She realised how limited her upbringing had been. Hugo had been to Russia: he knew. As a journalist, he got invitations to receptions and press tickets to everything. Everywhere he took Ruth there was this wonderful sense of togetherness and adventure. Everywhere she was accepted as his woman. If marriage were mentioned at all, it was only to disparage it as an antiquated bourgeois institution.

Ruth introduced Hugo to her brother Max. They took to each other immediately. 'But keep quiet about him at home,' Max advised her.

It was not easy. Ruth loved her parents and wanted their approval in the way they approved of her brother, who was training to be a doctor. It was never openly admitted, but Ruth knew quite well that her parents thought Max was more important than her, simply because he was male. The best she could do as far as they were concerned was to find herself a husband they liked. She was frustrated at being made to feel inadequate in all sorts of unstated ways. It made her say 'I'm not stupid, you know!' far too often. She had tried to do the right thing with the school doctor but, yes, the parents had probably been right there, he would have been a boring husband. How ghastly if she'd married him and never met Hugo!

Hugo was everything Ruth had ever hoped for. Everywhere he'd touched her she felt a golden glow. Her hands tingled with the feel of his skin, rough in some places and unbelievably smooth in others. When they made love, she would massage his back right down to his flat bottom, so unlike hers which stuck out rather unfashionably. Then he'd turn over and make love to her again, and she would forget everything except that she was fully alive – forget who was who, they were so completely one. If ever she believed in God, she believed in Him then, in those moments of absolute letting go, every last shred of inadequacy dropping from her. It beat going to synagogue!

But as soon as she got back to the Friedrichstrasse from a blissful occasion with Hugo, going up the backstairs like the maid, managing a large key without making it squeak, the whole business of inventing a life for herself acceptable to the parents would begin again. She did not really want to have to pretend; she would toss and turn at three or four in the morning, working out something plausible in case they asked questions. It never occurred to her that she could leave home and find some little room she could afford out of her salary. She knew that Hugo could not afford to set her up, a phrase she hated anyway. She would stay free in relation to him, even if she could not free herself from her parents' money. There was plenty of it, after all, and she sometimes felt impatient with the way it was spent. Everything had to be top quality and guaranteed to last for all eternity.

'Those'll come in for you and your children some day,' her mother would say, pointing to stacks of unused sheets and towels done up in shiny red silk ribbons. When Ruth did not respond – how could she say she did not particularly want children? – Elisabeth was quick to add, 'Of course, you'll want to choose your own things when you get married; tastes change, I know' – meaning that perhaps she might like to have her sheets done up in blue silk ribbons.

Ruth managed on remarkably little sleep, buoyed up by one day's excitement and looking forward to the next. She loved her teaching and got on well with the girls. In fact, life was being exactly what she wanted it to be and, apart from the money, it was a life she had made for herself. The parents would never have allowed her to go in for gym, but once it was a *fait accompli* they had come round. They would come round to Hugo as well. Ruth's heart beat faster – he was another *fait accompli* without any of the hoo-ha of a wedding ceremony.

Ruth did not have the very least yearnings for veils and bridesmaids and the whole Jewish palaver under the Chuppe. She had been to a couple of Orthodox weddings where, after the ceremony the men had danced with the men and the women with the women in separate rooms, bride and groom only being allowed out together at the end of the celebrations. She must remember to tell Hugo – it would make him laugh.

Theodor looked at his daughter on a morning when she had only had four hours sleep and said, 'You've got circles under your eyes, are you quite well?' The concern in his voice made her feel again that she would like to tell her parents everything that had been happening to her – to say she was very, very well and to tell them why. But Max was frowning at her, so she stuffed the last bit of breakfast roll into her mouth, swallowed black coffee much too hot and jumped up.

'An early night tonight, I hope!' Theodor said.

'I'm not sure what I'm doing,' she mumbled, though she knew very well – she was going to a reception at the Russian Embassy with Hugo.

Dashing out of the dining room, she put on a black velvet cloche hat and a coat with rather bold checks, the sort of pattern everyone said was wrong for someone as small as her, which was why she had bought it. In fact, it suited her well.

'Put on galoshes, it'll be slippery underfoot; don't forget, it's February!' Elisabeth shouted.

But Ruth had gone.

On her way to the school where she taught, she tried to plan the rest of her day. Hugo was going to meet her at Rudi's, but he could not get there before eight. Perhaps she could get there a bit earlier to change. Rudi wouldn't mind, and it wouldn't even matter if he wasn't there; he had given her a key. There was always the risk she might run into Ferdinand or, worse still, Bella – Rudi's studio was quite close to their flat in the Savignyplatz. So far that had not happened. Ruth thought Ferdinand an absolute creep, though they hardly ever saw him now that Aunt Magda was dead. There was something distinctly odd about her dying like that, flourishing one day, dead the next. When she'd mentioned it to Hugo, he'd shrugged his shoulders and said,

'These things happen, you know.'

Ruth had stopped pestering him to invite her to his room.

'It's not up to much,' he'd told her, 'just a bachelor den – decent landlady who gives me breakfast; I supply cherry jam made by my mother, fruit from our trees at home.' There was a touch of nostalgia in Hugo's voice when he talked about their cherry trees.

Ruth could not imagine Hugo's home in a tiny Thüringen village, his father a stonemason who kept pigs and killed them himself. 'I'll take you there one day,' he had said, but Ruth did not respond to that any more than she had responded to her mother's piles of pristine bed linen.

When she got back to the Friedrichstrasse after her day's teaching, she ran a very hot bath and put some dark green pine essence into the water. It was her father's, but she loved the tangy smell; it didn't seem specifically masculine – why shouldn't women smell of pine? Besides, it was good for the muscle tone and, anyway, she was going to spray herself with *Quelques Fleurs* immediately she got out of the bath. Hugo had given her a cut glass scent bottle with a pale blue tasselled puffer – he did know the kind of thing she liked!

She got out a new pair of salmon pink *crêpe de chine* camiknickers with a black lace inset over the left breast. The silk felt delicious against her skin, but they were the very devil to do up. As for undoing the gusset when you needed to go to the lavatory... She clipped on suspenders and rolled on white silk stockings, stepped into patent leather shoes with heels a centimetre higher than the ones she wore during the day. That extra centimetre boosted her confidence. She clacked up and down the bedroom and got out a dark blue Cossack style dress with a yellow turn-down collar that set off her wavy black hair. She knew that Hugo would love her in it and that it was just the thing to wear to the Russian Embassy. She had decided it was too complicated to try and change at Rudi's; she would just pop her head in to say goodbye to the parents on her way out – she really did not have to say exactly where she was going: after all, she was a fully fledged adult!

Elisabeth was writing a letter, Theodor reading the paper.

'Na. Puppchen...' he said.

It made Ruth feel ridiculous and at the same time cosseted.

'She looks better than this morning, doesn't she?' Elisabeth said, and Theodor nodded.

Ruth wished they had noticed that she'd rouged her cheeks. It was so easy to fool them!

Though she was quite early, she picked up a taxi to Rudi's studio and tipped the driver generously, because he'd given her an appreciative once-over. She found Rudi struggling with his black tie and tied the bow for him, enjoying the closeness of his taut body. Then the phone rang. It was Hugo to say he was held up;

he'd meet them at the embassy. Ruth felt put out. Just like her father, always ringing up to say he'd be late. Then she couldn't help grinning to herself because, really, it was hard to think of anyone less like Theodor than Hugo!

Rudi opened a bottle of champagne. They clinked glasses. 'Here, I want to show you something!'

He produced a portfolio and with great care unwrapped layers of tissue paper. Ruth enjoyed watching his long elegant fingers.

'Look!' He held up a small black and white drawing with the caption 'Akte im Walde'. 'It's the original, from a 1918 issue of *Die Aktion*, quite a find!'

Ruth put her head to one side. What she saw were crude white curves and crescent shapes against black splodges.

'What's it supposed to be?' The word 'Akte' made her look for naked figures but she could not discover any.

'Look, look carefully…' He outlined certain shapes with his little finger, until it dawned on Ruth those were meant to be naked women.

'I can see you don't think much of it!' Disappointed, Rudi put the drawing back into the portfolio. 'It's by Karl-Luis Heinrich-Salze. But guess what – that's a woman really, Katharine Heise. Astonishing, eh?'

'Interesting,' Ruth said.

She wished she could have liked the drawing. Rudi was beginning to make her feel out of her depth.

They downed another glass of champagne, then Rudi flung a coat over his shoulders and they went out to hail a taxi.

Hugo waved as they drew up at the embassy. He looked terrific in evening dress.

Even more than going out with him, Ruth enjoyed her times alone with Hugo. Rudi often left them to themselves in his studio; Hugo would talk about Darwin, about Havelock Ellis, about the Hirschfeld Institute for Sexual Research. She never minded asking him to explain things if she didn't quite understand them. Unlike Rudi, Hugo never made her feel uncomfortable.

Their lovemaking achieved greater and greater erotic intensity. Afterwards, lying back on Rudi's wide couch, chain-smoking gold-tipped cigarettes, Hugo would sometimes talk about his childhood in Thüringen; about his father who had beaten him when he was a boy and had not forgiven him for joining the Communist party; about his mother who could barely read; about his young brother who was better with his hands than with his head; about his sister whose fiancé had been killed in the war.

'Tell me about the war!' All Ruth knew was that Hugo had been buried in a trench and had had to dig himself out.

'I don't want to talk about it, except to say that it's up to us to see that it never happens again! You've no idea...' He stubbed out his cigarette.

Ruth ran her hand along the scar on his back. 'Does it still hurt?'

'Sometimes, when it rains.' Then he added, 'But now I've got you, I shan't feel it so much!' He stroked her shiny black hair and looked into her dark brown eyes. 'What's so good about you,' he went on, 'is that I can take you anywhere! You fit in wherever we go!'

'I do when I'm with you!'

Life in the Friedrichstrasse seemed remote.

Hugo would not take her to the Communist anti-war demonstration because he was afraid there might be violence from the Nazis, as well as from their own people – it was difficult to hold them back. In fact, things passed off quietly. But when he told Ruth he was going to the Sportpalast to hear the ghastly Gauleiter Goebbels, she insisted on going with him.

'We've got to know what those idiots are up to, but I must say Goebbels has got a hope thinking he can fill the Sportpalast!'

In the event, there were ten thousand people. Hugo waved to some of them. 'Quite a few of ours here,' he said.

'But hardly any women!' Ruth was pleased to be one of the few.

Goebbels limped onto the platform and seemed to swallow them up with his enormous bellowing mouth. His rabid oratory almost lifted him off the ground and the audience with him.

'Actually, what was he on about?' Ruth asked when the applause had died down and people were moving away in a trance-like state.

'Slogan after vapid slogan, one cliché after another. But he's no fool. The joke is, he started off a Marxist!'

Some of the comrades came up to Hugo. 'What did you make of all that?' they wanted to know.

Hugo said again, 'He's no fool!' He added, 'But then, neither are we!'

They laughed. 'Come on, Hugo, let's go for a beer!'

Then they noticed Ruth. 'Bet you're not a beer drinker,' one of them said to her.

'Of course I drink beer,' she insisted, going red.

The boys moved off. 'See you around, Hugo,' they shouted.

'So you can't take me everywhere after all!' Ruth said.

'Wait until they're in love.' Hugo hooked his arm through hers.

He bought her a copy of the new women's magazine *Die Dame*.

'Look at that!' Ruth pointed to an advertisement for Vogue perfume; when they passed a perfumerie, he went in and bought her a bottle.

It was the acme of luxury in its green, gold and black drum. What would the comrades think of that?

> 'Man lebt ja nur so kurze Zeit
> Und ist so lange tot!'

Hugo began to sing, and together he and Ruth skipped along the pavement not caring who stared at them.

Soon after that they went to the opening of Brecht's *Dreigroschenoper*. It was not quite the glorious occasion they had hoped for, because Peter Lorre and Helene Weigel were ill and Lotte Lenya's name had been left off the programme. But the house rose to Weill's 'Mackie Messer', and they went back to Rudi's studio humming.

Hugo wrote a glowing review of it, one of a sheaf of raves, except for the Nazi one which called it an absolute nothing.

'It's the fool who wrote that who's an absolute nothing!' Hugo said.

They also went to Piscator's production of *Der Gute Soldat Schweik*. Ruth didn't enjoy that as much as the Brecht. Afterwards Hugo, who liked to see her sparkle, said, 'I'll take you *somewhere!*'

'Somewhere' was the Eldorado in the Motzstrasse. Ruth's eyes nearly fell out of her head. There were beautiful people everywhere concealing their gender behind make-up, with one or two unmistakeable men wearing nothing but bow ties and bathing trunks.

'Those two have wandered in by mistake,' Hugo told her.

'And what about us?' Ruth enquired.

But there were other couples making a hedge of spectators.

One of the beautiful transvestites got up and began to sing in an engaging falsetto:

> 'Eine Mietzekatze hat se
> Aus Angora mitgebracht
> Und die hat se hat se
> Mir gezeigt die ganze Nacht…'

Sometimes Hugo felt a twinge of guilt because he was neglecting his pals in the Party. In fact, the only friend he saw at all regularly now was Rudi, who was still letting them use his studio, accepting any press tickets Hugo could dole out.

Rudi was far from being one of the comrades. He liked nosing around galleries and auction houses, indulging his good taste and perceptive eye with a pretty inexhaustible cheque book. Occasionally, he stretched a canvas of his own.

'I know mine's minor stuff, very minor,' he would say.

He and Hugo knew each other far too well for Hugo to contradict him. But Rudi managed quite a passable pastel sketch of Ruth and Hugo. She wore a primrose yellow linen dress with a short pleated skirt and royal blue trimmings; Hugo wore a pullover with brilliant orange, brown and blue stripes.

'Marvellous colours!' Rudi said.

'Concentrate on our faces,' Hugo told him.

Rudi caught them looking at each other with total adoration. But it was the last time Ruth would look quite like that.

To her dismay, she found she was pregnant. She had given herself so completely to the newfound ecstasies, it had never for a moment entered her head that they might lead to a baby. How could she go on being her wonderful new self in midnight cafés and dawn bars with a bulging belly? How could she go on being her professional self in the gym?

The first person she told was not Hugo, but her young aunt Hannah. They met at Krantzler's.

'Now you've gone and done it!' Hannah said. She had gone quite red. On no account would she be instrumental in allowing history to repeat itself – not that Ruth knew how Magda had died. 'What are your parents going to think of a penniless journalist for their son-in-law?'

'Son-in-law? You must be joking! Hugo... I... we... don't believe in marriage! Out of date institution!'

'Babies aren't though, are they?' Hannah spoke sharply.

'But I don't want to...'

'Want to or not, that seems to be what's happening to you, isn't it?'

Ruth's mouth turned down. Her chin began to tremble.

Hannah put a hand over Ruth's. 'You must tell Hugo. He's a decent sort of chap, isn't he?'

Of course he was. Still, he was taken aback. Hugo had not intended to start a family. He was captivated by Ruth's spontaneity, her gift for giving herself to the moment; she was the sort of girl he had always dreamt of and then been lucky enough to find, but...

'We'll go and see your parents,' he said. 'It'll be all right; don't worry!'

He took her to the newly opened Theater am Schiffsbauerdamm to cheer her up.

'I'd like you to meet a friend of mine,' Ruth said to her parents. Unable to hold back any longer, with tears streaming down her cheeks, she told them she was pregnant.

Her mother's reaction amazed her. Elisabeth took a lace-edged monogrammed handkerchief out of her pocket and wiped away Ruth's tears. 'We'll just say it's premature; it doesn't have to be a grand wedding.'

Theodor took Ruth's hand. 'Are you feeling well, child? No morning sickness?' He stroked her hair.

It made Ruth feel so odd to be called 'child' when she was about to have one herself. Where was the father who had forbidden her to marry the school doctor? The parents hadn't begun to ask about the baby's father.

The three of them sat on the green plush drawing room sofa, Ruth wedged tightly between Theodor and Elisabeth. They were very quiet; it was a soft and healing silence.

Ruth could see Hugo was not at his best when he came to the Friedrichstrasse clutching a bunch of chrysanthemums for Elisabeth. Theodor was formal and fiddled with his watch chain. Elisabeth did her best to put Hugo at ease with generous slices of cake. Ruth was willing him not to say he didn't believe in marriage.

Presently, Theodor got up and invited Hugo into the study.

Elisabeth stroked Ruth's hand. 'It'll all be settled. I can see your Hugo is a good man!' The way her mother said 'your Hugo' made Ruth feel safe.

'Max likes him,' she said.

Elisabeth did not show how surprised and disappointed she was that her son had known all about Hugo while she and Theodor had not. What she said was,

'We'll have to think about the layette.'

Ruth scarcely knew what that word meant.

Theodor and Hugo came out of the study. 'How soon can you manage the wedding breakfast?' Theodor asked his wife.

Later, lying on Rudi's couch surrounded by abstract paintings, Hugo said to Ruth, 'We won't have to come here any more. We'll have a flat of our own. Your father's a generous man.'

He put his hand on Ruth's stomach in a new, unerotic way.

She removed it. She did not want to begin thinking about the baby yet.

Ruth looked charming on her wedding day in ivory shantung and a wreath of tiny yellow roses in her jet black hair. She felt most peculiar, unreal. Hugo, with a yellow rosebud in his buttonhole, his bow tie slightly askew, had his hand on her shoulder. 'It's all right: no one can see you're pregnant – it doesn't show in the least,' he whispered.

Grandmother Laetitia was there at the reception in the Friedrichstrasse, still wearing grey suede gloves. Great aunt Rebecka eyed her condescendingly. Ferdinand showed up; he had a pretty good idea what this rushed and totally unsuitable wedding was about. Luise held her father's hand; Bella had the twins in tow; Stephanie followed behind. Elisabeth gave her a kiss – how lovely the girl looked when her face lit up! she had the same dark eyes as Ruth. Richard came with Beate, both looking well and prosperous. Hermann and Hannah were a little late.

'And Eduard?' Elisabeth looked astonished they had not brought their son.

'Put him in the icebox for the day!' said Hermann, who loved teasing his serious sister-in-law.

He shook Hugo warmly by the hand; it was good to have another Gentile in the family – he would soon forget those lefty ideas now he was a family man. Hermann kissed Ruth on both cheeks; she did look pretty.

The twins recited a poem which Ferdinand had composed for the occasion. God, Mercy and Blessing occurred frequently in it, though he had been tactful enough to omit any reference to Jesus Christ. Hugo caught Max's eye; the brothers-in-law winked at each other.

Hugo's Thüringen family were not there, but Rudi was, as well as Hugo's more presentable journalist colleagues. There was also a sprinkling of comrades, all in Sunday best. Elisabeth enjoyed plying them with black caviar rolls and oyster mayonnaise and thought them altogether agreeable; her fears about Ruth falling in with the wrong set had been quite unfounded. She was sorry that Hugo's parents, brother and sister had not come; Ruth had referred to them as country bumpkins, but that was neither here nor there – Hugo was surely not ashamed of his family! Elisabeth did not dwell on the fact that the wedding was what people called a 'shotgun' affair; she felt really delighted at the prospect of becoming a grandmother.

She kept a careful eye on Laetitia, who was patting Hugo's cheek with her gloved hand. He, the yellow rose in his lapel shedding some of its petals, was beaming all over his face. What could Laetitia be saying to him?

'I like the look of you, young man,' was what she was saying, 'though I can't remember your name. But you'll be a tonic in this family!'

Hugo thanked her for kind words and went to ask Ruth who she was. 'She's my mad grandmother Laetitia; leave her alone!'

'She didn't strike me as particularly mad. Said nice things to me!'

'She's got a past,' Ruth said, though she had no very clear idea exactly what Laetitia's past amounted to. Vaguely she remembered Hannah beginning to say something about it years before but never quite coming to the point. Now Laetitia was treated like a piece of superfluous antique furniture.

Theodor tapped his champagne glass with a pearl-handled fruit knife and people stopped talking. He had spent days thinking about what he was going to say at his daughter's reception; he wanted to be totally genuine on such a momentous occasion. It was not easy. If he were completely honest he would have to say that he would have preferred a well-heeled Jewish son-in-law in a reputable profession with moderate political views and a family one would be pleased to know. Above all, he would have preferred a son-in-law who had not presumed on honeymoon rights for several months before the wedding. In spite of that, Theodor had seen to it that the flat Ruth and Hugo had found in Steglitz was furnished in style. Things could have turned out worse: Hugo could have backed out of marrying Ruth; another abortion in the family so soon after poor Magda was out of the question, though these things could be arranged and were sometimes the best way out if seen to early enough – not necessarily life-threatening at all. Theodor did not have cast-iron views on the sanctity of unborn life, but to acquire a grandchild that only had one parent struck him as absolutely unacceptable: he did have cast-iron views on that. So he concentrated on the fact that he liked Hugo better every time he saw him.

None of these thoughts were suitable for a wedding speech. He had scribbled a few notes which he pulled out of his pocket, but as he looked at Hugo and Ruth standing with their arms round each other, everything he had thought out so carefully went out of his head and he simply said, 'Long life and all happiness to both of you,' and clinked glasses with Elisabeth.

During the last months of her pregnancy, Ruth read an unusual amount. Elisabeth lent her the copy of *Buddenbrooks* that Theodor had given her years ago – Thomas Mann had just got the Nobel prize. Hugo had given Ruth the complete works of Gorki, but she found him a bit long-winded. Ferdinand had given them Rilke's poems, which Ruth found pretty incomprehensible, except for the one about the round-about in the Luxembourg Gardens with the refrain, 'Und dann and wann ein weisser Elefant'. What she enjoyed most was the novel by Thomas Mann's less famous brother Heinrich, *Professor Unrath*; having seen it in its film version, *Der Blaue Engel*, made it all come to life again for her.

 The baby inside her was very much coming to life as well. Ruth's labour pains started before she had finished the novel. It was a long and strenuous labour and, in the end, to her regret, Laura was born by Caesarean section.

 Laura was a large, bald baby, more like Hugo than Ruth in physique. It would be hard to pretend that she was premature. The nanny, carefully vetted by Elisabeth, who had moved into the Steglitz flat with them, held Laura up and said, 'What a corker! You can tell she's a real love child!'

 Laura was an easy baby. She was put on the bottle almost straight away – Ruth did not have enough milk to satisfy so lusty an infant; besides, she wanted to get herself back into trim as soon as possible. She could hardly wait to get back to the school gym. 'Don't be in such a hurry; the child needs you even if you aren't feeding her,' Elisabeth said.

 'But Minna's the perfect nanny!'

 Ruth felt quite ready too to go back to her old life with Hugo, but to her surprise he was not quite so ready to take her along with him. 'Our daughter needs you,' he said kissing her on the top of her head. It was as if he were in collusion with Elisabeth. Reluctantly, Ruth agreed to delay going back to her teaching.

 The family celebrated Laura's first birthday in the Friedrichstrasse. After they had sung 'Hoch Soll Sie Leben' and blown the candle out, talk turned to the new Chancellor Brüning and the fact that the Nazis had gained a catastrophic number of seats in the Reichstag – from a mere dozen to a hundred and seven.

'Better than a hundred and seven Communists!' Ferdinand said.

Hugo went red. 'Have you any idea what miracles they've achieved in Russia?' he asked as mildly as he could manage.

'You can't trust them!' Ferdinand and Hermann said together, and Hermann added, 'Hitler's a world class politician now; people have started calling him "Unser Führer"!'

'Without asking where he's going to lead – namely straight into another war!' Hugo got angry.

'His propaganda cuts more ice than your lot does!' Hermann was not going to be shut up.

Hugo said nothing more for the moment. Two or three friends of his had suddenly disappeared and surfaced completely cowed after a spell in a concentration camp with common criminals. Did Hermann really think Hitler was good for the country? Did they have a Nazi in the family? So all he added was, 'You know in Russia women are being given absolutely equal rights with men. Teddy Thälmann wants to do the same here.'

Before the women round the table had time to comment, there was a wail from the far corner of the dining room, where Laura had been sleeping in Ruth's old cradle. It was Elisabeth who rushed to pick her up.

'Time to take her home to Steglitz,' Hugo said and took his daughter from Elisabeth.

'What are we doing this evening?' Ruth asked.

'Having a nice quiet night at home,' Hugo said.

Ruth pouted.

'Enjoy your lovely child!' Theodor said to her and, although he smiled as he said it, there was a hint of sternness behind the words.

Quite often Ruth would arrive at the Friedrichstrasse and leave Laura with Elisabeth.

'I need time to myself,' she would say abstractedly and rush out again into the taxi she had kept waiting.

Elisabeth had qualms but said nothing.

77

She was quite right to have qualms, for the taxi would be taking Ruth to the very place where she and Hugo had first made love. Now she was making love with Rudi.

Ruth did not pretend to herself that she had found the real thing with Rudi, though he was very attractive and no longer made her feel embarrassed. Besides, she continued to believe in free love, even if Hugo did not – believed in it and needed it.

She was angry with Hugo for treating her like a conventional wife – for preventing her from going back to her job which had now been given to someone else. She had enough erotic energy for a lover and a husband. Anyway, Hugo now seemed more interested in his little daughter than in his wife. All too often, he would come home from work at the paper dead tired, go to bed early and start to snore the minute his head touched the pillow. He had taken on a good deal of freelance work so as not to be indebted to Theodor for everything.

'Wouldn't have been necessary if I'd gone back to teaching,' Ruth told him several times a week.

'No wife of mine has to go out to work,' Hugo would say and stroke her cheek.

Ruth would push his hand away.

She hadn't wanted to be his wife. He seemed to have forgotten that marriage was an out-of-date institution. Well, she had not, even if he did come home expecting a hot meal on the table every evening. Not only that, he liked to know when he left in the morning what they were going to eat in the evening. Ruth would say the first thing that came into her head – chicken with Hollandaise sauce maybe – there was bound to be a recipe for it in the cookery book Elisabeth had given her. But after a session with Rudi, there was only just time to pick Laura up from the Friedrichstrasse and buy a couple of smoked flounders if she wanted to be back in Steglitz before Hugo. He loved flounders, she knew. Laura, who was now walking and talking and making an intelligent nuisance of herself, would want to stay with her granny and made a great hullabaloo when Ruth just picked her up and bundled her into a taxi. She would still be yowling when Hugo arrived.

'Nanu?' he would ask and pick her up. Laura would go instantly quiet.

Ruth could have killed her. When she put the cold flounders on the table, Hugo pushed them away.

'What the hell are these?' he yelled. He picked the fish off the plate, opened the window and flung them out onto the pavement.

He had come home exhausted and discouraged. The news was terrible. The Nazis were responsible for one political murder after another, and nothing was being done about it. In all likelihood, they would gain even more seats in the Reichstag.

Hugo apologised to Ruth, who was sobbing uncontrollably clutching a recalcitrant Laura. He tried to explain the reasons for his black mood, and over a glass of Sekt Ruth began to cheer up. She had no conscience whatsoever about her affair with Rudi, who was discretion personified, and she was still fond of Hugo, especially when he wasn't on about dreary politics.

They would make love on such evenings with almost the old abandon. But Ruth was determined not to put up with another flounder flinging scene.

Ruth and Hugo and Laura went as usual for Sunday lunches with Theodor and Elisabeth and Max. Max was a qualified doctor now, working in a fever hospital. When he managed to get time off for Sunday lunch in the Friedrichstrasse, he would bring his fiancée with him. Theodor did not consider that the dowry she was likely to bring would measure up to what Max would need to set himself up in practice, but he could quite see what had made his son fall for this pretty, lively Jewish girl.

They all enjoyed Elisabeth's roast chicken with Leipziger Allerlei, a mixture of peas, carrots, asparagus and mushrooms. There was lemon soufflé for pudding; then the maid would bring in the electric coffee-maker, and Laura was allowed to turn on the little tap – she loved watching the coffee trickle into the rose-bordered Meissen cups. Elisabeth would get out some chocolate-covered marzipan and pop a little piece of it into Laura's mouth; Laura would snuggle up to her granny. Grandparents, parents and uncle would all beam at her.

'Won't be long before she's drinking coffee with us!' Theodor said.

But long before Laura had got to like coffee, Max suddenly

died, overnight. He had caught infantile paralysis from one of his patients.

Elisabeth was shaken to the core of her being. Her son – her only son! Nothing, nothing would ever make her happy again. How could God allow… The all-knowing, benevolent God in whom she had believed all her life had covered His face. Elisabeth did not think she would ever see it again.

Theodor paced up and down in his study wondering what sin he had committed to bring such a terrible punishment. But God's face had hidden itself from Theodor too. He could do nothing but sigh and, when he looked at his grief-stricken wife, could not prevent tears from running down his face.

Ruth too was shattered. She felt lost without her brother, the only person in her life with whom she had been able to be entirely open. She had even confided her affair with Rudi to him.

Hugo wrote a moving poem in Max's memory. But his personal feelings were being eroded by the ever worsening political situation… The Nazis now had almost two hundred seats in the Reichstag. Hugo could hardly bear meeting Hermann at the Friedrichstrasse; Hermann was so sure things were looking good for Germany.

Ferdinand took a more measured view. He had been deeply shocked that the Deutsche Christen had pro-Nazi leanings. Trying to put a picture of Hitler on the high altar of the Gedächtniskirche was overstepping the mark by several degrees. Ferdinand felt considerable sympathy for Pastor Jakobi, who had got into a fight with the rabid Pastor Hauk about it. Jakobi belonged to the Dahlem Group, with pastors Niemöller and Bonhoeffer. Ferdinand had no doubt which was the path to true spirituality. How could anyone calling themselves Christian join those mindless Nazi slogan-chanters, who prided themselves on their pagan roots?

Ferdinand made a point of going to Max's funeral at the Weissensee Jewish cemetery. That young man's death had touched him deeply. How could a just God, Jewish or Christian… but that kind of questioning was sinful. God's ways were inscrutable; you accepted them with humility.

Hermann and Hannah sent flowers to Weissensee and apologies for their absence – their young Eduard had the measles.

Hugo was strangely moved by the Hebrew prayers. They would make no difference to the disintegrating corpse in the coffin; it would rot away with all the others in the cemetery. But he could not help seeing how the prayers sustained Theodor and Elisabeth. And Ruth was leaning against him in the old trusting way.

The day after the funeral, he tried to take her to a showing of the film of Remarque's novel *Im Westen nichts Neues*. If that did not stop men from ever fighting each other again, nothing would. But when they got to the cinema, there was a picket line in front of it. The film could not be shown.

'Pacifist pigs!' the picketers shouted.

'This cannot go on!' Hugo was outraged.

But it did.

Ruth, still raw with grief over her brother's death, needed to get away from everything and everyone, including herself, though she could hardly formulate that thought, she was so crushed. She did not enjoy being with her little daughter, who was much happier with her granny. Hugo, afraid that his job on the paper was threatened, spent even more time picking up odd jobs. There was still the occasional reception to which Ruth insisted on being taken, but it took more and more Sekt to give her the sensation of being fully alive.

She had got fed up with Rudi – he talked too much about new movements in art and that perhaps there was a general tendency away from the abstract. Ruth did not care one way or the other. Instead of helping to eke out Hugo's dwindling income, she spent some of the allowance Theodor still gave her on new clothes and started another affair with someone she picked up at one of those parties – no one very special, but he had an Opel sports car in which he whizzed her about.

This time Hugo found out. It was Rudi who tipped him off – he was miffed that Ruth had stopped coming to his studio and knew quite well who his successor was.

Rudi had never seriously thought about marriage for himself, but he was not quite sure how far a married woman with a child should take her enthusiasm for free love.

'Are you looking after that young wife of yours?' he asked Hugo pointedly. 'Doesn't do to let politics take over too completely!'

'Well...' Hugo admitted that he had rather been neglecting Ruth.

Without mentioning that he had enjoyed himself with her, Rudi told Hugo with whom Ruth was having an affair.

When Hugo confronted her, Ruth did not deny it. 'It's because you've ruined my life!' she yelled at him.

'I've ruined your life!' Hugo yelled back

'All that talk about free love was so much hot air, wasn't it? All you want now is a Hausfrau – well, go and find one! And I thought you believed in equal rights for women, like your beloved Russians. But no, not for me, only for other women! I'm not allowed to be a teacher!'

Hugo stared at her. She looked very pretty, all pink and flushed. He could not believe that any mother of a young child would go to bed with a man who was not that child's father. So, getting a hold on himself, he asked quietly, 'And Laura?'

Ruth began to sob. She did not say that Laura too had ruined her life. But she had – Laura even more than Hugo.

Ruth wrung her hands and fell on the Persian rug which had come with all the other things Theodor and Elisabeth had given them. 'I want to die, to die!' she shrieked.

'Pull yourself together; we'll talk when you've calmed down'. Hugo left the room and walked out of the house.

He walked into the Steglitz Stadtpark. A group of brownshirts were shouting themselves hoarse: 'Clear the streets! Wake up Germany! Death to the Jews! Blood must flow! Smash the goddamned Jews' Republic!' Hugo waited for something about Communists, but they just went on chanting the same words over and over again.

Hugo's faith in Communist ideals, in the struggle for peace among nations, was as strong as ever. But his faith in the KPD, the German Communist Party, had taken a battering. *Die Rote Fahne*, to which he contributed regularly, had urged them all to be at the Bülowplatz in January when the NSDAP was honouring the young Nazi Horst Wessel, who had unfortunately been killed by a Communist. No one would have heard of either Horst Wessel or the misguided Ali Höhler who had killed him if the incident had not given Hitler a wonderful opportunity for his rabble-rousing propaganda. The SA in front of the Karl Liebknechthaus in the Bülowplatz far outnumbered the Communists, who were only represented by a few desperate unemployed. The Communist Party leader Thälmann did not even turn up; that was the real stab in the back. There were rumours that Stalin actually wanted Hitler in power! But did anyone really want peace? want it more than power? Hugo began to think out an article about power – personal and public. But who would print it?

It began to rain. He turned up his coat collar and made his way home. Thank God Laura was spending the night with her grandparents! He suddenly thought how odd it was that, long after one had stopped believing in any God, one went on invoking Him. As soon as his thoughts turned back to Ruth, hot waves of jealousy shook him. So his wife was giving someone else a good time! Couldn't leave it alone, could she!

'Where are you?' he shouted as he unlocked the front door.

No answer. He tried the bathroom door; it was locked.

'Come out of there, will you!'

He went on rattling the handle until he heard the bolt pushed back. Ruth emerged, her face covered in cream. She walked straight past him into their bedroom; a pillow and an eiderdown came flying out at him.

'Sleep on the couch; I never want to sleep in the same bed as you again!' Her voice was thick with suppressed sobs.

Hugo rather felt she had stolen that line from him. After all, wasn't it she who had been unfaithful to him? He felt pretty close to sobbing himself when he thought of losing Laura.

'And what about our Laura?' he asked as she was about to close the bedroom door in his face.

'Laura is perfectly safe and happy in the Friedrichstrasse,' Ruth told him, as if that were where she belonged.

And it was true. Laura was safe and happy with her grandparents.

Quite soon Ruth moved back with them herself. Nor would it

take long for the divorce to come through.

Elisabeth accepted it calmly – nothing could really touch her since Max had died. But Theodor was shocked. After all he had done for them! He was disappointed that having a child had not given Ruth a greater sense of responsibility.

'Hugo's agreed to say he's the guilty party,' Ruth told her parents.

'And is he?' Elisabeth asked her daughter.

Ruth said nothing.

'We'll discuss that later,' Theodor said.

He knew quite well that Hugo was not the guilty party, but he did not want to dwell on his daughter's insouciant way of life. He couldn't help sighing and wondering where he had gone wrong to deserve such... such... but all he could do was to sigh again and devote himself to his patients – there was a young man with severe stomach problems whom he seemed to be helping.

It would never have occurred to the young man that the Herr Doktor had problems of his own. Hard to believe he was a Jew – he seemed such a kind, intelligent man. He would certainly continue with the treatment, never mind what the Nazis said about Jews. Well, anyway, he would go on coming until the pains in his stomach had quite disappeared. They were much better already.

Little Laura sat at her grandparents' large dining-room table dropping brightly coloured boiled sweeties into her hot milk and watching it turn mauve or green. 'Divorce' was a new word in her vocabulary, a word she heard repeated over and over again in the conversations people thought she could not understand. She understood that it meant that her father and mother did not love each other any more, though they kept on telling her that, of course, they both still loved her and always would.

When her father said it, she believed him, but not when her mother said it. Lying in the twin bed which had been her father's in the Steglitz flat, Laura felt plunged into ice-cold dark loneliness. She slipped under the eiderdown, made a groove for herself and tried to go to sleep. But she could not. She wanted her Daddy; wanted to feel his cheek against hers, to hear his voice, just to know he was there. But he was not.

Nor could she get rid of the other new and nasty words that

kept cropping up in the adult talk: 'swastika', 'anti-Semitism', 'concentration camp'. The strangled voices in which they were said hardly left space for the words to come out. And whenever the radio was turned on, there was all that roaring: 'Sieg heil! Sieg heil! Sieg heil!'

VII

1933-1936: BERLIN & THÜRINGEN

Hitler was the new Chancellor.

Hugo arrived at the Friedrichstrasse out of breath.

'They're burning books, all the best...' He stopped for a quick cup of coffee and rushed out again.

Ruth had found a teaching job at a Jewish school in the Grunewald. Almost at once she got involved with the headmaster. He was called Klaus. Laura thought that was another ugly word.

Elisabeth, still in mourning black for Max, went on providing everything as always, but the light had gone out of her eyes. Very occasionally, they lit up a little when Laura put her arms round her neck and said, 'Granny, I do love you!'

The Reichstag went up in flames.

'They did it and now they're blaming us!' Hugo said.

Laura knew 'they' were bad and 'us' were good 'They' were the Nazis and 'us', when her father said it, were the Communists. She knew that when her granny and grandpa said 'us' it mean 'us Jews'. And yet they were all Germans, as well. She knew that, too. Those divisions troubled her. She wondered who would be her 'us' when she was grown up.

Hugo thought Laura was the best thing that had ever happened to him. He missed her terribly now he was back in the same old bed-sit with the same old landlady. He went to see his daughter in the Friedrichstrasse two or three times a week. He could not understand Ruth at all, though he missed her too. Perhaps the comrades were right – perhaps it did not do to put so much of oneself into personal relationships. He was badly in need of a change, a rest from inner and outer turmoil. He took a break and went to see his parents in their Thüringen village.

Hugo had not been home since he and his father had fallen out about his left wing politics, but he had had a letter from his sister Anna telling him that all was forgiven and that it was high time he came. He would have loved to take Laura – she ought to get to know her other grandparents – but it was just too awkward now that he and Ruth were divorced. In his village people did not get divorced: when you got married, you stayed married; 'for better or worse' meant exactly that. Besides, in the present political climate they were bound to think that it had something to do with Ruth's being Jewish, when that was the very last reason. The only Jew who had ever come to their village was the peddler who made his round twice a year selling everything from shiny buttons to cheap novelettes. As far as Hugo's family were concerned, that was what Jews were like – not that they had anything against old Moyses personally.

Hugo admitted to himself that he shied away from taking Laura to the house where he was born, with its tiny rooms and earth closet in the yard with pigs rootling about. What would his daughter think of all that after the opulence of the Friedrichstrasse? Maybe when she was a little older, he would take her.

He sighed as the train steamed through the gentle green Thüringen landscape. Under the present régime the outlook for journalists with left wing views was pretty bleak. It might not be long before he was reduced to writing little pieces like 'Ant-eating Butterflies' – that sort of thing. In truth, the prospect, apart from the fact that it would leave him strapped for cash, did not bother him so very much. If the war had not scotched his plans, he would have gone on to university to read natural history. That was the basic stuff of life, but no one ever got a lot of money for concentrating on the basic stuff of life. So he thanked his lucky stars for Theodor and Elisabeth. What would have become of Laura if it weren't for them?

He cheered up when he saw his sister waiting for him on the

platform at Sommerda. 'Not before time,' she said and hooked her arm through his as they walked to where she had left the horse and cart behind the station.

The cart was loaded with sacks of potatoes. 'Let me!' Hugo took the reins.

The cherry blossom was out, the blackbirds were singing, cowslips gleamed yellow in the sunshine. Anna put her hand over his. 'Just steer clear of politics and everything'll be fine!'

'You're sure?' Hugo was sceptical.

'Of course I'm sure, just don't rub father up the wrong way!'

'But look at all this!' Hugo pointed at the swastika flags waving among the cherry trees. 'I can't believe my eyes!'

'Hitler's birthday coming up,' Anna said.

They clattered over the cobbled market place, past the inn with the golden horse's head glinting above its door. That horse's head meant home.

The cart stopped outside their front door and Hugo's mother, wearing a long white apron, came out smiling. Hugo kissed her on the forehead, and for a moment she held him against herself – for a moment Hugo was a boy breathing in his mother's smell of earth, sweat and freshly baked bread.

The table was laid with the best blue and white china. Hugo sat in his old place by the window.

'Here are the men,' Anna said.

Hugo's father and brother Joachim came in. Joachim was carrying a large swastika flag. Hugo swallowed hard when he saw it.

'Well, son!' Hugo and his father shook hands.

'We'll go and wash,' Joachim said. He barely greeted his brother.

When they had cleaned up under the pump in the yard, they sat down and slurped their coffee, cooling it first in their saucers. Hugo's mother cut a yeast cake into generous slices.

Hugo felt them looking at him, uncertain what to expect of him. Only Anna had ever been to Berlin. As far as his mother was concerned, Berlin might as well be the other side of the ocean. She and her cronies used to think nothing of lifting their skirts along country lanes, planting their feet wide apart and making water while they went on chatting. He wondered if they still did that.

Hugo opened his briefcase. He had an ashtray with a replica of the Brandenburg Gate for his father, a cushion cover with 'Nur ein Viertelstündchen' embroidered on it for his mother, a bottle of 4711 cologne for Anna and a book about Berlin for Joachim. There was a second book, which he slipped back into the briefcase.

'What's that then, let's have a look!' Joachim stretched out his hand.

Hugo hesitated; he had promised to steer clear of politics. 'Oh never mind, it doesn't matter. Have a look at the Berlin book!'

'Come on, hand it over. It's not a bomb, is it!'

Hugo gave his brother the second book. It was Marx's *Das Kapital*. His father said, 'Give that to me!'

Anna looked accusingly at Hugo. 'This cake's delicious,' Hugo said to his mother.

'1 will not have that book in this house,' Hugo's father said.

'Have you ever read it?' Hugo asked him.

His father raised his voice. 'I have not and will not!'

'Well then, I'll just have it back,' Hugo said quietly. He did not, did not, want a row. He wanted a holiday.

His father held on to *Das Kapital*.

'I'll take your things upstairs,' Anna said. She had gone quite white.

'Hugo will not share a room with Joachim,' his father shouted. 'He can sleep in the summerhouse, and he can take his own things out there!'

'Father!' Anna looked at him aghast, but she could not breach the wall of prejudice.

Hugo could not restrain himself any longer. 'I shall be glad to get out of a house that is about to fly a swastika flag!' he shouted, wishing he sounded less pompous.

'But he's only just arrived,' his mother said. She was almost crying. That cut no ice with her husband. He crashed his fist on the table so that the china rattled.

'I stretched out my hand in friendship,' he bellowed, 'and what does he do? He tries to pervert his brother's mind with this Jewish communist filth!' He waved *Das Kapital* in the air. 'And then he insults our Führer's flag, a flag under which we shall at last be able to hold up our heads again!' he stopped for breath and then turned to his younger son. 'Come, Joachim, help me hoist it!'

Sounds pretty pompous himself, Hugo thought; that's where I get it from. He grabbed his things and walked out of the front door which he had only just entered.

As he stepped into the street, the front door of the house opposite opened and four small black ponies trotted out, followed by Herr Morgenroth, the coalman, who began hitching the ponies to a cart standing nearby. Hugo had helped to groom Herr Morgenroth's ponies when he was a boy and had earned the odd sack of coal for it. He crossed the road.

'Remember me?'

Herr Morgenroth looked startled, then clapped Hugo on the shoulder. 'Hugo, boy, good to see you! But where are you off to?'

'The summerhouse,' Hugo mumbled and could not stop himself from telling Herr Morgenroth what kind of a welcome he'd come home to.

'Jump up into the cart, we'll take you!'

The summerhouse smelt musty. An old camp bed was still there with a cold, damp mattress on it; no bed clothes. The oil stove was rusty; there were damp patches on the walls.

'This won't do – no one's been here for months; you can't stay here, Hugo boy!' Herr Morgenroth said.

Hugo could not remember when his own father had spoken to him with such affection.

'These damned politics!' Herr Morgenroth shook his head. 'As far as I'm concerned, the Führer will have to celebrate his birthday without a flag waving from my house. Ridiculous. Mind you, one has to admit...' And he went on to say how unemployment had virtually disappeared since Hitler had taken over, how good it was not to see all those beggars propping up the walls.

Hugo shrugged his shoulders. 'But people aren't allowed to think or say what they want; books get burnt. And what about the anti-Semitism?'

'Oh, he's out of order there, but you see, he needs a scapegoat for all the misery we've been through. But don't worry, all that'll settle down. The country can't do without its Jews. Everyone knows that's where the brains are. By the way, how's your wife?'

Herr Morgenroth clucked his tongue when he heard Hugo was divorced.

'Pity, what a pity!'

Hugo pulled a photograph of Laura out of his wallet. 'She's so bright!' he said with immense pride.

'Poor child!' Herr Morgenroth said.

That remark hurt Hugo more than anything else that had happened on this home-coming day. It had never occurred to him that his lovely daughter might be the object of pity in anyone's eyes, least of all in the eyes of someone as remote from her as Herr Morgenroth.

'Oh, she's well looked after; lives with her grandparents, they're very good to her…'

'I'm sure,' Herr Morgenroth said, 'but where will she belong later on?'

'To the human race, like the rest of us,' Hugo said, piqued.

Herr Morgenroth patted him on the shoulder. 'You know, Hugo, if you hadn't brought that book, everything would have been all right!'

'I wasn't going to give it to my brother; I promised Anna not to get into politics, but he more or less snatched it out of my hand!'

'I know your father was looking forward to having you back in the family. He wanted…'

'To have everything his own way, as always! No one's allowed to have an opinion that doesn't fit in with his. I looked forward to it as well, you know!'

'I'll get that sister of yours to bring some dry bedclothes and oil for the stove. Lovely girl she is; rotten shame her man got killed. Still, maybe God will send her someone else!'

'You still believe in God?' Hugo asked.

'Of course, my boy, and always will.'

'Hitler or no Hitler?'

'What's he got to do with it?' Herr Morgenroth was contemptuous.

Hugo saw him and the ponies off.

'All the best, Hugo. I hope you'll bring your little girl to see us soon!'

Hugo knew quite well that the trouble between himself and his father stemmed far less from their political differences than from the fact that he lived in his head and not in his hands; he had not followed the family tradition of becoming a stone mason. He cursed himself now for bringing that copy of Karl Marx.

In spite of the musty smell and the damp, he felt quite at ease in the summerhouse. He might even have suggested coming here himself; it was better than sharing with Joachim who would have regaled him with the latest village gossip – who had got whom pregnant, who would do the decent thing by their girls. Now there would be the additional tittle-tattle about who had and had not joined the Party. If only he could find a way of making his father and brother see through all that Heil-hoo-ha that made your chest swell and your brains shrink! But how? When they could point to decent wages, all he could do was look at his down-at-heel shoes...

He needed a beer. As he thought it, Anna arrived with just that. Their mother came in behind her clutching a feather bed.

'All this politics gone to their heads,' his mother said. 'And that flag is big enough to wrap right round the house! I hate all politics; splits up families and where does that get you?' She looked at Hugo with a mixture of reproach and affection because, after all, politics had gone to his head too.

Left, right, who cared?

'Are you going to apologise to your father?' she asked.

'For what?'

'For bringing that book!'

'Do you believe in muzzling people, in controlling their thoughts?'

Off he goes, she thought. It's no good, best leave it alone.

'He ought to apologise to me!' Hugo said.

Worse and worse.

Anna was pottering about making the summerhouse habitable. She lit the stove and soon had a kettle simmering on it.

They drank coffee out of enamel mugs in companionable silence, resentments ebbing away.

'This beats that acorn stuff we put up with during the war!'

His mother buried her face in the mug.

Hugo thought he saw tears mingle with the steam.

Once he got back to Berlin, Hugo looked up Rudi. When he complained to his friend that he was not getting enough work, Rudi told him to join the Party.

'If people like us join, things won't ever get too bad,' Rudi said, but Hugo thought they were too bad already.

There was the tiniest swastika in Rudi's lapel and the abstract paintings had disappeared from his studio walls.

'What happened to all the art?' Hugo asked as he was leaving. The couch had been replaced by two single beds, but he did not ask about that.

'That rubbish,' Rudi said, though he had the grace to blush. Then, with a grin that almost turned him back into his old self, he added, 'Made a pile out of them, though!'

At the Friedrichstrasse, Laura bounced into Hugo's arms. She rubbed her cheek against his and asked for a story. Elisabeth listened with them, laughing about a little girl who insisted on having everything coloured purple, including her bath water.

Later, when Theodor had joined them, they talked about the recently formed Jewish Cultural Association which they had been invited to join. 'Ghetto mentality,' Hugo said. 'Berlin hasn't had one of those for two and a half centuries!'

'Don't exaggerate; they're offering an excellent programme.' But Theodor was not as enthusiastic as he was trying to sound.

Theodor had been affronted by the fact that the announcement of a production of Schiller's *Die Räuber* had a big CANCELLED BY ORDER stamp over it. The government did not deem Schiller appropriate for Jewish audiences. Not long afterwards, Goethe was added to the proscribed list.

Theodor was somewhat reassured by what he read in *Der Schild*, the paper for Jews who had been in the army; there was a move to get them exemption from the anti-Jewish laws. But how outrageous that it was something for which they had to plead! Over 70,000 Jews had died for the Fatherland and now... Now Leo Baeck, a Jew Theodor had not heard of before, was urging all German Jews to unite. Surely that was ghetto mentality? What kind of future were they living towards?

He patted his little grand-daughter on the head. Laura leant her head against his stomach. 'You're fat, grandpa.'

'Comfortable, is it?'

'Very!'

Oh, by the time she was grown up, Hitler would be long forgotten. 'Come and sit on grandpa's knee!'

She climbed onto his lap. 'Do "This is how the ladies ride, this is how the gentlemen ride"...'

For the moment, politics were forgotten.

They went through the sliding doors into the rose-carpeted drawing room past the grand piano with its brocade cover. Laura could never resist passing her hand over that to feel the hard nobbliness of the fruit and flowers embroidered in metallic thread. 'Play something, grandpa, please!'

'Shall I?'

He took the cover off the piano, raised the lid, sat down and began to play Mozart's 'Rondo alla Turca'. Laura marched up and down making the china figurines in the rosewood vitrine tremble. As he played, Theodor felt convinced things would soon settle down again. Mozart was a great raiser of spirits; Theodor couldn't help feeling optimistic.

But his optimism took some knocks.

Röhm's S.A. were getting too big for their boots. With a sinking feeling, Theodor read the news that Hindenburg approved of Hitler's action in ordering the S.S. to shoot his old associate. Schleicher and his wife with nineteen others had also been shot; it was called 'state emergency defence'. Well, were the S.S. any better than the S.A.? True, there had been rumours, some of them substantiated, that Röhm's brownshirts had been behind a good many of the political murders...

Worse was to follow. Hindenburg died, the last figurehead who had had something in common with the old order. To people's amazement, Hitler had himself declared Supreme Head of State. The Army had to swear allegiance to the Führer. What had been the 'Reichswehr' became the 'Wehrmacht'.

On the Saturday following Hitler's inauguration as head of state, Theodor went to the Oranienburgerstrasse Synagogue. No one was going to pray for Hitler as they had for the Kaiser before his abdication, but Theodor wanted to find out how his friends in the congregation were reacting. After the service, they normally gathered for a chat outside; but today most people went straight home.

'Chin up, Theodor,' a lawyer friend of his said. 'As far as I'm concerned, we German Jews are totally bound up with the Fatherland. And now that he's got where he wanted to be, Herr Hitler will modify his policies.'

'Your words in God's ear!' Theodor said; then he too went home, where Elisabeth was waiting with a lunch of Wiener Schnitzel.

She took his hand. 'Sit down and eat, Schnucki,' she said. And he did.

The time had come to decide on a school for Laura. Elisabeth made sure Hugo was there when the subject came up. Laura could already read quite well and was bored with the Kindergarten run by a school friend of Ruth's where they did paper cut outs, wool embroidery on cards and modelled plasticine birds and beasts. Laura was not good with her hands, but she loved anything to do with words.

'She will have to go to a Jewish school.' Ruth was unexpectedly assertive.

Hugo nodded. 'It'll be best; we can't have her exposed to Jew baiting. I've seen the new laws. Every single subject on the timetable has to have an anti-Semitic slant. And you know, teachers and children are having to say "Heil Hitler" instead of good morning and so on. The Hitler Youth boys and the BDM girls are supposed to inform on anyone who...' Hugo did not need to finish the sentence.

'And to think that Hannah's boy, our nephew Eduard is...' Elisabeth did not need to finish her sentence either.

Eduard was in the Hitler Youth. He and Hermann hardly ever came to the Friedrichstrasse now, and they saw a good deal less of Hannah.

'You know what happened along the Kurfürstendamm, don't you?' Ruth said.

'You spend too much of your time on the Kurfürstendamm!' Theodor retorted sternly.

He did not want to hear the details of the anti-Semitic demonstration there. The papers had been full of it – 'Berlin Judenrein'. It was all too unspeakably painful. His family had lived in Berlin for over two hundred years.

'So it'll be the Auguststrasse school for Laura, won't it?' Elisabeth said. She was always the first to channel things back to normality as far as possible.

'Yes, and quite soon she'll be able to walk there by herself – there aren't any big roads to cross,' Ruth said and added: 'The sooner she learns to be independent, the better!'

'I shall take and collect her for the first year!' Elisabeth said anxiously. Hugo nodded gratefully.

Ruth had not finished with her political news. 'Have you heard what they intend doing with the mentally ill? They want to liquidate them!' Liquidate was not a word Ruth normally used, but it made her feel important in a macabre kind of way.

There was a heavy silence after she had said that – they were all thinking of Laetitia.

On Laura's first day at school, Hugo came round at 7.30 in the morning with a large bag of sweeties – raspberry drops, chocolate pastilles with hundreds and thousands on them, soft toffees, mauve and pink fondants, fruit jellies, all jumbled together. He put them into the enormous Schultüte Elisabeth had bought.

'Enjoy yourself, big girl,' he said and looked round for Ruth.

'Mummy didn't come home last night,' Laura said.

Holding her granny's hand, Laura went to school through the passage that led from the Friedrichstrasse to the Oranienburgerstrasse and then just a short way along to the Auguststrasse.

'I'll be there at the end of the morning.' Elisabeth watched Laura skip away with the other children, all clutching their cones full of sweeties.

Laura loved it at school. 'You know, we do Hebrew,' she told Hugo when he enquired what they'd been learning.

Ruth was hardly ever at home, but when Laura heard her mother's four staccato rings at the front door, she felt a hot rush of love and hugged her fiercely as she came in. Nearly always, that was followed by a sense of disappointment – something that should have happened and did not. Laura wasn't quite sure what.

Elisabeth was always there. 'Come and help me count the linen, my little goldfinch!' Her granny had such nice names for her.

They went down the long corridor at the end of which there was a large cupboard. Elisabeth would open it and take out bundles of sheets and pillow cases tied with red silk ribbons. Laura noticed that the bath towels and the drying up cloths were the same as they had had in Steglitz.

'Did you give Mummy those?' she asked, passing her grubby hands over them. 'I did, and if we're careful, there'll be enough left for you, too!'

'For me?'

'When you get married!'

Laura couldn't help smiling. Of course she wanted to get married, but she could not imagine to what sort of a person it might be.

There were two long, steady rings at the front door.

'It's him, it's Daddy!' Laura yelled and flew along the corridor through the dining room into the hall. She opened the front door and Hugo hugged her.

Elisabeth brought coffee and yeasty plumcake and a mug of milk for Laura. Theodor joined them between patients, wearing his white coat. Laura loved to see him in that; in fact, he never seemed quite real to her when he was not wearing it.

'How are things?' Theodor asked Hugo, who was looking tired and seemed to have lost weight.

Hugo shrugged his shoulders.

Elisabeth helped him to a second slice of cake and said, 'Stay for supper, won't you?'

Laura looked at her grandparents and her father and saw their faces go sad. Even though she was a schoolgirl now, she crept under the dining table. It was safe there with that roof over her head. If she tapped on it, they would laugh, but if she didn't, they might forget about her. She could hear what they were saying, though their voices were muffled by the folds of the tablecloth and she could not really understand what they were talking about. But the undertow of apprehension, the sense of dread, got through to her.

'Whatever happens here,' she heard her father say, 'and I'm afraid a lot more is going to happen that we won't like, you can always count on me. I shan't allow anyone to make me say black is white!'

Laura loved her father very much for saying 'You can always count on me'. Then she heard his fist crash down on the table.

'Things'll get worse before they get better. We simply have to hang on by the skin of our teeth. And you can count on me!' He said it again, almost ashamed to be saying it, but it had already become an act of courage and defiance for a non-Jew to visit Jews.

Laura could bear it no longer. She tapped her hand against the table top.

'Whatever can it be?' Hugo said. He felt five hot fingers scrabble up his trouser leg. 'It must be a mouse, or perhaps it's a squirrel!'

Laura emerged from under the table giggling. 'Let's play Ludo!'

She went over to the sideboard where there was a drawer full of games for her. They played, and Laura won.

Round about this time, Ferdinand called Luise and Stephanie into his study and at last told them who their real mother had been. He simply said she had died suddenly, tragically young.

'So it was all true!' Stephanie said. She felt immensely relieved; something inside herself fell into place.

Luise, who had just left school – it was this that had decided Ferdinand not to wait any longer – was not as moved as her sister. 'I shall go on thinking of Bella as my mother,' she said.

'Of course, of course.' Ferdinand put a hand on each of his daughters. 'Your mother, Magda, was a wonderful companion and colleague.'

He avoided any reference to the circumstances of her death. Then he unlocked a desk drawer and took out two photographs of Magda. Luise and Stephanie saw tears in his eyes.

'I loved her beyond words,' he whispered.

Stephanie put the photograph of her real mother up in her bedroom and stood looking at it for a long time.

Luise went to find Bella and put an arm round her. 'Papa has just told us about our mother. But you're much more real,' she said and kissed Bella on both cheeks. 'You've never minded about us being baptised Jews, have you?' she asked.

'Would I have married your father if I had?'

Bella felt warmed by the girl's affection. She did not go into the fact that marrying Ferdinand had meant a permanent rift with her parents – her father was now a high horse in the Nazi party. The twins, Lola and Frieda, came rushing in. They had both just joined the BDM and looked smart in their short brown jackets. So far no questions had been asked about their racial origins.

Stephanie was longing to leave school, to get away from home in the Savignyplatz. She knew that her family found her difficult. The twins were just plain nasty to her – wouldn't walk on the same side of the street as her because she looked so Jewish. Every night now before she went to bed she knelt in front of Magda's photograph and prayed for help. 'Let someone love me,' she prayed. Ferdinand too was feeling the need to be loved, and so father and daughter grew closer.

'The state is interfering more and more in church affairs.' he told Stephanie, 'and the Bekenntniskirche is threatening to break off relations with state run churches.'

'And?' Stephanie was not at all sure what that implied.

'And seven hundred clergymen of the Bekenntniskirche have been arrested for opposing racist laws, and various independent theological colleges have been closed down. There is nowhere safe left, nowhere at all!'

Stephanie went over to her father and held his hand in hers. 'We have to find safety inside ourselves,' she said. She had had to do that all her life.

'I shouldn't really worry you with such thoughts.' Ferdinand looked at her with opened eyes. He kissed her gently on the forehead, and she leant her head against his for a moment.

Luise had noticed that recently Stephanie and her father spent more time together than usual. It had something to do with going to church. Luise went to please her father, but Stephanie went because it really meant something to her. An all-powerful God made no sense at all to Luise; it was obvious to her that the only power which counted was held by people who had elbowed their way into positions of influence in all sorts of dubious ways. She decided that quite soon she would find an excuse to stop going to church. The break would come quite naturally when she left for Madrid to look after the children of a doctor's family, with whom Ferdinand had put her in touch.

On the day he had finally told his daughters who their real mother was, Ferdinand asked Bella to come to his bed for the first time in many months.

She came obediently. 'I'm glad the girls know about their mother at last; I hated all that pretending, you know!'

'It's not always easy to know where reality ends and pretence begins,' Ferdinand said, but that was beyond Bella. It was the kind of thing Magda would have taken him up on; they would have talked till dawn and then he would have made love to her – love, not an act of physical desperation. And yet he would be entirely lost without Bella now.

He stroked her hair and tried to think of something nice to say to her. He could not, but it did not matter because she had dropped off to sleep. He could not fall asleep, so he got up, sluiced his face in cold water and tiptoed out of the bedroom into his study.

He got out a notebook and pencil and waited for the first line of a poem which would express... express... he was not quite sure what. But as he waited in the silence of the night hoping for inspiration, the only image that came to him was of his father's enchanting smile. It was a long, long time since he had thought about Louis, the father whom he had never really got to know; but he could not turn that image into a poem.

He woke at dawn, his head slumped on the desk, a crick in his neck. Bella was just waking up when he got back to the bedroom. 'Couldn't sleep, may as well get to the lab early,' he said.

Bella jumped out of bed; it would not do to let him go out of the house without his roll and cup of coffee. But when he had finished his breakfast, Ferdinand suddenly said:

'No, I can't go in today!'

'Why ever not?'

'I just...'

Bella looked at his ashen face with concern. 'Well then, take the day off. You've been working too hard; spend the day with Luise – we won't be seeing her for a whole year once she's gone to Spain!'

'I can't; I must...' Ferdinand said and, although his legs felt like lead beneath him, he made himself get up.

'Your tie isn't quite straight.' Bella fiddled with it and, unusually, Ferdinand patted her cheek.

Life at the lab had become increasingly difficult. He had not yet ever said 'Heil Hitler' when he arrived in the mornings, and the omission was beginning to cause comment. Still, he thought, while his research was going so well they would leave him alone. He had sent off a paper summing it all up and was waiting to hear when it was to be published. His new assistant, a bright young man, was most enthusiastic about the work. He was also an enthusiastic Party member.

Although it was earlier than usual when Ferdinand arrived, the assistant was standing outside the laboratory door. 'Hallo there, are you locked out?' Ferdinand asked.

'Heil Hitler!' the assistant said.

'Yes, yes, let's get going.' Ferdinand tried to pass him.

'One moment please. Herr Doktor, the Director wants to see you!'

'Can't it wait? Are you sure he's arrived yet?'

'Yes, I'm sure and, no, Herr Doktor, it cannot. This way, if you please!' As if Ferdinand did not know the way, as if they were total strangers, the assistant with whom he had shared all his ideas, pointed to the other end of the corridor.

'Question of your antecedents, you know.' The Director was quite affable. 'Had this directive from the powers-that-be. Baptised Jews are just Jews in their book!' He scrutinised the bit of paper he was holding to hide his embarrassment. 'Hm, hm, you see: father Jewish, mother Jewish...'

'But...' Ferdinand had not taken the offered chair. 'What difference does my race or religion make to my research?'

'Don't follow the reasoning behind it all myself, but the long and the short of it is, and I can't see a way round it much as I'd like to, we'll have to let you go.'

'Let me go?'

'Your assistant is about ready to take over from you, I believe...'

'But I am not in the least ready to go.' Ferdinand was trembling with rage.

The Director got up and put his hand on Ferdinand's shoulder. 'I've seen it coming; we've got to safeguard the work of the Institute. If they find me employing people of Jewish origin...' The Director passed a hand across his throat; then he went on, 'We've got your things ready for you to take away; there's no need for you to go back into the laboratory...'

'My laboratory!' Ferdinand almost choked on the words.

'By the way,' the Director mumbled, 'this came for you yesterday.'

He handed Ferdinand a brown foolscap envelope. His paper had been returned.

'It only remains for me to say...' The Director was struggling for words.

'Nothing, nothing remains to be said!' Ferdinand replied in a voice that did not seem to belong to him.

'Nothing personal; you know that, don't you...' The Director stretched out a hand, then thought better of it, raised his arm and said, 'Heil Hitler!'

Ferdinand thought that if he stood quite still he would perhaps wake up from the nightmare.

The Director propelled him towards the door. As he opened it, a lab boy appeared with two neatly done up parcels.

'Heil Hitler. Herr Doktor, your personal property – books in this one, lab coats in the other. Heil Hitler!' The boy was outdoing himself with efficiency.

The nightmare went on as Ferdinand took the parcels.

'Sign here, please, Herr Doktor.' The boy held out a receipt book.

'A mere formality, just to keep our records straight,' the Director murmured. Then he told the lab boy to call a taxi for the Herr Doktor, turned on his heel and went back into his room.

The address Ferdinand gave the taxi driver was his mother's. He did not realise what he had done until they stopped in the Oranienburgerstrasse.

'This is it, guv,' the driver said.

'Yes, yes, of course.' Ferdinand did not have the presence of mind to tell him to go on to the Savignyplatz.

He got out and paid.

'Don't forget your parcels, guv – talk about absent minded! Do you know the one about the professor who kissed his egg and banged his wife on the head with a spoon. Ha, ha, ha!'

Ferdinand stared at the man. 'I... I... I,' he began helplessly.

'Don't forget yer change!'

'Thank you, thank you. I'm a little...'

'Have a good day, guv,' and the taxi drove off.

It did not occur to Ferdinand until some time later that the driver had not said 'Heil Hitler'.

His mother let him in, her sleeves rolled up, a flowered apron over her dark grey dress. 'Whatever brings you here at this hour? We're polishing the silver!'

'We' were Rebecka and her factotum Helga.

'And what are those?' Rebecka eyed the parcels.

'Mother, I need to sit down!'

Rebecka realised something quite out of the ordinary had occurred. She rolled her sleeves down, untied her apron.

'Helga will do us a little lunch presently. There's a nice bit of calf's liver...'

Ferdinand shook his head. 'I need a drink!'

'At this time of day?' Rebecka couldn't help saying. But she gave her son a large cherry brandy, the only kind of alcohol she had in the house. 'And now tell me what on earth's the matter?'

'I'll have another drink first, please!'

Rebecka gave herself one, too.

Then Ferdinand told her what had just happened to him.

'Fat lot of good getting baptised did you!' Rebecka said and burst into tears. 'What is happening? What are we to do, what are we to do? What have we done to deserve it?'

Ferdinand took her hand, speckled with the brown spots of age, and stroked it. 'Nothing, mother, nothing at all! It's this insane government!'

'Liver's nearly done, shall I lay the table?' Helga called from the kitchen and, before they had time to say anything, she came rattling in with a tray full of crockery. When she saw the state Rebecka was in, she stood stock still.

'Has someone died, Gnä Frau?'

They shook their heads.

'Well, thank God for that, then it can't be so dreadful!'

'My son has been dismissed from his post at the Institute for reasons of race,' Rebecka said, suddenly quite in control of her voice.

'Reasons of race?' Helga started laying the table.

'I don't suppose you realise…' Ferdinand began.

'Realise?' Helga straightened the cutlery and then turned to face them. 'I realise that those brownshirts can go and… go and…' She did not finish the sentence but went on, 'I would like you to know, Gnä Frau, Gnä Herr, that you can count on me to be here whenever you need me. And if the worst comes to the worst…'

None of them knew exactly what that could turn out to be.

'Yes, if the worst comes to the worst, I have some savings…'

'I'm deeply touched,' Ferdinand said.

Helga brought in the food; neither Rebecka nor Ferdinand made a move towards the table.

'Eat, eat before it gets cold.' Helga pulled the chairs out.

They sat down to please her, but neither of them ate more than a mouthful.

'It's the humiliation, the utter humiliation – and the Director had the nerve to say "nothing personal"!' Ferdinand wiped his mouth, though it hardly needed wiping.

'That's what they want, of course, but to push you out after all these years, it's quite unbelievable! After all you've achieved! And without the least warning…' After a short pause, Rebecka went on, 'Let me know how much you need! We won't have to touch Helga's savings just yet!'

In spite of the seriousness of the situation, mother and son smiled at each other. Ferdinand realised Rebecka must have more behind her than he knew. But he said, 'Oh, I expect we can manage for the moment. Bella is wonderfully economical – though what she'll say when I tell her.'

'I'm glad you came to me first,' Rebecka said.

'Well, but now I must go home and tell her.' Ferdinand kissed his mother goodbye.

Suddenly she said, 'God will give us strength.' It was some time since she had thought about God.

'We shall need all He can give!'

When he arrived back at the Savignyplatz, Ferdinand did not feel in the least strong. Bella was not for taking it sitting down. She asked to see his baptismal certificate.

'Baptism does not change racial origin,' he told her.

'There must be something we can do!'

But there was not.

A month later Ferdinand discovered that the substance of his research on diabetes had been published under his assistant's name, which was embellished with a swastika in bold print. There was nothing he could do about that either.

'My life's work!' Ferdinand said over and over again.

'Have you been to see Theodor?' Bella asked.

She had kept clear of the Friedrichstrasse, feeling somehow unforgiven there for having taken Magda's place. It did not occur to her that Theodor and Elisabeth might think she was avoiding them because they were Jewish. Perhaps in her heart of hearts Bella did fear it might jeopardise the twins if she were observed going to the Friedrichstrasse. At any rate, there was no reason for Ferdinand to stay away. Theodor had been very good to him in the past. But Ferdinand was pessimistic.

'What could Theodor do for me? He'll have problems of his own now, I expect. I'm finished, done for, it's the end of the road for me!'

Bella took it all in her stride. What Ferdinand called 'drastically reduced circumstances' were still streets ahead of what she had been brought up to.

Ferdinand did go to see the pastor about what had happened, but all he got from the man of God was some mumbled, anodyne formula. The poor man was obviously afraid of saying something that might be misinterpreted by the government. You never knew who might be listening.

Nor could Ferdinand discern God's will in the fact that he was suffering from a severe bout of jaundice. He spent most of his time stretched out on the *chaise longue* in his study, sighing, pencil and notebook untouched. His skin itched madly; his limbs felt heavy. He kept asking if there were thunder in the air, but the storm was inside himself. He felt a hurricane of guilt sweep over him, feelings of remorse he thought he had dealt with years before: dear, sweet Magda... how could he have failed her so... owed her everything... Yes, perhaps that was what God was punishing him for, his blindness *vis à vis* his first wife. He prayed for forgiveness, but for the first time in his life he was not quite sure who or what he was praying to. A shadow of doubt had cast itself over everything.

'Don't fret so. We'll manage,' Bella said.

But managing was not what Ferdinand had intended his life to be about. 'I want to live!' he wailed.

The women in his family found his anguish hard to bear.

'Would you rather I didn't go to Spain?' Luise asked Bella.

'Of course you must go. He'll recover, from the jaundice at any rate, and then we'll have to see what we can find for him to do. I do wish he'd get in touch with Theodor; I don't think they even know yet at the Friedrichstrasse what's happened!'

'I'll be calling round there to say goodbye before I go to Madrid. I'll tell them, though I don't suppose Theodor will be able to do anything about it, will he?'

Bella shrugged her shoulders and then, quite unexpectedly, put her head on the kitchen table and began to cry.

'Don't Mummy, please don't!' For the first time in her life Luise was seeing Bella out of control. It embarrassed her.

'Oh, let me be, just for a minute...'

Gradually, Bella calmed down. She wiped her eyes with a handkerchief that had a fine crocheted border, which Elisabeth had made for her.

'I won't go to Madrid, I'll stay,' Luise said again. 'I'll start the dress-making course straightaway.' Bella had arranged that for her; it was the kind of skill that was always needed wherever you were.

'You're going!' Bella said firmly. Then, with a rare gesture of physical affection, she stroked Luise's cheek, 'You're a good girl; you always have been!'

Theodor was very nice to Luise when she came. He made all sorts of encouraging noises about travel broadening the mind and gave her a generous cheque to help the process.

'I know your father can't do all he'd like to.'

'Then you know, Uncle Theodor?'

He nodded. 'That kind of news travels fast. I should have liked to talk to him, but I thought I'd wait for him to get in touch with me. Besides, there's very little I can do for him.'

In fact, Theodor had done nothing about seeing Ferdinand because he did not want to embarrass him by forcing on him contact with a family that had never pretended to be anything but Jewish.

'Papa would love to hear from you,' Luise said, though she was not quite as certain as she sounded.

Ferdinand's jaundice did not get better. He languished on the *chaise longue,* pretending to read, pretending to write, but most of the time he lay there with his eyes closed. When Bella came in with tempting morsels of roll-mops or salami, he waved her away. When the twins tiptoed in, all he could do was murmur, 'My poor little girls, my poor little girls!' And they crept away again feeling miserable.

Stephanie, who had set her heart on going in for nursing, hoped that in spite of everything her father might help her find a place at a teaching hospital, but he refused absolutely. 'I should only harm you; leave me right out of all that!'

Without telling him what she was doing, Bella got in touch with Ferdinand's old director at the Institute. She knew he was quite a decent man, in spite of what had happened; his hand had been forced.

'Such difficult times we live in!' he said on the telephone. But he did find a place for Stephanie to begin her training.

It was the difficult times that had given Bella the courage to get in touch with him in the first place. Nothing ventured nothing gained, she told herself; they would survive. The twins were surprised to be given extra large cones of vanilla ice cream when they got home from school that day. There was one for Stephanie as well, but Bella did not give herself one.

On the Sunday before Stephanie moved to the nurse's hostel, Ferdinand roused himself from his invalid's couch, opened a bottle of Sekt and said something about 'Henkersmahlzeit' – hangman's meal, an expression that went back to well before the Third Reich in connection with meals before departures. Stephanie wished there were a more lighthearted way of putting it. In fact, it was not long before she was eating with the family again.

Luise had unexpectedly arrived back from Madrid; the Spanish Civil War had broken out. 'It was awful,' Luise told them. 'One day you were friendly with your neighbours and the next you weren't supposed to know them, they were the enemy. The children just couldn't understand it!'

'Those damned Bolsheviks!' Ferdinand said.

Both Luise and Stephanie thought their father looked worse. Where before he had walked ramrod-straight, he now slumped about. To avoid Bella's silent reproaches – she had given up telling him to go and see a doctor – he dragged himself from home to science library to church and back again, though he could not concentrate on books or prayers.

One day he walked all the way to the Nikolaikirche, the oldest church in Berlin, only to find swastikas daubed all over the outside and Hitler Youth yobs prowling round. He did not attempt to go in. When he got back to the Savignyplatz bathed in sweat, he collapsed on to his bed and did not get up again.

His temperature rose. He became delirious and called for his mother. When Rebecka appeared, puffing and blowing – she had put on a good deal of weight – he did not recognise her.

'When's the doctor coming again?' she asked Bella.

'He won't see any doctor!'

'Get a doctor at once!' Rebecka shouted. And then, more calmly, 'No, wait, I will!'

She got Dr Herzfeld to come. He had looked after her ever since she had had Ferdinand. When he arrived, he got Rebecka and Bella to leave him alone with the patient.

After he had examined Ferdinand, who lay supine on his bed, the doctor said, 'Ferdinand, can you hear me?'

Ferdinand opened his eyes but said nothing.

'Listen to me: You could get better. If you wanted to. You're quite ill, but not desperately ill. You have a wife and mother and daughters who will look after you, but you will have to help them. If you don't want to get better, then you won't. Of course, it's in God's hands, but God needs your assistance!'

Ferdinand shut his eyes again.

Dr Herzfeld wrote out a prescription. 'If you die,' he said as he left the room, 'it will be yet one more feather in the Nazi's cap!' He gave Bella the prescription.

'Well?' Rebecka asked.

'He may pull through,' Herzfeld said. He did not add: 'And he may not.'

Rebecka's chin trembled. 'You'll come again?'

He put his hand on hers. 'The day after tomorrow we sail for Tel Aviv,' he said, his face transformed with joy.

'You too!' Rebecka said.

The medicine did not help Ferdinand.

Bella telephoned Stephanie in her nurse's hostel. 'Your father's on his deathbed,' she said.

Stephanie did not quite believe her but, when she saw Ferdinand, his hands on the bedclothes in utter abnegation, she knew it was true.

'Where's grandmamma?' Stephanie asked.

'He asks for her and, when she comes, he doesn't recognise her. It's too upsetting for her. And the doctor's gone to Palestine!'

'Then Papa should be in hospital,' Stephanie said.

Bella shook her head. 'Let him be, perhaps it's all for the best!' Stephanie was shocked.

'How can you say that?'

'Well, what is there left for him?'

Ferdinand opened his eyes and whispered, 'Call Luise.'

When Luise had come, Ferdinand asked Bella to leave the room. He looked first at Luise, then at Stephanie and with immense effort stretched out his hands towards them. 'Your mother...' he said so softly that they could hardly hear him, 'Magda...'and he sighed deeply. A smile appeared on his face which was quite like his father Louis's, but Rebecka was not there to see it.

He died peacefully.

Bella and the twins did not see him alive again.

Bella resented the fact that he had sent her out of the room; she had always done her best for him and felt she had deserved to be there at the end. Quite soon after the funeral, she told Luise and Stephanie exactly how their mother had come to die. They ought to know that Magda had not been the saint Ferdinand made her out to be. All the same, Bella knew it was wrong of her to have told them, wrong and very unkind. But then, there was a great shortfall of kindness everywhere.

'Did you believe her?' Stephanie asked Luise.

Luise nodded.

They never talked about it again.

For some weeks after Ferdinand died, Bella avoided calling on Rebecka. She was busy hatching plans about protecting the twins from Nazi snoopers. They were 'Mischlinge Ersten Grades'. When she finally got round to going to see her mother-in-law, Rebecka held out her arms.

'I hoped you'd come, my dear. I know what you've been through and what you're still going through! And of course your twins come first. If it now embarrasses them to visit their Jewish grandmother, they need not!'

'But they're very fond of you!' Bella said.

'That's neither here nor there, things being what they are,' Rebecka said crisply.

As she kissed Rebecka goodbye, Bella remembered Ferdinand's clothes. 'What shall I do with them?'

'Hugo,' Rebecka said. 'They would fit him perfectly. I hear from Elisabeth how good he is to his little Laura – and to them, for that matter. And he has a very hard time making ends meet these days.' After a short pause, she went on. 'You'll see, this madness will pass. Germany is one of the most civilised countries in the world!'

But the madness was not passing. It was gathering impetus.

Hugo received Ferdinand's clothes with mixed feelings, but he was chronically strapped for cash – his friend Rudi only managed to get him very minor commissions. One day, though, Rudi turned up with tickets for the Olympic Games. How the tables had turned! In the old days it was Hugo who had been the one to hand Rudi free tickets.

'Take your kid.' Rudi said to him. 'Chance of a lifetime!'

They had a beer together. You couldn't help liking Rudi in spite of the swastika in his lapel.

He saw Hugo eyeing it. 'Means nothing to me,' he said. 'By the way, do you know who's Hitler's favourite painter?'

Hugo shook his head.

'Alfred Ziegler. Master of the pubic hair!'

They had a good laugh, almost like old times. Almost, but not quite. You never knew who was listening. Then, with a sense of nausea, Hugo wondered if Rudi were sounding him out. Of course not! What horrendous times that allowed one even to think along those lines!

The next time Hugo arrived at the Friedrichstrasse, he brandished the Olympic Games tickets.

'Guess what, we're off to the Stadium!' he said to Laura.

Theodor and Elisabeth looked worried. 'Are you sure it's alright to take the child?'

'What do you mean?'

Hugo knew perfectly well what they meant. Jews were not allowed in the Stadium anymore than they were allowed in theatres or cinemas. But if anyone said the least word against his daughter he would... Hugo did not specify to himself what he would do.

Walking next to each other, they looked like any other German father and daughter. It hurt him so much that he could not make Laura feel proud of being German!

Laura, too, knew what her grandparents had meant when they wondered if it were alright for her to go to the Olympic Stadium. She kept looking round from side to side as they were finding their places and, when she thought she saw a couple of brownshirts staring at her, she took hold of Hugo's hand. Above their brown shirts they looked quite ordinary and, when they noticed Laura's nervous gaze, they smiled at her. She smiled back – and immediately felt guilty. Jews did not smile at Nazis. But, of course, they did not know she was half Jewish; it would not occur to them that anyone might contravene the law prohibiting Jews from entering.

There was a fanfare, a swirl of swastika flags. The Führer. Everyone got up and raised the right arm: 'Sieg Heil! Sieg Heil! Sieg Heil!' they roared.

Hugo did not get up. He put his hand firmly on Laura's knee. 'Sit,' he said as if she were a little dog.

Dangerous, but nothing happened.

Laura watched the events with intense interest. She had never seen black people before and was astonished by what they could do with their beautiful lithe bodies .

'Mummy would enjoy all this, wouldn't she?' Hugo said.

Laura nodded, but she was relieved Ruth was not with them. She felt terribly uncomfortable when her parents were together, knowing they did not love each other any longer.

VIII

1936-1939: BERLIN

Just opposite Laura's Jewish school was one for Gentiles. In her second year Laura was allowed to do the ten minute walk from the Friedrichstrasse to the Auguststrasse by herself. The Jewish children and the others never walked on the same side of the street. There was no law against it, but all the other laws channelled the children into that behaviour pattern. Sometimes Laura looked across the road and sometimes she met someone's eyes and there were ghost flicker smiles. She could not understand why they had to be so separate. But once her eyes met the stony stare of three brawny boys, and one of them yelled 'Judensau' across at her. His friends roared with laughter. Laura stopped looking at the children on the other side of the road.

She always mentioned to her friends that her parents were divorced, in case it made them not want to play with her. Everyone else's parents lived together. But she did not say her father was not Jewish because then they were bound to think he was a Nazi. She was not at all sure how saying he was Communist would go down with her class mates. It also meant keeping quiet about going to Shirley Temple films, the Circus, the Olympic Games. One break time, someone in her class asked why her parents were divorced. Laura wished she had never mentioned it. She shrugged her shoulders and turned away to play hopscotch with her best friend Sonya.

'Your father's a goy, isn't he?'

How had they found that out?

'Yes, he's a Nazi goy, isn't he!'

'He is not a Nazi, he's a Communist!' Laura said.

Everyone in the playground stared at her. She wished she had not let that slip out, but it was hard not saying things all the time. She felt like crying; she never seemed to be the right sort of person. Never mind where she was, it was always awkward.

'Shut your lousy trap; mind your own shitty business, you piddlearse!' Sonya shouted as loud as she could.

Laura loved Sonya. What terrific words she knew! The two little girls put their arms round each other and skipped away.

Sonya often came back to the Friedrichstrasse. Elisabeth encouraged that; Laura needed company of her own age. One lunchtime when they were chewing their way through the statutory Eintopfgericht cooked in one saucepan to save fuel, Sonya's mother appeared unexpectedly, hair flying, face puffed and red.

'At once, Sonya, I beg you, come home; they have taken your father!'

Laura, as well as listening to the sense of the words, heard the foreign-sounding German, the rolling r's, words not quite in the right order. Sonya's parents had come from Poland quite recently.

'But what's he done – whatever's the matter?' Elisabeth asked.

'Nothing, nothing has he done... kicked down the stairs, don't want us Polish Jews in Germany. Where, where they want us?'

'But it's against...' Theodor was about to say 'against the law'.

But it was not. He felt deeply ashamed that he had ever allowed himself denigratory thoughts about recently arrived Jews from the East. He wiped his mouth with the damask table napkin and said, 'Allow me to take you back home!'

Elisabeth beamed at him.

During the summer holidays Ruth took Laura to a pension in Thüringen run by a Gentile woman who, amazingly, had no objection to Jewish guests. When Hugo heard how close they were going to be to his village, he was tempted to ask Ruth to take Laura. But in the end he decided against it; the times were not right. Elisabeth had embroidered a white *batiste* dress for Laura; Ruth had bought her a new bright blue bathing costume with a red goldfish in one corner.

'By the time we come back, you'll be able to swim, there's a marvellous open air pool quite close to where we're going!'

Learning to swim with her mother was fun. They went to the pool every day and got browner and browner in the August sunshine. Every day Ruth watched Laura practise her breast stroke, with a cork belt round her waist. In the second week she managed to get her feet off the ground without the belt, while the swimming pool attendant walked round the edge in front of her holding a metal loop on a stick which she could grab. But she did not need it.

Laura was so pleased to have her mother there all the time, smiling at her. She saw more of Ruth during that holiday than for the whole of the rest of the year. What was more, there seemed to be a respite from all the political talk; no one they met said disturbing words like 'anti-Semitism', 'concentration camp', 'storm troopers', 'emigration'.

Ruth and Laura went for walks in the Thüringer Wald and picked wild raspberries and bilberries. One day, after a sudden shower, they heard a rustling in the undergrowth and there was a salamander, brilliant black and orange. Ruth held Laura's hand. They both felt really happy. Then the salamander disappeared.

In the train on the way back to Berlin, they sat in the dining car the whole way. There were four officers eating at the table the other side who chatted to them. Obviously the officers did not realise they were Jewish. Laura had not thought about that for two whole weeks. The holiday was over.

Hugo desperately needed work. He owed the landlady several weeks' rent. Though he knew she would not throw him out, he also knew that she relied on his rent for part of her livelihood. He rang Rudi several times, but Rudi was never in. Then one day Hugo ran into him in the street.

'Any ideas?' he asked and was annoyed with himself for sounding so needy.

'Can't stop!' Rudi said. '*Sauve qui peut!*' he muttered and with a quick pat on Hugo's shoulder rushed off.

Hugo stared at the back of his old friend as he disappeared around the corner.

How to save body and soul? Not that Hugo believed in souls as such, but the terminology seemed appropriate. What weighed most heavily on him was knowing that, if things went on as they were, he might have to do something about getting Laura out of the country; he was not going to have her grow up a second class citizen or worse. As he walked the Berlin streets, 'Juden unerwünscht' notices everywhere, copies of the *Völkische Beobachter* with its rabid anti-Semitism posted at every street corner, with more and more Jewish businesses folding and people getting the hell out, he realised there might be no other way. He had taken a break at the Quaker centre in Bad Pyrmont – they ran holidays for war veterans and, though that was a label Hugo hated, it applied to him. He had met an elderly English woman there who had looked him in the eye and said he could count on them if the need arose. He was not quite sure what those words covered. Time to find out.

He got his landlady to iron a few shirts and sew on a few buttons – he'd been able to catch up with the rent because there'd been an unexpected cheque in the post for an article he'd written months before, which had never been published. He put on one of Ferdinand's suits, a tweed one with a herring-bone pattern, the sort of thing he had never been able to afford himself.

On the bus on his way to the station, Hugo noticed a young nurse staring at him. She had remarkable brown eyes which reminded him so much of Ruth's that he had to look away. The time when he had looked into those eyes with love and confidence seemed as mythical as the Garden of Eden. The nurse got up and touched him on the shoulder.

'Hugo? I recognised my father's suit! How nice you look in it!' It was Stephanie. She knew that Bella had passed on her father's clothes.

Hugo hardly knew her; he had only met Ferdinand's daughters occasionally at the Friedrichstrasse. He shook her hand warmly and, when he got off the bus at the railway station, Stephanie waved until he was out of sight.

Stephanie had been on her way to the Jewish hospital to be interviewed as a trainee midwife. She had passed the initial nursing exam. To be the first to hand a newborn baby to its mother seemed a blessed way to spend one's life. Her thoughts about having babies of her own were less well-defined.

The interview was sticky. The sister, who eyed the cross round Stephanie's neck suspiciously, began probing into her background. No, Stephanie told her, she was not Jewish; she was a practising Lutheran.

'Not Jewish?' The sister looked at her with an ironic twist to her lip.

'My father converted…'

'Oh, I see…' More irony.

'Both my parents are dead!'

'Oh, I see,' the sister said again, more gently this time. 'Well of course, under the present laws you are Jewish, so you can start the course. But it might be better for you not to live in our hostel which is for Jewish girls only.'

Stephanie went straight to the Friedrichstrasse. Theodor and Elisabeth might allow her to stay with them; they had been so good to Aunt Hannah before she married. On no account did she want to go back to live in the Savignyplatz now that her father was dead.

She found the family assembled in the Friedrichstrasse and Theodor pacing up and down the dining room clutching a sheaf of papers. Elisabeth, looking ashen, told him to sit down; all the pacing was not going to change anything. Only Laetitia was placidly chewing a large piece of sultana cake.

Richard was there with his Beate. So was Hannah, but not Hermann. Ruth was not there, either.

They all looked abstracted as Stephanie came in.

'Sit by me,' Hannah patted the chair next to hers.

'Yesterday at the Kulturbund,' Elisabeth said as she poured coffee into Stephanie's cup, 'a Nazi official appeared in the interval to tell us that Mozart's music is not suitable listening for Jews!' Her bosom heaved, and she burst into tears.

'But that's not really what it's all about,' Hannah whispered to Stephanie. 'Theodor is not to be allowed to practise, and they have to give up this flat. They're to move somewhere more in keeping... more in keeping with...' Hannah's voice faltered, 'with their racial status.'

Stephanie noticed that Hannah said 'their'. As if she wasn't... But then she asked herself what she would have said? Hadn't she just denied being Jewish?

Laetitia held her plate out towards Elisabeth. 'More of your delicious cake, my dear, if you please!' She was not wearing her dentures but looked a good deal more alert than in the past. Living in the Berlin Home was obviously suiting her.

'What can we do?' Richard asked, making himself sound as matter-of-fact as he could. He and Beate had sold the flat behind the Tiergarten some time before; it was just too large for them. They had found something far more modest near his office, not far from the Alexanderplatz.

Beate got up and took a slice of cake over to Laura who was reading in the corner. Laura looked up from her book.

'You're not Jewish, are you, Aunt Beate? Are you a Communist?' she asked.

Everyone looked at her startled.

'What an idea!' Beate managed a smile.

'Child's father's a Communist; that's why she asks!' Laetitia said with her mouth full of cake.

The family were even more startled by this contribution to the conversation from someone they thought was only interested in her food.

'And I don't want to move! I live here!' Laura got up to join the grown-ups at the table.

'The child knows everything!' Elisabeth said.

'Understands everything.' Theodor sounded immensely grieved. He spread out the various papers he was holding and, like a school boy with learning difficulties, put his index finger under each word as he read out the protocol.

'I feel so ashamed!' Beate burst out.

Richard put his arm round his wife. 'You have nothing whatsoever to be ashamed of!' he said and kissed her full on the lips.

Laura grinned with embarrassment. But it was very reassuring to see people loving each other.

Richard had much reason to kiss Beate. It was she who had persuaded the manager at the button factory, now a big shot in the Party, to see to it that his friends did not relieve Richard of his directorship. 'Since it's you who're asking!' the manager had simpered and promised to use his influence. For the moment things were all right, but no one could be sure of anything for long. The manager had found it necessary to add, 'A beautiful woman like you married to...' Beate had finished the sentence for him: 'The best and most honourable man in the world!'

The best and most honourable man in the world felt totally helpless in face of what had just happened to his sister and brother-in-law. All he could do was look at Elisabeth and say, 'What a blessing Papa did not have to live through all this!'

Laetitia, who, when she had finished eating, had slipped her teeth back in, said, 'Would have been water off a duck's back for Oskar. Like everything else, everything else!'

'The things she comes out with!' Hannah looked at her mother censoriously She was glad her Eduard was at home with his father. Hermann kept him well away from the Jewish side of the family, and Hannah regretfully thought that was all to the good, considering the difficult times they lived in.

But Beate asked, rather pointedly, 'And where's Hermann?'

'Probably at a Nazi meeting!' Richard muttered. Then he put his hands in his pocket, 'I almost forgot!' He pulled out sample cards of buttons – glass, enamel, horn, brass, copper, silver – and gave them to Laura. 'For you, my dear!'

Laura gave her great uncle Richard a big hug. She loved his smell of lily-of-the-valley pomade, and she loved the buttons – she had quite a collection of them. But Hannah turned her head away when she saw them.

Ruth did not get back home until after the relations had left. When she heard the awful news, she looked away from her parents. Her chin trembled, but she stopped herself from crying. Her mother was not crying.

'We must trust in God,' Elisabeth said.

'What God?' Ruth asked. She had stopped believing in God when her brother had died.

'Your mother is right.' Theodor put his hand over Elisabeth's.

'We have three months to find something round the Bayrischeplatz – they seem to think that district is in keeping with our racial status.' Theodor could not keep the bitterness out of his voice.

'It'll be easier for visiting Laetitia,' Elisabeth said. She had not lost her way to finding an up-side to even the most depressing news.

'Oh, marvellous!' Sarcasm helped Ruth to keep her tears at bay.

Theodor looked at her gravely. 'You and the child will have to find somewhere by yourselves. We will not be able to…'

'Somewhere quite close to us, of course,' Elisabeth added quickly.

'Oh yes, and nice and near Laetitia!' Ruth snapped. Then she changed gear. 'Have you told Hugo?'

Ruth quite missed Hugo. Her affair with the headmaster had petered out, though she went on teaching at the school. Laura was to go there at the beginning of the new year. Living at the Bayrischeplatz would make it easier to get to school in the Grunewald.

'We haven't seen Hugo for a few days,' Elisabeth told her.

'Oh?'

'He may have gone to see his Quaker friend in Bad Pyrmont.' They all three knew what that meant.

The move was arranged for January 1938.

'I can't quite believe it yet,' Elisabeth said two or three times a day as she emptied cupboards, put aside valuables for the government to confiscate, including a whole canteen of gold cutlery that had belonged to her grandparents, which she had hardly ever used. She had planned to bring it out when Ruth got married, but in the event that had hardly seemed appropriate.

'It can't be right, it belongs to us,' was another phrase she repeated over and over again.

'It's the law,' Theodor said.

He said nothing about it being right.

Two or three times a week Elisabeth telephoned Hannah and Beate to ask them if they would like this or that – Persian rugs, hand engraved champagne glasses, cobalt blue china coffee cups and so on and so forth.

Beate refused everything. Again and again she said, 'I feel so terribly ashamed!'

But Hannah accepted. At least some of the things would stay in the family.

Ruth stayed out of the way while the upheaval was in progress. She was not attached to all the clobber; parting with all that did not hurt her in the least. What hurt her were her parents' drawn faces and the fact that she would have to get used to looking after Laura a good deal more than in the past.

She had found a tiny two-room flat in a recently built block five minutes walk from where the parents were going to be living. Ruth was not even there on the day the government agents came to confiscate Theodor and Elisabeth's property, though most of the family looked in to see if they could help.

Elisabeth felt her daughter's absence keenly. She needed her – or rather, she needed a daughter. Ruth had never quite fitted into that slot; perhaps one day Laura might fill it, but today Elisabeth could not concentrate on the child, who was running about among the packing cases in febrile excitement.

Elisabeth tried to realise what was being asked of her on this ghastly day. She felt herself failing as a hostess, but surely today no one was expecting coffee and cake? She was immensely touched when Hugo called in with a bunch of mimosa, its fragrance softening the fraught situation.

In fact, what Elisabeth found hardest of all to bear was Theodor's cast-iron expression, his stiff back, his clipped sentences. All he had tried for and achieved was in ruins. She thought back to the winding up of the house in Upper Silesia after Laetitia's committal: harrowing enough, but a family affair, property intact, future assured. Then, for some unaccountable reason, she had a sudden image of Laetitia's little dachshund Karlchen, who had come to Berlin with them, and her beautiful mare Cyganka, who had not. For a moment she stood quite still by herself in the bare bedroom, enveloped by the past.

Hannah, who was running her hand nervously over the packing cases, could hardly bear the commotion either. She wanted to go back home to Hermann and Eduard, where she could forget about being Jewish. But she was part of this family for whom things were going so badly. Had it all begun with Magda's death? even years before that, with her mother's lashing out at Oskar? Those were entirely private affairs; but Ferdinand being dismissed from his Institute and dying of grief and shame was not. She knew, too, that Richard's position at the factory was under constant threat. Theodor and Elisabeth being turned out of their home seemed the last straw. What did these faceless men in overalls think they were doing requisitioning family property?

And yet it was true, Hannah had to admit, that Hitler had brought prosperity to a lot of Germans. And though it was not true that Hermann attended Party meetings, he did take care not to fall foul of the Party line. He was doing pretty well with his motor cars. Hannah knew he had had a qualm or two when the new law about special number plates for Jews came out – they meant harassment, if not worse, for the least little traffic offence – but what was he supposed to do about it? He never let on to their Gentile friends that Hannah was Jewish. Thank God she did not look it, not like her nieces Ruth and Stephanie. One day Eduard had come home from school and told them that the teacher had pointed him out to the class as the typical Aryan dolichocephalic type! That only went to show what rubbish it all was! But that kind of thinking was dangerous.

Hannah felt uncomfortable visiting them when Theodor and Elisabeth were installed in their new flat near the Bayrischeplatz.

There were practically only Jews in the district now and, quite apart from that, it was painful to see them in such reduced circumstances. The furniture they had been allowed to keep was crammed into rooms half the size of those in the Friedrichstrasse, and there were far fewer of them. Suddenly she and Hermann – the passed-on Persian rugs elegant in their sitting room – had caught up with and overtaken what had been their rich relations. Occasionally Hannah still arranged to meet Ruth for a cup of coffee along the Kurfürstendamm; there was still some of the old rapport between them, but they avoided talking about the past. Instead they talked about emigration. Should Theodor and Elisabeth, like so many others, be thinking along those lines?

'It's different for me,' Hannah said. 'Mixed marriages aren't affected so much. What a pity you and Hugo got divorced!'

She asked Ruth how she enjoyed having Laura all to herself, but Ruth avoided answering, and Hannah could not help feeling sorry for the little girl. One day recently Laura had asked Hugo exactly why he and Ruth had got divorced. All he could do was to reassure her again that they both loved her and that they never wanted her to think about it. Laura had just looked at him with her big brown eyes. She was far too bright to have any wool pulled over them, nor did he want to deceive her in any way.

'You're the very best thing in my life,' he had told her and put a hand on her head.

Hugo could hardly bear the thought of parting with his daughter. His Quaker friend at Bad Pyrmont had promised she would provide the necessary guarantee of a thousand pounds for Ruth and Laura to come to England, but Hugo had not yet quite made up his mind whether it was really necessary.

One brown, wet November morning Laura was standing at the stop waiting for tram number 57 to take her to school in the Grunewald. She was wondering what her granny would have for lunch when she got back. She always ate with the grandparents; they were just round the corner from where she was living with Ruth. Laura was getting used to the new school, though going to gym lessons taught by her mother was very embarrassing, particularly as she was not good at it! She had not yet found anyone she liked as much as Sonya, though when she had invited her over there was nothing to talk about and they had felt at sea with each other. Now, standing at the tram stop, Laura thought about the book her father had given her called *Alice in Wonderland*. She loved it when Alice found the 'Drink Me' bottle. Her father had said that one day she might be able to read the Alice book in English, but she would much rather have had a bottle of the stuff that made Alice grow and shrink than learn English well enough to read about her in the original.

Laura came out of her reverie as the tram rattled towards her. As she got on, she noticed a lot of broken glass on the pavement and in the road. Half a dozen shop-fronts were shattered. When she got to school, hardly any of the masters were there and a good many of the children were absent. There were no proper lessons; they were sent home early.

'The time has come,' Hugo said after Kristallnacht. When Laura heard him say that, she felt most peculiar. Something she could not imagine at all was going to happen to her.

Not long after this, Hugo called round to see Ruth with an important letter from England.

'I knew she'd be as good as her word!' he said excitedly 'Read it, Ruth!'

Ruth took it from him and read it, frowning. 'Mmn. Mmn, she writes good German, I see, but she says I'd be their housemaid to begin with. Surely, you don't expect…'

'Think of Laura,' Hugo said, and for the first time since they had got divorced he took her hand and held it. 'She'll be sent to a first-rate boarding school as soon as her English is good enough. And we here would know that you two were in safe hands. Now, time's of the essence, you know that as well as I do!' Hugo took the letter from her.

'I'll think about it,' Ruth said. 'I'll talk to the parents tomorrow.'

'There's no more thinking to be done!' Laura saw her father's face go very red. 'I have talked to Theodor and Elisabeth; everything's agreed. They're going to pay for the journey and transportation of whatever things you decide to take. All you have to do now is go to the authorities here for the various papers…'

Ruth hung her head.

Next day, Laura decided to enjoy Sunday lunch with her granny and grandpa as usual. She skipped all the way there, hoping there would be chocolate pudding for afters – either in the fish mould or the melon mould. The fish mould was nicer.

'I want the tail,' she said when it turned out to be exactly that.

She sat next to her granny at the old dining table, which they had been allowed to keep. It seemed even bigger here than in the Friedrichstrasse. Laura was pleased, too, to see the old coffee maker on the table. She turned on the tap and filled everyone's cup to where the little flower was on the inside. Elisabeth opened a box of Sarotti chocolates. Laura loved the lid with the two little black boys in red and blue and gold turbans carrying things on trays. She had a collection of those boxes, which she kept her button cards in. Probably she wouldn't be able to take them to England.

'Will you be coming to England as well?' she asked her grandparents.

'Probably not.' Theodor said, lighting his Sunday cigar.

Elisabeth stroked Laura's head. 'You won't be gone for so very long, my little goldfinch; it's just to make sure that in case…' Without finishing her sentence, Elisabeth turned to Ruth. 'Hugo showed us the letter. You could not be in better hands!'

'As their housemaid!' Ruth said bitterly.

'It won't come amiss for you to learn how an English household is run. We've a lot to be grateful for to Hugo. Besides, it's only an interim arrangement!'

'As soon as the dates are settled, as soon as you've got all your papers, I'll book a passage on one of those American liners – they dock at Southampton before crossing the Atlantic – a little holiday for you both before the new life begins,' Theodor said puffing smoke rings.

Laura went on extended shopping expeditions with her granny to buy outfits, clothes that would be right for rainy England. At Tietz, at Wertheim, at N. Israel, they met other families getting ready to emigrate. Some people were buying clothes several sizes too big for their children.

'One is not preparing for untold years of penury!' Theodor

said.

'Besides, the things will look hopelessly dated by the time the children have grown into them,' Elisabeth added.

'You'll be safely back in Berlin long before that!' Hugo said.

At school, there were fewer and fewer people, though Dr Fisch, the music master, still played Mozart's 'Rondo alla Turca' every day as they filed in and out of assembly. At lunch time, when the noise got too much for the headmistress, she would bang her knife against her plate and tell them that once they were in England they would not be allowed to talk at table at all. Laura wondered if that was true. She had began to doubt almost everything that adults said where before she had taken all things on trust.

'But we're going to America!' someone shouted.

'Chile!'

'Shanghai!'

'Australia!'

And so the classrooms thinned out.

It was time for the Christmas fair at the far end of Unter den Linden. When she was younger, Laura had been pulled by Hugo on her sledge, but she had got too big for that now. This year she and Hugo walked hand in gloved hand, their shoes squeaking on the snow.

The fair was not as much fun as usual. There was the same smell as always of Pfefferkuchen mingled with sizzling sausages, and the Christmas tree baubles sparkled in the lamplight. But there were a lot of brownshirts about rattling Winterhilfe tins, and boys in their Hitler Youth uniforms were standing by all the stalls, which somehow dampened the festive atmosphere. When they got back to the Barbarossastrasse – Laura had not got quite used to the fact that that was where the grandparents now lived – Elisabeth had glasses of lemon tea and a plate of chocolate stars for them. Theodor was there as well and, unusually, Ruth.

The first Chanukah candle was ready to be lit in the Menorah. They sang the Chanukah song 'Mo-ow-sur' together as Elisabeth lit the candle Schames. Hugo hung back, but Laura could see he was enjoying it all. Lately her father and mother – she never thought the word 'parents' because that made them a pair, which they were not any longer – had been getting on better. Hugo was helping Ruth sort out what papers she still needed for emigration. Emigration! That word undermined the nicest occasions.

There had been a parcel from England with a Christmas pudding. It weighed a ton and looked quite inedible, nor could they make out the English cooking instructions.

To Theodor and Elisabeth, it seemed only moments later that they were getting ready for Ruth's and Laura's farewell supper.

To Ruth, the three months waiting for permit, passport, visa, hurrying from one government department to the next had seemed endless. Now she was longing to get the goodbyes over. The time all that was taking seemed endless, too. She would have preferred to spend her last evening in Berlin quietly with her parents and Hugo – she realised that without him the emigration (did that word really apply to her?) would not have become possible. But Elisabeth insisted that the family would never forgive her if they were not allowed to say goodbye.

The strain of leave-taking was masked by the fuss over laying the table. Laura enjoyed watching her mother and grandmother doing things together – folding napkins, straightening knives, polishing glasses. It hardly ever happened. She went to make sure her new red velvet dress was still on the hanger which had 'For the Good Child' printed on it. On the reverse, her father had written in indelible pencil 'For the Naughty Child' so that she could use it every day! They had giggled together as he wrote it. She was certainly going to take that hanger with her to England.

Hugo was the first to arrive. His eyes flickered towards Ruth; she looked him full in the face. The circles they had skated round each other at their first meeting made shadowy spirals around them.

The front door bell rang again. Richard and Beate came in. Elisabeth looked at them with great affection. At least they would still be about when the children had gone. Losing sight of her grand-daughter was almost more than she could bear; it was almost like having another death in the family. Elisabeth pulled herself up sharply: it was wrong, quite wrong, to think like that. After all, how far was England? No distance at all! Elisabeth remembered very vividly that medical congress she and Theodor had gone to before the war. She went into the kitchen to give the sauce a stir. While she was stirring, she suddenly had an image of her mother Franziska with a grey kitten on her knee; and she remembered taking Richard's hesitant hand in hers and guiding it towards the kitten's head, and Franziska had put her arms round both of them...

'Well, well... so...' Back in the drawing-room, Richard was patting Laura on the head.

He had been relieved of all responsibility for, and income from, the button factory There was nothing more to be said or done. Beate was setting up a little haberdashery shop – anything, everything, from darning needles to shoe horns and shoulder pads. Oh yes, with Beate by his side he could survive anything, Richard thought. He looked at Theodor. Would he and Elisabeth survive?

Hannah arrived by herself, mumbling excuses for Hermann. She hugged Ruth. This time, they did talk about the past. Some of the old warmth between them was rekindled They remembered leaping about the large rooms in the Friedrichstrasse, remembered talking about boys. All before Magda had died.

Luise arrived and a little after her, rather out of breath, Stephanie.

Stephanie was out of breath and flushed because she had just run into Hannah's Eduard – or rather, to her immense surprise, he had been waiting for her outside the Jewish hospital, where she was doing the midwifery course. Eduard had left school when he was sixteen and was helping his father with the motor car business. With his good looks and charm he was already turning out to be a successful salesman. He was taking quite a risk coming to the Jewish hospital, but a friendship had grown up between cousins. He felt he could talk to Stephanie about his problems. His main problem was that he was half Jewish and having to hide it.

'Dad just tells me to forget about it, but it's not as simple as all that!'

They had walked together to the bus stop, though Eduard had no intention of joining his relations for Ruth's and Laura's leaving party.

'I'm fully Jewish and a Christian; that's not so very easy either! The Jewish girls think I'm a traitor!' Stephanie had told him.

Taking her arm, Eduard had said, 'You see, when all the others go on about shitty Jews, about how Germany needs to get rid of every last one of them, I find it hard to be as vocal as they are, and when I do join in, I think: but that's my mother I'm talking about!' At that point Eduard had actually burst into tears.

'We mustn't let all this ruin our lives!' Stephanie had pressed his hand. Then, to her astonishment, he had put both his arms around her and kissed her full on the mouth.

Stephanie was three years older than Eduard, but it was the first time she had been kissed like that. She knew it was wrong, not only because Eduard was her cousin but because she enjoyed it so much. Now, she let Eduard's mother peck her on the cheek without mentioning that she had just seen him. She noticed how like Hannah Eduard was – they were both very beautiful.

Luise said, 'Mummy sends her very good wishes; she's had to take the twins somewhere!'

Elisabeth thought that it wouldn't have hurt Bella to have brought them for a moment. And she still resented hearing her niece call Bella 'Mummy'.

When Rebecka arrived, they all stood up.

'The child? Where's the child?' she asked as soon as they had helped her off with her coat.

Laura came running up to her. Rebecka put a little red leather box in her hand. When she opened it, Laura found a pearl and enamel brooch with *A L'Amitié* engraved on it. She bobbed a curtsey to Rebecka, who bent down and kissed her on the forehead. 'It means *To Friendship*,' Rebecka said and thought: what a pleasant little girl; why has she got to leave the country? What madness! It's all quite beyond me! Poor Elisabeth, how she will miss her grand-daughter! Then she asked whether Laetitia was coming and, when Elisabeth told her that going out in the evenings had become too much for Laetitia, Rebecka allowed herself a little smirk. It was not too much for her! and she had a good deal further to come. She was still where she had always been, in the Oranienburgerstrasse. No one had interfered with her yet – they tended to leave widows alone for longer.

'And so,' she began to speak again rather slowly because she did not enjoy what she was saying, 'Luise, too, is to leave for England in the very near future!'

'Yes, grandmamma, they sound a nice family with a large country house, and they've written to say my dressmaking skills will be most welcome!'

'When you've finished scrubbing their floors,' Ruth interrupted.

'But I haven't got all my papers yet,' Luise went on, ignoring Ruth.

'Don't worry, they'll come!' Hugo said.

He was feeling rather isolated, but then he noticed Stephanie also standing apart from the others.

He went over to her and reminded her of their meeting on the bus, when he had been wearing her father's suit. He was wearing something of his own this evening and a blue silk bow tie Ruth had once given him.

Elisabeth joined them. 'Do they work you very hard at the hospital, my dear?' she asked. She thought the girl was looking rather dazed. She was not to know that Eduard's unexpected kiss was still hovering round Stephanie's lips.

'Yes, it is hard work at the hospital, but I love the midwifery.' Stephanie paused and then added, 'When Luise gets to England, she's going to try and help me get over as well.'

They went to sit down for the Henkersmahl.

Ruth looked at her father. She could not imagine not being able to look at him. But tomorrow... 'Come, Puppchen,' Theodor said and hooked his arm through hers.

After the meal, Laura fell asleep on Hugo's knee. He carried her to bed. She and Ruth were spending their last few days in Berlin with Theodor and Elisabeth; their little flat was empty.

In the morning Elisabeth woke Laura with a hug; it felt like old times in the Friedrichstrasse. Laura could not imagine not being able to hug her granny.

It was awful at the station.

It was awful for Theodor, who knew he was seeing his daughter and grand-daughter for the last time. Of course there was always hope, but beneath the hope there was the certain knowledge that he would not.

It was awful for Elisabeth, because she knew that added to her own grief she would have to carry Theodor's. She knew what he was feeling and knew she would have to try and dispel those feelings when just now she herself... Elisabeth remembered God. Trust in God, right here, on the Anhalter Bahnhof.

It was awful for Hugo, because he did not believe there was a God to trust in. He believed in trusting people, though that belief had taken quite a battering lately. But when he looked at Laura leaning out of the train window he knew that, of course, he trusted his English friend to look after his daughter. No matter what was coming to him, he had seen to that.

'Auf Wiedersehen!' he shouted as the train pulled out of the station and waved his handkerchief. 'See you again quite soon!' But he could not be sure they could still hear that.

In the train, Ruth and Laura sat close to each other, their legs touching. It was awful for them, too.

Once Ruth and Laura had left, nothing seemed quite real to Elisabeth. She wandered about the flat picking up odds and ends the children had left behind – a pencil box with a broken lid, a black velvet jacket of Ruth's, a game of Ludo... Elisabeth stroked the lid. What fun they'd had playing, how excited Laura got when the six came up on the dice! Elisabeth could still see her rosy cheeks and hear the shriek of delight as she chased the little men round the board. Elisabeth's tears fell on the brightly coloured cardboard box.

Theodor found her crying.

'I can't... I can't...' she sobbed. She meant she could not help him in his grieving.

'That's not like you!' Very gently, Theodor wiped her tears away.

He had been given a new lease of life with a blue metal plate up on the front door allowing him to treat Jewish patients. The room that Ruth and Laura had slept in during their last few days in Berlin was converted into a consulting room.

Elisabeth watched for the postman eagerly. Ruth's letters when they came were miserable, and Elisabeth did her best to write encouraging replies. But Laura wrote cheerful, vivid accounts of the country house and garden, the dog and cat. She included household hints: in England they don't have table-cloths, just mats; in England they don't do the drying up, the plates drip dry on a funny rack. She told them she was eating lots of apples that grew on trees in the orchard, that she had seen cows in a field and picked up horse dung – yes, really truly – to fertilise the flower beds. And she was having English lessons every day.

Laura wrote to Hugo as well. He was very proud of his daughter's writing skills. He called in to see Theodor and Elisabeth every day, sometimes twice a day, to exchange letters. Gradually, Ruth's letters too sounded a touch more settled. The post was a great comfort. Elisabeth began to cheer up and put her mind to the housekeeping, to making life as comfortable as she could for Theodor – as always.

Then in September 1939 war was declared.

It seemed unbelievable to Theodor and Elisabeth that their daughter and grand-daughter were in the country Germany was fighting. The enemy. Who was whose enemy?

Hugo still came every day. 'It can't last long,' he said.

'They said that last time,' Theodor spoke sadly. 'That war lasted four years!'

'We'll see. I mean, the sooner this dastardly dictatorship is finished off, the better!' Hugo needed to cheer himself up. He missed Laura terribly.

A few more letters trickled through after war had broken out, then stopped altogether.

Elisabeth wept into the crocheted kettle-holder Laura had sent for her birthday just before the war had begun. She treasured it like a talisman.

'You mustn't cry so much, my dear; it's not a bit like you,' Theodor told her.

'That's because I'm not like me any longer,' Elisabeth said.

She knew Theodor's cheerfulness was only skin deep. The practice was falling off; more and more patients came for the last time saying they were going away. Now that did not mean they were emigrating, it meant…

Theodor and Elisabeth looked at each other apprehensively

every time someone came to say goodbye.

They saw a good deal of Stephanie on her days off from the hospital. She preferred coming to them rather than embarrassing Bella and the twins in the Savignyplatz. Luise had managed to get to England just before war broke out, but it had been too late to arrange anything for her sister. 'She's quite one of us now,' Elisabeth said to Theodor, meaning that in spite of the cross round her neck, Stephanie belonged to the Jewish part of the family.

Stephanie had met a young Jewish doctor at the hospital. She knew he was the man she would marry. When she was near him, she came fully alive in a way that had begun the day Eduard had kissed her. Her young doctor did not object to the fact that she had converted; he told her he loved every Jewish little bit of her, converted or unconverted, and made her laugh a good deal in spite of all the difficulties.

One day Stephanie decided to call on her grandmother. She had not seen Rebecka for quite a while. When she got to the Oranienburgerstrasse, there was Helga, Rebecka's factotum, in tears. She had just found Rebecka dead, slumped in her armchair with her deportation order crumpled on the floor beside her.

'It's all so wicked – so very, very wicked!' Helga said over and over again.

'Thank God she was spared the deportation,' Theodor said, when Stephanie came to tell them.

'Why should they want to deport an old woman?' The sense of unreality around Elisabeth intensified.

'I only wish,' Theodor went on, 'that Laetitia would go the same way. I don't know how much longer they will allow those two ladies to run their house!'

To hear her husband, a doctor, wishing someone, their own relative, dead, felled Elisabeth completely. She did not even offer Stephanie a cup of coffee. Not that that was a great deprivation – the sort of coffee they had these days was barely drinkable. Jews had such restricted shopping hours they only came in for the leftovers.

'Don't worry,' Theodor said when he saw Elisabeth's ashen

face, 'they'll leave us alone. After all, I was in the army during the last war!'

'But they haven't left us alone!' Elisabeth couldn't help saying.

'I mean...' Theodor said.

Elisabeth knew he meant that they would not be deported. But they were.

They stood wedged in a crowd of Berlin Jews waiting for the train. Theodor, sweat trickling down his face, patted his coat pockets, his jacket pockets, his trouser pockets. He hoped to come across his small metal box of instruments. How could he act as medical supervisor of the transport (transport? us?) without his instruments?

'Don't,' Elisabeth said to him, 'you know they've gone astray!' She still thought in such civilised phrases.

The instruments had been stolen. They had managed to get word to Stephanie – perhaps she could bring replacements before the train left? Theodor went on patting his pockets. There was nothing else to do.

The train arrived. Men in uniform shouted; people were bundled in.

'There!' Elisabeth pointed into the crowd. 'I knew she'd manage it!'

Stephanie reached her uncle and aunt and, before they had disappeared into the train bound for Theresienstadt, gave Theodor a small metal box of instruments.

'All sterilised,' she said.

He wanted to say 'Thank you' but could not. He patted her on the cheek.

Elisabeth managed to kiss her. Stephanie handed her a large package wrapped in grease-proof paper.

'Sandwiches. From Beate. She thought you might need them on the journey; she didn't want you to go hungry...'

'Please thank her, thank her very much,' Elisabeth heard herself say. It sounded like someone else. She was thinking: 'Why can no one prevent this from happening to us?'

'You'll be all right,' Stephanie said and left before the train pulled out. What else could she have said?

She had to hurry back to the hospital where the young doctor whom she loved had said he was going to kill himself now that the Nazis had taken the hospital over.

She would not let him do that. But when she arrived back, there was a commotion in his department. People made way for her. He was not quite dead – she could have tried to resuscitate him. Fighting all her human instincts, she did not try.

Slowly she injected more and more morphine into his unresisting arm, until he had stopped breathing. She closed his eyes, stroked his warm face. Then she walked out of the hospital as far as the Weidendammerbrücke, flung her nurse's cap into the Spree, tore the yellow star off her coat and made for the next train to Cologne. Bella had given her an address – 'a safe house, if you ever need it'. Stephanie needed it.

Bella had no idea whether Stephanie reached the friend in Cologne, who had promised to provide her with false papers. She dared not make enquiries. Nor was there news from Luise in England. She felt pretty certain, though, that by now Theodor and Elisabeth would have been sent out of Berlin. She hardly knew Richard and Beate: they had certainly not been in touch with her – people pretty much kept themselves to themselves these days.

Bella had to have her wits about her to keep going, scratching and scraping to make sure there was enough to eat for the three of them. Lola and Frieda were working in a factory that tinned corned beef for the troops. She had got a new birth certificate for them, proving the twins were the illegitimate offspring of a pure Aryan. She had had to pay the man handsomely for allowing her to use his name.

Then one afternoon Hannah turned up on her doorstep, quite out of the blue. Bella had not seen her for over a year.

Hannah looked undernourished and frightened. Bella produced a tiny cache of coffee beans and ground them. They inhaled the delightful aroma of real coffee.

'Now, tell me what's been happening!'

Hannah swallowed her coffee much too hot and told Bella that Hermann had been taken for interrogation three days before, since when she had heard nothing. 'They found out that I'm

Jewish, you see. Hermann always lied about it!'

Bella put her hand over Hannah's. 'But they've left you alone?'

'I don't understand it myself.' Hannah said. 'They're a law unto themselves, aren't they!' She added, 'I won't stop long – I don't want to compromise you' What a deranged way for relatives to have to talk to each other!

Hannah asked Bella if she'd heard the news about Laetitia – she could not bear to say 'my mother', even now. Bella shook her head, so Hannah told her of the Jewish old age home being hit by a bomb. There had been no survivors.

Bella asked Hannah if she had heard from Eduard, who had been sent to the Russian front. There had been no news from him for months. 'You'd have heard if...' Bella did not finish the sentence. She could see Hannah was trying hard not to cry.

The two women sat there saying nothing for quite a long time. 'Come again soon, you're welcome any time,' Bella said finally. 'I'm sure they'll let Hermann go in a day or two: he's too useful repairing all those army vehicles!'

'Yes, I'll come, air raids permitting!' What a good sort she is, Hannah thought.

'I live in fear and trembling of that siren,' Bella said.

'Well, they're getting as good as they give!' Hannah still believed Germany would win the war.

And Luise? And Ruth and the little girl?

'Over there?' Bella whispered.

Hannah shrugged her shoulders.

Hugo, too, was shattered by the constant bombing. He carried snaps of Laura about in his wallet. From time to time he spread them out on his writing table, though he knew she would have changed almost beyond recognition by now. He decided it might be a good idea to send all the photographs and Laura's letters, which he'd read so often they were falling to pieces, to his sister in Thüringen. He looked forward to the time he could look at them with Laura when she came back; it was thinking about her return that kept him going.

If the bombing did not let up, he would probably be safer in Thüringen himself; but he was reluctant to leave Berlin, where he had friends who hated the Nazis as much as he did. During raids, he crept under the dining room table with his landlady, though that hardly seemed adequate now the bombing had increased in ferocity; so he accepted a friend's offer to shelter in his cellar. He posted the photographs to his sister on the way there, just as the siren began its nightly wail. Hugo should have stayed under his landlady's table – his friend's house was razed to the ground by British bombers that night.

Richard and Beate escaped the bombing. Richard worked in a munitions factory, and Beate ran their little shop on skeleton stock. They managed every now and then to send a small parcel to Theodor and Elisabeth in Theresienstadt. They got a card in Theodor's handwriting acknowledging it, saying things were well organised – he attended lectures, Elisabeth was 'working'. It wrung Richard's heart. What work was his sister being made to do? Encouraged by the acknowledgment, they sent off another package. Some months later, came a printed card. Elisabeth had prefixed her signature 'Widow'. After that, nothing.

They got in touch with Hannah to tell her that Theodor had died. 'He was quite an age, wasn't he?' was all that Hannah said. Hermann had not come back home; there was still no news of Eduard.

The widow Elisabeth, half starved, in rags, was rounded up in one of the last transports to Auschwitz. She both knew and did not know what was about to happen – she had not been in her right mind since Theodor had died of pneumonia, infested with lice. He, the doctor! 'Oh God! Oh God! Oh God!' she mumbled to herself incessantly without the least idea what those words referred to. She clung to whoever was jammed against her in the cattle truck, trying not to suffocate.

Somewhere along the line towards extinction the train stopped. Suddenly there was a breath of fresh air, and Elisabeth inhaled deeply – it smelt of childhood, of conifers in the rain, of smoke from a wood fire, of apples, honey and fresh horse dung. The word 'Cyganka' and an image of her lovely mare floated to the surface of her clouded mind. Something in her expanded until she felt she must burst. The train began to move again – it was only a few miles from her Silesian birthplace. As fast as it could, it carried its cargo towards Auschwitz. Quite soon, Elisabeth would be one among a pile of corpses.

On the day Elisabeth was gassed, Hermann suddenly reappeared. Hannah had never seen him look so cowed.
'In the end, I just had to sign a few things,' he told her.
'And that took all these months?'
He shrugged his shoulders. He never said anything more about his time away, just as he had never talked about what he had done in the first World War.
On that same day too, Eduard deserted from the army. No one had ever questioned his status as an 'Aryan' when the call-up papers came. This tall, handsome, fair-haired young man was a credit to the Fatherland. Before he had been sent to the front, girls buzzing round him, he had fathered a little girl. It was an affair of high passion which had blotted out all labels – German, Jew, Nazi, Communist, ally, enemy, soldier, civilian. He was human, fully alive. Then, fully alive, he had been sent to the Russian front. It was when the German army was in full retreat that Eduard had managed to desert. Better to fall into American hands than Russian. He knew where Stephanie was hiding in Cologne, running a children's home under an assumed name. Starving, in rags, with bleeding feet, Eduard made it.
On that day, Hugo's brother, Joachim, was taken prisoner by the Americans. He was shipped to South Carolina where he spent the rest of the war cotton-picking alongside the descendants of black slaves.
On that day Ruth, who was working in a munitions factory in London, had to take time off – her gallstones were playing up. She'd had a card from Luise announcing her marriage to an Englishman. Ruth threw the card into the wastepaper basket. Marriage! She was having an affair with a motor mechanic. He was not good-looking; he had little money, but he was a decent sort and kept her sane. It would be difficult when Laura came to stay with her during the holidays from that posh boarding school.
On that day, Laura was walking up to the platform in the assembly hall at school. It was speech day. She was getting a prize

for English literature, a volume of Tennyson bound in green leather. 'I must write and tell Granny,' Laura thought.

§ § §

Becoming English

for my daughters
Judith, Catherine & Sarah

Outside, a fierce February wind whistles through the trees. Inside, a little girl sees her pale face reflected in the mirror of the station waiting-room.

'Is this me?' Laura asks herself.

A woman is sitting beside her, shivering. Ruth is her mother, but Laura cannot make her feel quite real now that they are in Somerset and not Berlin. She will *not* cry; she is nearly ten years old. If only her granny and grandpa and her father were there, too! Her grandpa said he was much too old to change countries; he was German first, Jewish second, no one would touch him. And, of course, her granny would not come away without him. Her father, who is not Jewish, will not abandon the country he loves. He has arranged for Laura and Ruth, from whom he is divorced, to stay with his English Quaker friend Miss Tate.

Here she is, tall and thin and white-haired, coming to pick them up. She smiles towards them.

'Ruth, Laura, meine Lieben!' She speaks good German.

It is dusk by the time they drive up a cinder path through a white five-barred gate.

'Welcome to Meadow House!'

A light comes on above the front door. Two tall figures emerge, one with a brown knitted hood hiding her face, the other with silvery hair shining like a crown under the light. They go inside, where a little dog with silky blond hair is wagging its tail.

'His name is Barney,' the woman in the brown hood says.

Laura pats him and he licks her hand. *Feels lovely*, she thinks.

'These are my friends Miss Harvill and Miss Croft; we all live in Meadow House,' Miss Tate says. Laura's mother shakes hands with them; Laura bobs a curtsy. The three old ladies smile. Has she done something funny?

A little later, still clutching the raffia chimney sweep her father gave her for good luck just before the train pulled out of the Anhalter Bahnhof, she goes to sleep next to her mother in the servants' bedroom. When she wakes up, she is not quite sure where she is. Of course, she is in England!

Every morning she has an English lesson with Miss Tate. They read a book about a girl called Rhoda who goes to boarding school, is a good sport and plays lacrosse, which she calls 'lax'. Laura has no idea what sort of game that is.

'As soon as your English is good enough, you'll go to a school rather like that,' Miss Tate tells her.

'And play lacrosse?'

'I think they play netball and hockey at Mentmore House, where you'll be going.'

At least Laura has heard of those games. In Berlin they played handball; she was not much good at it.

Miss Croft and Miss Harvill speak English to Laura all the time. When she does not quite understand, Miss Tate translates. There is a list of new words for Laura to remember every day. Usually she remembers them quite well, except one or two, like *promise* and *suppose*. For some reason she finds those difficult.

'Promise to remember *promise*,' Miss Tate says.

The old ladies give her English children's books to look at. She gets to know Moly and Ratty in *The Wind in the Willows* and the Philosopher in the *Crock of Gold*. She already knows *Alice in Wonderland* and *Little Lord Fauntleroy*: her father gave her those in German.

One afternoon two real English girls come to tea. They are called Penelope and Angela and talk very fast, saying things like *Don't be pernickety* and *It's all higgledy piggledy*. Laura has never heard the name Penelope, but Angela is familiar, except that at home it is pronounced *Anghela* with a hard g. She is getting used to sounding her g's soft like j's. Not always, though. English pronunciation is hard to get right all the time. With a start she realises she has just thought *at home* meaning Berlin, meaning her granny and grandpa, her father. But that is not *at home* any longer. Where is that now? She falls silent; Penelope and Angela go on talking to each other.

Laura's mother Ruth has hardly stopped crying since they arrived. She cries most when there are letters from Berlin but also because she does not like being the old ladies' housemaid.

'I'm not a housemaid. I'm a physiotherapist!' she sobs.

Ruth got herself trained in Berlin and talked enthusiastically about how she would help people recovering from injuries. There was such a glow about her then! Laura knows her mother hates housework, but it was the only condition on which she was allowed into England.

Miss Harvill shows Ruth how to lay a fire in the grate with twists of newspaper and twigs under the rectangles of peat.

'One match should be enough!' Miss Harvill says, but Ruth needs at least half a dozen matches to get the fire going – in Berlin there was central heating. Quite soon, Ruth asks permission to go to London: she wants to find work with a Jewish family. She has to ask permission because she needs the train fare. They were not allowed to bring any money out of Germany and she only gets a pound a week for the housework she hates doing. Most of that goes on cigarettes from the village shop. Sometimes Ruth gives Laura threepence to spend on those cushion-shaped peppermints called humbugs. The three old ladies look disapproving when they see Ruth light a cigarette; Laura decides she will not smoke when she grows up.

'Perhaps you will be happier with your own people,' Miss Tate says tersely. Laura knows Miss Tate means other Jewish people. She thinks: *I'm only half Jewish.* She has not thought that since she arrived in England and she does not want to think it now; she is fed up with not being quite this or that. At her Jewish school in Berlin the others would say incredulously: *your father's a goy?* She never got to know *his* parents, who live in Thüringen. In case her being half Jewish might have been embarrassing for them. Here in England she can grow whole.

Ruth hugs and kisses Laura as she leaves. 'Very, very soon I come to fetch you!' But Laura does not want to be fetched: she likes it where she is.

When Ruth has gone, Miss Tate, Miss Croft and Miss Harvill say they would like Laura to call them Aunt Ann, Aunt Edwina and Aunt Tessa. They seem to feel she might be missing her mother, but Laura is relieved. Having Ruth about was making it much harder to try and become English. How long will it take?

The honorary aunts take her to a fête at the Women's Institute. Aunt Tessa – the one with the silvery hair – wins first prize for her flower arrangement. Her cheeks, which are like chamois leather, go quite pink. Laura wishes her granny were with them. A parson in a long black cassock comes up to them.

'So this is our little refugee girl,' he says and takes her by the hand. 'Are you coming to gamble with me?'

Does he know she is half-Jewish? That she has never been in a church? At the shove-a-ha'penny stall the parson quickly loses all the ha'pence he rolls onto the oilcloth marked out in squares.

'Now we shall never mend the church roof,' he says cheerfully. When he hands her back to the honorary aunts, he pats her on the head.

'Poor mite!' he says.

Laura has no idea a mite is, but she can feel it has something to do with being a refugee. In the car on the way back home (yes, Laura has thought *home* about Meadow House) she asks, 'When will I stop being a refugee?' She does not feel like one. She feels like her grandpa's 'little rascal', like her granny's 'darling goldfinch', like her father's 'big girl' who is allowed to ask him any questions she likes. She wishes she could ask *him* how long it will take to stop being a refugee. And then she smiles to herself, thinking of the child-sized coat hanger he gave her. It has *For the good child* printed on one side (in German, of course); with indelible pencil her father printed *For the naughty child* on the other side. *So you can use it every day,* he said and kissed her on the forehead. She has brought that hanger with her. Laura notices tears are trickling down her cheeks. When they get back to Meadow House, Aunt Tessa asks if she would like to give Barney his supper.

Every morning, indoors in the workroom or, if it is fine, outside on the terrace called the sun parlour, Aunt Ann brushes the tangles and burrs out of Barney's coat. Laura helps pull the burrs out as gently as she can, but Barney always yelps. When the brushing is done, he jumps off Aunt Ann's knee, shakes himself and turns round and round. Aunt Ann hands Laura two bone-shaped biscuits.

'Make him sit!'

Laura says 'Sit' as sternly as she can.

Barney sits: she gives him the biscuits; his warm tongue lollops over her palm. *Barney likes me,* she thinks – *Barney hat mich gerne.* It doesn't matter whether she thinks it in English or German, Barney likes her anyway. She runs out into the garden with him.

Picture postcards arrive from her father, long letters from her granny asking for details of all her doings; her grandpa adds a few lines in spidery writing that Laura finds it hard to read. Aunt Ann gives her writing paper and envelopes and she switches back to thinking in German in her replies. There is a letter from Ruth calling her *My darling independent daughter* and telling her that soon, soon they will be together again. That letter makes Laura's heart sink. She is looking forward to going to a school like Rhoda's in the book which she can now read by herself. She writes to her mother saying how much she likes it in Meadow House and that she can't wait to go to school; so, when, just before the beginning of the summer term, Ruth reappears, Laura is not pleased.

'You come viz me to London now, you come vair you belong viz your muzzer!' Ruth is speaking English.

'But I'm going to boarding school!' Laura bursts into tears.

The honorary aunts ask Laura to come and visit them in Meadow House whenever she likes. She wishes and wishes she did not have to leave.

So then she is on a train to London with her mother. Ruth has found a job as house help with an Orthodox Jewish family in Stamford Hill. Laura is allowed to sleep there, but she has to be out during the day. Émigré friends from Berlin who live in Golders Green have offered to look after her. Laura travels across London by herself. 'You haf to learn to be independent,' Ruth tells her, not for the first time. Laura got to hear that quite often, even in Berlin. She has to change buses; the conductor tells her where to get off; then she asks a policeman the way. You don't have to be frightened of policemen in England; they're called Bobbies.

There is chocolate pudding for afters which the friends have made as a special treat.

'Just like your granny used to make,' they say; but it is not in the least as delicious as her granny's.

'At Meadow House we had spotted dick or treacle tart or apple crumble for pudding; the apples were from the garden,' she informs the family. When she sees them look rather crestfallen, she wishes she had not mentioned it.

Ruth picks her up in the evenings. When they get back to Stamford Hill, there are always men washing their hands and mumbling Hebrew prayers. They smile at Laura and go on praying. She has never met people like them before. In Berlin the family only went to synagogue on High Holidays.

After two or three weeks of this to-ing and fro-ing, Ruth tells Laura she has found a family in Northolt, just outside London, who want to look after a little refugee girl. That phrase again!

'But why can't I go back to Meadow House?'

Laura misses life in Somerset. Most of all she misses Barney. The family who want to look after a little refugee girl have a dog, too, a black Scottie called Trixie. And they have a son the same age as Laura, called Arthur. His father plays cricket with them in the long narrow garden at the back of the house. Laura has never seen anyone play cricket; she learns to bowl with a soft ball when Arthur shouts *ploy* (she knows it means *play*). They go to watch a cricket match, and Laura enjoys looking at the men in their white flannels, but it goes on for a very long time and she does not quite follow the rules, though Arthur's father explains everything. Laura notices that Arthur is totally absorbed in the match, so she tries not to feel bored.

She goes to the same school as Arthur, but he does not walk with her. He has his own friends – boys, of course. She walks a little way behind them.

'She's got to take a test with MD children,' she hears Arthur tell his friends. She catches up with him.

'What's MD?' she asks.

'Loonies!' Arthur taps his forehead.

There are questions like: *a violin, a drum, a flute, a cauliflower, a piano – which does not belong to the group?* She passes the test, but she does not mention it when she writes to her father and her grandparents. She tells them about weaving a tea cosy with a thing called a *heddle*, about country dancing, about singing *If all the world were paper, and all the sea were ink.*

Occasionally, Laura is first back in the house after school. Only Trixie is there. She takes the dog into the garden, where the raspberries are ripe on their canes. Arthur's mother makes delicious jam with them, which they quite often have for tea. *I'll just have a few; it won't matter,* Laura thinks. There is something so special about eating fruit you have picked yourself. She is still stuffing them into her mouth when Arthur's mother comes home.

'Arthur doesn't do that,' she says gently.

Laura wishes she had not eaten so many raspberries, but she has. She starts to cry. Arthur's mother hugs her.

'Never mind now, dear,' she says. 'Worse things 'appen at sea,' Arthur's father says when he hears what she has done. Laura is not quite sure what that means, but she can tell he is not angry with her.

At the beginning of the summer holidays, Ruth arrives one Saturday afternoon to say that now, because almost certainly there will be war, Laura is to go back to Meadow House. Laura is delighted: it feels almost as if she is going home. She will see Barney! Though she has made friends with Trixie, she knows that the Scottie likes Arthur best. By the time she leaves that kind family who have taught her the rules of cricket, her English is fluent and she thinks in German only when there is post from Berlin.

Ruth tells Laura about a pamphlet she has been given called *A Helpful Guide for Every Refugee,* published by British Jews. There are lists of things refugees must and must not do: *don't speak German too loudly in the street; don't read German in public; don't criticise government regulations; don't take part in political activities; don't dress conspicuously; remember the English attach great importance to modesty; understatement in speech rather than overstatement.*

'Ze English Jews tell us how ve have to behave. Zey sink ve give zem a bad name!' Ruth says.

The Golders Green friends who looked after Laura did speak German in the street quite loudly and, even when they spoke English, Laura thinks, it *sounded* like German. But, no, they did not dress conspicuously.

Ruth puts Laura on the train to Bridgwater at Paddington and asks the guard to keep an eye on her.

'Just arrived over 'ere?' he asks Laura.

She tells him she has already been in England for six months.

''Ave yer an' all,' he says and winks at her.

She tries to wink back but cannot quite manage it. The guard laughs, and Laura laughs with him. He helps her off the train with her case.

All three honorary aunts are on the platform to meet her. Laura hopes they will be pleased with the way her English has come on, but she notices that they look at each other in a peculiar way when she asks if she should shut the *gite* and tells them about *ploying* cricket.

'You've turned into a proper little Cockney, haven't you?' Aunt Ann says.

Aunt Edwina pats her on the head and explains that Cockney is a particular London kind of English. They do not say that it is not good English, but Laura knows from the way they correct her that it is not. She begins to realise that there are different ways of being English.

War is declared at the beginning of September. They listen to the Prime Minister Neville Chamberlain broadcast: *I prayed that the responsibility might not fall upon me to ask this country to accept the awful arbitrament of war... We have no quarrel with the German people, except that they allow themselves to be governed by a Nazi government. As long as that government exists and pursues the methods it has so persistently followed during the last two years, there will be no peace in Europe...*

Ruth is staying in Meadow House for a few days. She has found a new housekeeping job.

'Viz educated people, also from Berlin.'

The aunts are very kind to her, call her *Ruth my dear* and look serious when the grandparents are mentioned; all German Jews who have not got away are in grave danger now.

Laura is relieved when Ruth goes back to London: it is so much easier to turn into her new English self without her mother. She sits with the honorary aunts round the peat fire sewing brass rings on the inside of the black-lined curtains so that they can be stretched tightly across the windows and fastened on to hooks that Ben the gardener has screwed in. No chink of light must be seen from the outside; there will be air raids. Laura does not feel frightened; inside herself she feels safe.

'We remember the outbreak of the first world war,' Aunt Ann says.

'We hoped and prayed it would be the last!' And then she adds 'Your father will not have to fight. He was injured in the last war.'

'My father's not a Nazi!' Laura says hotly.

'Unthinkable! We tried so hard to persuade him to come out of Germany,' Aunt Ann goes on, 'but he would not, he loves his country. We understand and respect that.' Aunt Ann speaks with great affection about him.

They go on to talk about their local MP who got elected as an Independent. 'Such an astute man,' Aunt Tessa says. *Astute* – a new word for Laura to look up in the dictionary.

'I wish we had more Independents,' Aunt Edwina says, and then, looking at Laura, 'It means he doesn't have to vote with either of the main parties. Still, now there's a war on, we'll almost certainly have a coalition government.'

Coalition – another new word.

'We'll have the best brains in the country working together!'

Laura begins to feel it is her country.

§

Towards the middle of September Aunt Ann says, 'Beginning of term next week!'

Laura has got her school uniform – royal blue tunic, white blouse, royal blue jumper, royal blue bloomers for gym. *Bloomers* – what is the connection between blooms and knickers? There isn't any; it's just that English is so peculiar. She has black stockings, indoor shoes, outdoor shoes. Her navy blue coat from Berlin still fits her.

'And we'll get second hand Sunday uniform for you at school, and a blue velveteen dress for Friday evenings.'

Sunday uniform? Friday evenings? Laura says nothing, but she is puzzled. Friday evenings are Jewish; Sundays are Christian. Which are for her?

Aunt Ann and Aunt Edwina drive Laura to Mentmore House School in Weston-Super-Mare on a Sunday afternoon. Aunt Edwina has come with them because she was at school with the younger of the Misses Thomas, the sisters who are the headmistresses. Laura cannot imagine Aunt Edwina at school; her skin is so wrinkled and her mouth a bit crooked, because she has had a stroke. Only her blue eyes set deep in her face have stayed young. She and Aunt Ann, who is driving, are arguing about whether driving fast or slowly uses less petrol. Going downhill, Aunt Ann turns the engine off and they coast along.

'Just as well we know our way about,' Aunt Ann says as they pass two men taking down signposts.

'You don't really think there'll be an invasion?' Aunt Edwina asks.

Laura can tell from the way she asks that she is not at all sure. Aunt Ann does not answer. Laura is disappointed not to be wearing her new school uniform; the dress from Berlin she has on is getting a bit short for her.

It is tea time when they arrive at the school, which takes up three buildings in a Queen Anne Crescent. They walk up a short path to the front door of the middle house, and Aunt Edwina pulls the brass bell. A fat smiling woman opens the door, a fat grey and white cat streaks out past her.

'George, George, come back at once, you naught boy!'

'Hallo, Vera. Still keeping the school well fed?' Aunt Edwina says, laughing.

'I do my bit! They're expecting you in the drawing room,' Vera says. 'Sorry about the cat,' and then, looking at Laura, 'So this is our other little refugee girl!'

That phrase *again*. Maybe if she'd had her school uniform on, she would not be called that?

There are three women in the drawing room. The eldest, who

has three rows of beads dangling over her bosom, stretches out her hand.

'How nice to meet you, Laura,' she says, and Laura only just stops herself from bobbing a curtsy. You don't do that in England.

'This is Miss Thomas,' Aunt Edwina says and then, turning to one of the others, 'And this is Miss Elizabeth.'

Miss Elizabeth says, 'Hallo there,' and smiles warmly. Laura likes her at once. She is wearing pointy shoes a bit like the ones her granny wears.

'And this is Matron.' Miss Thomas introduces the third woman in the room. 'We call her Mademoiselle. She looks after all of you!'

''Allo thair, Laura my dear,' Mademoiselle says. She says hallo without an h but it does not sound like Cockney. And she says *Lowra* in the German way.

'Mademoiselle comes from Switzerland,' Miss Thomas says and goes on with a sigh, 'I don't suppose we'll be able to take the girls to Lausanne next summer, with this awful war going on!'

It's all right to be Swiss, Laura thinks, *but not German – and Jewish?*

'Never mind about that now,' Miss Elizabeth says. 'Let's get this young lady settled in!'

'She's a good settler,' Aunt Ann says and bends down to press sixpence into Laura's hand.

'You're to have sixpence pocket money a week,' she says.

As she leaves the drawing room with the Swiss Matron, Laura hears Miss Thomas ask how good her English is. She is proud to hear Aunt Ann say, 'Surprisingly good. She's got a lively brain; she'll be a credit to the school.'

Mademoiselle tells Laura she has been put in the bird room. Laura has no idea what that means until she sees the wallpaper with swallows swooping up and down the pale orange frieze. How nice!

'We sought you'd like to be in ze same room as our ozair little refugee, Traudl. She's from Vienna; you can speak German togezair.'

Laura does not want to speak German; it's the language of the enemy now, isn't it? Then she remembers one of the last things her grandpa said to her: *Don't forget your mother tongue.* No, of course she will not forget, but for now... For now, Laura turns her head away from Traudl, who is unpacking her case. She will *not* speak German to her; don't people know that Austrian German sounds quite different? Two English girls, Molly and Betty, are also unpacking. Laura smiles at them and they smile back; then they turn to each other and giggle.

In the mornings after breakfast they go for a walk along the seafront in 'croc', two by two. Laura is expected to walk with Traudl; they do not talk to each other. Quite soon Traudl gets moved out of the bird room and a girl called Sheila has that bed instead. So now Laura is with three English girls. She does not feel so different from them, except when Mademoiselle, who takes them for French, says 'Isn't Lowra clever! She 'as only just learnt English and now she is doing so well in French!' She hates the way the others stare at her. Laura does not want to be clever; she wants to be like them.

At needlework, which Miss Ingram takes on Saturday mornings, Laura is worse than the others. She enjoys choosing scraps of stuff on which to try out different kinds of stitches, but they have to be very neat and even to earn a *Nicely done* from Miss Ingram. More often than not Laura gets to hear *Try another row of chain stitch* or *What a lazy buttonhole!* Miss Ingram has dark sallow skin, dark brown eyes and grey hair, which she does up in peculiar sausages. Sheila whispers to Laura that Miss Ingram is half Indian. How does she know that? Sheila says it's obvious. Laura shrugs her shoulders. Is it obvious she is half Jewish? half German? Sheila also says that everyone new sooner or later gets called into Miss Ingram's room for a heart-to-heart chat.

Eventually Laura gets called. After the preliminary *How are you getting on* kind of remarks and a rather stale chocolate biscuit, Miss Ingram gazes earnestly at her.

'You know, child, you have it in you to make everybody happy, a great and precious gift!'

Laura wriggles uncomfortably. How could Miss Ingram possibly know something like that about her? And it isn't true: she didn't make Traudl feel happy, did she? She is relieved when, after a little pat on the head, Miss Ingram tells her to run along.

Laura is chosen for the junior inter-schools gym competition. She has always been quite good at headstands and handstands, somersaults – she can do eight in a row. Hanging upside down from the wall bars is fun; climbing a rope is harder, but she makes herself do it. The hardest thing, though, is balancing on the bar; it's like walking the plank, and you have to do it without wobbling. She feels sicker and sicker as the bar gets raised higher and higher. Yes, yes, yes, she *will* do it!

One morning, a week before the competition, she wakes up to find all her bedclothes on the floor and matron bending over her with a concerned expression.

'Lowra, dear, are you all right?'

'You were sleepwalking,' Sheila says.

'You were trying to balance on the bed rail,' Molly says.

''Ave you evair walked in your sleep before?' matron asks.

Laura shakes her head. Everyone thinks it is too much of a strain for her to be in the competition. Another girl takes her place. Laura watches her school win and claps hard.

On the last day of term, packing day, they sing *Hills of the North Rejoice* at prayers, yelling the line *Shout while ye journey home* at the top of their voices. Laura can see Miss Elizabeth, who takes prayers, smiling. *Home!* Laura cannot help still thinking *home* is her granny and grandpa's large flat in the Friedrichstrasse in Berlin where she lived for five years after her parents were divorced. She remembers the year Chanukah and Christmas coincided – they lit candles on the Menorah in the drawing room and then moved into the study to light candles on the Christmas tree. That was before the Nazis made them move into a smaller flat in a Jewish district. Laura does not remember that flat nearly so well; it never became home.

She wonders if there will be a Christmas tree at Meadow House. The others have been talking about holly and ivy and giggling about mistletoe which Laura has never seen. They are all expecting a stocking filled with little presents on Christmas morning. She has made felt egg cosies for the honorary aunts, as well as one for her mother in her favourite colour, royal blue. But even as she was making it, Laura was afraid Ruth would only pretend to like it, which is why the buttonhole stitching is not very even.

Aunt Ann picks Laura up from school and on the drive to Meadow House tells her to expect a big surprise. The surprise turns out to be that Ruth is already there, her arms stretched out wide as Laura comes through the front door. Laura wishes she were as pleased as the grown-ups expect her to be.

'You're in the spare room this time,' Aunt Ann says.

It's because my mother isn't their housemaid any longer, so we don't have to be in the servants' room, Laura thinks.

When she wakes up on Christmas morning she sees a bulging grey stocking with sprigs of holly sticking out of it dangling at the end of her bed. *Good,* she thinks, *I've got one like the others.* She unwraps the little packages; is very pleased with the box of crayons, the India rubber, bar of lavender soap, three red and white marbles, a whipped-cream walnut and, in the toe of the stocking, a piece of coal.

'Vot's zat for?' Ruth asks. Then she gives Laura three handkerchiefs with a blue L embroidered in the corner.

'It's not much, dahlink, but it's viz all my love,' and she strokes Laura's hair. Laura wishes her mother would not say things like that. She gives her the royal blue egg cosy. Ruth looks at it with her head on one side.

'An egg cosy,' Laura says.

'I sink it's a nose varmer,' Ruth says and slips it over her nose. Laura smiles a bit.

At breakfast the honorary aunts explain that the piece of coal is for luck. Laura gives them their egg cosies.

'What's this, my lamb?' Aunt Edwina asks.

Laura goes pink with pleasure. Being called *my lamb* is almost as good as her granny calling her *my little goldfinch.*

'Purple is my favourite colour,' Aunt Tessa says.

'So beautifully stitched,' Aunt Ann says.

'I have a blue one,' Ruth says, 'but I sink zey are nose varmers!' And she slips hers on her nose again.

The three old ladies smile a bit; Laura looks into her lap. Aunt Edwina turns to Laura.

'We don't have a Christmas tree, but after breakfast you and I will go into the garden and pick the first Christmas roses to put on the table for lunch!'

Barney comes with them wearing his new blue and green plaid coat, which Aunt Tessa has given him because he is getting quite old and shivers in the wind. The Christmas roses look lovely on the table.

There are visitors for lunch: Mr. Pocklington with his little boy Matthew – Aunt Ann has explained that poor Mr. Pocklington lost his wife when Matthew was born. And there is also Miss Martha Dearlove who lives by herself in the cottage up the lane. When she arrives, Laura does not think she has a *dear love* kind of face: it is too pointy and her grey hair is done up in a tight bun. Laura sees her mother look up expectantly at Mr. Pocklington. When they sit down to lunch he talks about the windy weather; a new bird-feeder he has found which the squirrels have not yet mastered; that his golf course is likely to be turned into pasture and, with a delighted smile, that Matthew will be going to school in January. Laura sees Ruth's interest waning. She tries to talk to Matthew who is sitting next to her, but he does not respond, just crams forkfuls of turkey, sprouts and potato into his mouth. Martha Dearlove talks, almost regretfully, about the fact that in spite of what they were told to expect, there have not been any air raids; and that the evacuees in South Petherton are making a nuisance of themselves.

'Poor mites,' Mr. Pocklington says.

Laura is gratified to know that English evacuees can be *poor mites* as well as refugees. Mr. Pocklington does not seem to think that *she* is *a poor mite*. After lunch, he asks her to look after his little Matthew. She shows him the three marbles she had in her stocking.

'Oh, look, Matthew, they're splendid oxblood ones,' Mr. Pocklington says, but Matthew is not very responsive. Laura did not know they were called that.

They go for a short walk across the fields to see Martha Dearlove back to her cottage. Mr. Pocklington carries Matthew on his shoulders; Laura remembers how her father used to do that when she was younger. Ruth does not come with them, she has a headache.

At teatime Laura likes the marzipan icing on the cake better than the cake itself but she knows she has to eat it all. Her granny used to say: *Eat everything on your plate and the sun will shine tomorrow!* The honorary aunts say nothing of the kind, but Laura knows what is expected of her. She likes the way hardly anyone ever says *You must... you mustn't... you ought to...* And yet ground rules are quite clear.

Ruth has reappeared.

'You look well rested, my dear. Your cheeks are quite rosy!'

Laura knows Ruth has put on rouge. Can't Aunt Ann tell?

They play a card game called *Red Nines* with two packs of cards. Matthew is allowed to win. Laura minds a bit, but then she is rather proud to think that she is not the youngest at the table.

Next day, Boxing Day – Aunt Ann explains why it is called that – there is a Quaker picnic a few miles away.

'A picnic? On a freezing day like zis?' Ruth looks out of the window at the grey sky and branches bending in the wind.

'It's quite a sheltered spot; we go every year, come wind, come weather!' Aunt Ann says.

Come wind, come weather. Laura thinks it sounds like the beginning of a poem.

'You are not obliged to come,' Aunt Tessa looks at Ruth rather sternly. Laura bends down to fasten Barney's lead on his collar.

'Zen I stay here,' Ruth says. Her *here* sounds like *hier,* Laura thinks, without being able to explain the difference to herself.

Aunt Ann gives Laura a bag of pink and white marshmallows to carry.

'We'll toast them over the bonfire, after these,' and she holds up strings of chipolata sausages.

There is quite a crowd when they get to the picnic spot which is down a steep path. People are throwing twigs on the bonfire, holding their hands over it and stamping their feet.

'You can hand the marshmallows round now,' Aunt Ann tells Laura. She recognises the girl called Penelope who visited Meadow House. They say hallo but Laura does not think Penelope is very pleased to see her.

'Sit down here with us, my dear,' a woman who is probably Penelope's mother says. Laura sees Aunt Ann waving so she runs back to her.

'That's the refugee girl,' she hears Penelope tell her mother.

'I know, you might have made more of an effort with her, Penny!'

Laura does not want people to make an effort with her; she wants them to *like* her. She toasts a pink marshmallow. It tastes delicious, but she is not quite sure whether all the kind people sitting round the fire are only nodding and smiling at her because she is a refugee.

Ruth goes back to London the next day. Laura wishes she were not pleased her mother has left – but she is. She can't wait for school to start again.

When she gets back, it is freezing cold in the form rooms; they take it in turns to warm their bottoms in front of the anthracite stoves. In English they are reading an abridged version of *Ivanhoe* with Miss Elizabeth. Most of the others think it is boring, but Laura reads on well ahead of where they have got to in class. Every day between the end of prep and supper there is an hour's free time. She takes *Ivanhoe* into the library and sits at the table covered with a tapestry cloth with long tassels that reminds her of one her granny and grandpa had. There is very little news from them now, or from her father, but Laura feels them safe inside herself. She knows they love her.

She wants to know whether Ivanhoe will marry Rowena or Rebecca; she so wants him to marry Rebecca, but in her heart she knows it will be Rowena. When he does, Laura feels as if he has turned her down personally. It was never good to be Jewish, was it? Why wasn't it? Laura shuts the book and stays in the library for a while. She is usually by herself, but surrounded by books she does not feel alone. Before *Ivanhoe* she read *Alice in Wonderland* in English; she already knows the story. She loves the Tenniel illustrations, and her favourite bit is the Mad Hatter's tea party. *Twinkle, twinkle little bat, / How I wonder what you're at, / Like a tea tray in the sky / Up above the world you fly!* She laughs out loud as she walks across to the dining room with the gong for supper clanging. You can't translate that into German! She has written a composition about the Mad Hatter. As she was writing, she found she was not only describing him but making him up in a new way as she went along. Miss Elizabeth asked her to read it out and to her delight everyone laughed.

She sits down in the dining room opposite the large reproduction of the *Mona Lisa*. The housekeeper Vera claps her hands for them to stop talking.

'Girls, you know food is being rationed because of the war. We won't starve, but there is going to be less of everything. Now I was thinking that if everyone gave up sugar in their tea, then cook could go on making her delicious puddings. Hands up everyone who is willing to do that!'

Everyone, staff and girls, puts up their hands.

Vera smiles. 'That's settled then!'

Every Saturday morning there is a letter from Ruth. Holding the unopened envelope makes Laura feel like the others; everyone gets post from their parents once a week, but when she has taken the letter out of its envelope she feels lost. It smells of cigarette smoke and is written partly in English, partly in German. She has not yet seen the furnished room into which her mother has recently moved. Ruth has stopped being a housemaid, has got a job as a waitress – a nippy in a Lyons Cornerhouse. In the last letter Ruth told her that she is to spend half the Easter holidays in London and half in Meadow House.

Laura travels to London with Molly, whose parents are picking her up at Paddington. Ruth is taking the day off from Lyons so she can meet the train. The closer they get to London, the more Laura hopes Molly's parents and her mother will not meet. Molly is hanging out of the window as the train pulls into the station.

'I can see them, I can see them,' she shouts and is out of the train in a flash.

Laura steps on to the platform. Yes, there is Ruth hurrying towards her, wearing the black felt hat that looked just right in Berlin, but here it looks sort of... Then Laura is caught up in a hug and for a few seconds everything is all right. When Ruth lets go, she looks round – Molly and her parents have disappeared. Good.

There is just enough space for two beds in the room in Golders Green. There is a sink and a gas ring behind a bead curtain. The little table by the window is laid for two. There are Frankfurters with potato salad for lunch, chocolate pudding for afters.

'I saved some sugar,' Ruth says.

Laura is just about to say that everyone at school has given up sugar in their tea when she feels her cheek being stroked.

Ruth gazes at her. 'Vell, is it nice to be viz your muzzer?'

The words get stuck inside Laura; all she can see are her mother's bright red fingernails. So instead of talking about sugar, she asks, 'When am I going to Somerset?'

Ruth's eyes fill with tears. They finish their meal in silence. Later on, going for a walk in Golders Hill Park, things relax a little. Then they go to see a Betty Grable film. Laura enjoys the Technicolor: she has not been to many films in colour, only some cartoons her father took her to in Berlin. Before they go to bed, Laura sees Ruth swallow some pills.

'Zey help me sleep,' she says.

Laura wishes they did not have to sleep in the same room and wishes she did not have to go downstairs to the bathroom, which might be engaged. Before she slips into her bed, Ruth bends over her and kisses her.

'You're all I have now,' she whispers. It makes Laura feel uncomfortable to hear her mother say that.

They have cornflakes for breakfast.

'Ve're quite English, aren't ve,' Ruth says with a grin. She has rearranged her shifts at the Cornerhouse so she will only be working from four to nine.

'Today you come viz me, and ze Belgian vill stay viz you!'

'The Belgian?'

When they get to Marble Arch, the Belgian turns out to be a tall man in khakis. He gives Ruth a smacking kiss and is about to do the same for Laura but she backs away from him.

'Zis is Louis,' Ruth says and disappears.

Louis finds a table near the band and orders a knickerbocker glory for Laura and a cup of tea for himself.

'Coffee 'ere is undrinkable,' he says. He sounds a bit like Mademoiselle at school.

Ruth, changed into her nippy's uniform, brings their order. Laura barely recognises her mother. She digs the long spoon right down into the knickerbocker glory. After about an hour Louis leaves.

'Your mozair is a grand leetle voman,' he says and pinches Laura's cheek. She disappears right inside herself. Presently, Ruth reappears with a piece of chocolate gâteau.

'You stay here and read, dahlink!'

Laura gets out *Little Women* and forgets where she is.

Back in the Golders Green room, Ruth is sitting on Louis's knee. Laura wonders when he will go; she is very tired. When he finally leaves, Laura hears him ask Ruth how long her daughter is staying. Laura longs to be with Barney in Meadow House.

'Now you know a bit of my life,' Ruth says as she kisses her goodbye at Paddington. She sees Laura into the compartment and does not get out until the guard is slamming the doors.

'I shall miss you, dahlink!' Ruth calls as the train pulls out. Laura does not believe her.

It is easy to talk to the honorary aunts; they understand about the Mad Hatter and Ivanhoe. They enquire with great concern about Ruth.

'She's a waitress in Lyons now.'

Laura does not mention Louis.

'That must be hard work,' they say.

They go for long walks with Barney. Laura learns to identify wild flowers with nice names like Herb Robert and Red Campion. Woody Nightshade is poisonous. There are some tiny pink berries called spindleberries with bright orange seeds inside; you can't eat them.

'I don't suppose your mother has news from Berlin?' Aunt Ann asks.

Laura shakes her head; she does not want to think about Berlin. She listens to Children's Hour with Auntie Doris and Uncle Mac. She loves it when he says *Goodnight children!* And after a tiny pause adds *Everywhere!* Then she wonders if he really means *everywhere* or only England.

Back at school everyone is talking about what they did in the holidays.

'My Dad took me and my brother to...'

'We went to see my granny and grandpa...'

'I had a new bike for my birthday…'

'I'm going to have a baby brother or sister in a few weeks time…'

'We had a family reunion, hundreds of cousins, most of them got leave, only the one in the navy wasn't there…'

When they look at Laura she says, 'I had a knickerbocker glory in a Lyons Cornerhouse!' She explains about the Cornerhouse. They don't know what she is not telling them.

She feels hungry all the time, but she does not like to mention it, because none of the others do; she realises how much more important food was in Berlin. She loved discussing what they were going to eat and going shopping with her granny, the fun of trying out new recipes like making waffles with a waffle iron. She longs constantly for sweet things. At breakfast, they have margarine and marmite on their bread; on Sundays there is toast and marmalade, one spoonful each. Laura knows quite well it means a teaspoonful, but one Sunday morning she takes a dessertspoonful – no one has actually ever said anything about it being a teaspoon. No one says anything now. So that's all right then? When she says something to her neighbour at the table, the girl turns her head away. When, a bit later, she asks Molly something while they are making their beds (with hospital corners), she starts talking to one of the others. On Monday, when she asks to borrow a rubber, it is as if everyone has gone deaf. Lessons go on as usual; the teachers do not leave Laura out when they ask questions, but none of the girls speaks to her. Not Tuesday, not Wednesday, Thursday or Friday – not even on Saturday, when they sit round the dining room table doing needlework. So on Sunday when the marmalade is passed round, Laura does not take any. As soon as the pot of marmalade has passed on to the next girl, her neighbour smiles at her and says something about the hockey match on the coming Friday. Later on, Molly comes up to her. 'How did you like being sent to Coventry?' she asks. Oh, so that's what it was!

Sometimes they are allowed into the drawing room for the six o'clock news; they sit on the carpet and listen to Bruce Belfrage or Alvar Liddell reading it. Winston Churchill is the new Prime Minister, and there is a coalition government. Laura remembers talk about that at Meadow House. Towards the end of May there is bad news: our troops are stuck in Dunkirk. Laura thinks *our* quite spontaneously. They have looked Dunkirk up on the map in geography – it is very near, just across the Channel. One or two girls have fathers there. They hear how everyone who has a boat, however small, is setting out for Dunkirk; the boats go there and back, again and again, picking up as many men as they can. When Laura hears they are rescuing dogs as well, she cries. Some girls are knitting scarves and balaclava helmets for our boys. Laura can knit quite well – her granny taught her in Berlin – but she knits the German way, which wouldn't do for our boys, would it! So she pretends she can't knit.

At prayers in the morning she closes her eyes and asks God to forgive her for telling lies. She wonders if it really matters and thinks of all those millions of people asking God for different things. Who is He supposed to listen to? When the bit about *Through Jesus Christ our Lord* comes at the end of the Lord's Prayer, Laura listens away (like one *looks* away). Jesus is not for her, He is for the others. She does not go to church on Sundays with everyone else because her mother has asked that she should not. In case she turns into a Christian? Not that Ruth ever goes to synagogue now.

'Not ze same wizout ze parents,' she tells Laura. Perhaps Ruth has stopped believing in God?

Laura hides herself away in the library when the others put on their royal blue Sunday coats and black velour hats to go to church. She meets them outside after the service to go for the walk; she feels she is somehow cheating to be wearing the royal blue coat when she has not been to church. There is never anyone left to walk with, so she has to walk with the mistress on duty.

The following holidays, Ruth has moved to a different room in Golders Green. It is a bit bigger than the last one, and they have their own bathroom. There is a different man, too; the Belgian has disappeared.

'Vell, he is in ze army...' is all Ruth says.

The new man has red hair and is called Erich, though he prefers the English version Eric. He lives quite close by.

'Intelligent chep, setting up his own electrical business,' Ruth says.

Laura does not much like him – perhaps he does not much like her? At least her mother does not sit on his knee. She has stopped being a nippy at Lyons and now works in a small munitions factory.

'Making bombs to kill zat beast,' she says, meaning Hitler.

Laura has brought Palgrave's *Golden Treasury* to show Ruth; she knows quite a few of the poems by heart. When she starts on 'The Lady of Shalott', she can see Ruth is not really listening, even though she says 'Lovely, dahlink' every time Laura stops for breath.

'Ve'll take you to a show,' Ruth promises.

Laura wants to see *Macbeth*. They are doing it at school, and she has been reading the part of the First Witch.

'Macbess?' her mother asks.

Laura nods hopefully.

'Without me,' Eric grunts.

Laura looks away from him. She really wants to see it.

'Zen I take my daughter by myself!' Ruth says.

So she does love me a bit, Laura thinks. Their brown eyes meet.

After the play, it is good to get back to the Golders Green room without Eric there. Ruth puts the kettle on and gets out some alphabet biscuits called *Russian Bread*, which Laura has no seen since Berlin. She dips her L-shaped biscuit into the topaz coloured tea and sucks it; her mother does the same with her R. They smile at each other and Laura feels confident enough to say, 'I don't really like Eric!'

She does not have to see him much more: he is being interned on the Isle of Man with the other enemy aliens. *Collar the lot*, Churchill has said. Ruth is outraged.

'Zey sink ve are Nazis? Vy zey sink ve came to zis country?'

Almost every night the sirens go, and they rush into the damp Anderson shelter at the bottom of the garden with the other tenants in the house huddling together as the bombs crash and the anti-aircraft guns respond. Laura is not frightened: she knows, though she does not know *how* she knows, that she will not be hurt. *The News Chronicle* carries photographs of bombed out people outside smouldering houses; the number of dead is not yet known. Churchill broadcasts again. *We shall not flag... we shall never surrender...* Laura so much wants to be included in that *we*.

The war goes on and on.

We survive the Battle of Britain.

We lug our gasmasks about and occasionally try them on.

We make do and mend, darn socks, patch elbows, tie knots in our knicker elastic when it wears out, because you cannot buy any new.

We take our baths in five inches of water and wash with one bar of soap a month.

We eat our reconstituted egg and Spam.

We allow iron railings to be removed and give up saucepans, to be turned into munitions.

We know that careless talk costs lives.

We welcome the Americans into the war as our allies after the Japanese bomb Pearl Harbor.

We hear with dismay that Hong Kong has surrendered to the Japanese.

We welcome the Russians as our allies when the Germans invade their country.

We grieve when Singapore falls to the Japanese.

We are jubilant when General Montgomery defeats Rommel at El Alamein.

§

Laura has just passed her thirteenth birthday. She goes on spending half her holidays with her mother, half with the honorary aunts in Somerset. But it is at school she feels most at ease.

When they go out for their walks in croc along the seafront after breakfast and before tea, they pass convalescing wounded servicemen in bright blue suits and red ties, some limping along on crutches, some with only one arm, some with a black patch over an eye. They always wave at the girls, and the girls wave back. *They can't tell I'm not English*, Laura thinks.

One night there is an air raid. German bombers on their way back from Bristol unload what bombs they have left on Weston-super-Mare. As soon as the siren goes, everyone rushes downstairs in their pyjamas, gasmask boxes slung across their shoulders. The air raid wardens have declared the basement of the school building even safer than the air raid shelters. It is quite fun seeing the staff appear in their nightwear; Matron has her hair down, and where are Miss Owen's teeth? You can see nearly all of Miss Hetherington's bosom because her dressing gown barely covers it. Miss Dutton is tapping the air, playing a spectral piano. Miss Thomas and Miss Elizabeth, one in a brown, the other in a blue-checked dressing gown, look composed, their hair tidy, teeth in place. Cook hands round lime green lemonade, made with powder crystals. There are also Garibaldi biscuits called squashed flies. Matron calls the register; they are all present and correct. The raid goes on longer than usual; there are loud thuds making the building shake. Molly, who is a weekly boarder and lives quite close to the school, has gone pale. Laura puts an arm round her. 'It'll be all right!'

At last the All Clear sounds. As they file back upstairs, there is a lurid glow against the windows. They pull back the curtains and see their town in flames. There is a screech of fire engines.

'Oh my God, I think that's our house!' Molly screams.

Laura puts an arm round her again. Molly pushes her away. 'I suppose you're pleased, you Jerry!' she yells.

Laura cannot believe her ears.

Miss Elizabeth is standing behind them. 'Time for everyone to get back to bed, quick as you can now!'

She turns to Molly. 'We will telephone your parents first thing in the morning, my dear.' But it is on Laura's shoulder that Miss Elizabeth has put her hand.

Back in her bed, Laura whispers the Hebrew prayer her granny used to say with her, but not the German one. In the morning Molly comes up to her.

'I'm really sorry,' she says 'I didn't mean it. I've just spoken to my parents. The incendiaries missed our house!'

'Oh, it's all right,' Laura says. But is it?

Miss Elizabeth gets Laura to come to her in the morning room. She takes her pince-nez off her nose and wipes it.

Then she says, 'Miss Tate tells me she has discovered a refugee doctor and his wife from Berlin who have settled in the town; it turns out his wife knew your mother. So we've got in touch with them, and Mrs. Karlsberg has said she will read some German literature with you. They've invited you to tea next Saturday.'

After a moment Miss Elizabeth adds, 'The war won't go on forever, you know, and it won't do for you to forget your mother tongue, will it?'

Exactly what her grandpa said.

The Karlsbergs live the other end of Weston. The letter Laura has from her mother that morning mentions that Hannah was one of the brainy ones at the Luisenschule in Berlin. With the breeze blowing in her face, Laura walks along the front expectantly, pleased that she, like a good many of the others, has been invited out for tea. Some of the girls go riding on a Saturday; Laura waves to them as they canter past on the sands.

She finds the Karlsbergs' house quite easily and when the door opens, there is a small woman with greying hair and large brown eyes who holds her hand out and says, 'You don't look very like your mother!' Then, after a moment, stroking Laura's cheeks, 'Well may be, a little, after all, round the eyes!' Her English is fluent, much better than Ruth's, but the intonation is German.

In the sitting room Dr. Klaus Karlsberg, a small round man with friendly eyes, shakes Laura's hand, asks how old she is, how she likes her school and whether she can still speak German.

'Ja, ja, ein Bisschen!'

After tea he disappears, and Hannah Karlsberg gets out a copy of Schiller's *Maria Stuart*.

'We'll take it in turns to read. Stop and ask if there's anything you don't understand.' Suddenly Laura realises Hannah is speaking German to her. They sit next to each other on the sofa. At the end of Act I, Hannah closes the book.

'That's enough for today. Did you enjoy it?'

Yes, Laura has enjoyed it. Then, to her surprise, she finds herself telling Hannah about the test she had to take with MD children at the elementary school in Northolt before war broke out. She has not talked about that anyone else.

'Well, I'm sure you passed that all right!' They laugh together. 'You'll come again next Saturday? And remember me to your mother when you write to her, won't you!'

Ruth has moved from Golders Green to a room in a large house in Muswell Hill. They have to share a bathroom again, but to Laura's delight there is a small room of her own with wallpaper that has illustrations of John Gilpin careering about on a horse. When she asks about Eric, Ruth tells her he has been released from the internment camp and has joined the Pioneer Corps, where he spends a good deal of time peeling potatoes. There does not seem to be another man about. While Ruth is out at the munitions factory with her hair tied up in a turban, Laura enjoys time by herself reading *Emma* and learning Tennyson's poem 'The Revenge' by heart. She is going in for a verse speaking competition at school.

Very occasionally there is post from friends in Switzerland. The news is sad: the grandparents have been deported to Theresienstadt, Laura's father is still in Berlin, *working hard* the friends write. They do not say what he is working at. One morning during that holiday the postman brings another letter from Switzerland. In it there is a red printed card from Theresienstadt which Laura's granny has signed *Widow*. Now they know that her grandpa is dead. Ruth and Laura stand hand in hand looking at the grandparents' photographs on the bedside table. They do not cry.

The next day, Ruth runs a temperature. Her left ear hurts badly. Laura goes down to the pay phone in the hall to let the factory know Ruth cannot come to work. The person she speaks to tells her to make sure Ruth brings a doctor's certificate when she comes back to work. Laura does not know whether Ruth has a doctor. Mrs. Wilson, their landlady, comes out into the hall.

'I couldn't help overhearing what you were saying, dear. I'm sorry your mother's not well. Let me know if she'd like a doctor. Our Dr. Jackson will come if necessary.'

She smiles at Laura.

'How do you like your little room with the Caldecott wallpaper?'

Laura has no idea who or what Caldecott is.

Ruth's ear gets worse. Dr. Jackson comes. Yes, the ear is quite bad; she will have to stay in bed a few days until her temperature has gone down.

'You'll look after her?' Dr. Jackson gives Laura a prescription. 'Get these from the chemist. She's to take them three times a day.'

He shakes Laura's hand and promises to look in again.

When the doctor has gone, Ruth says, 'Dahlink, I'm sorry, I spoil your holidays!'

Laura knows it is the red card from Theresienstadt that is spoiling the holidays.

'Give me a kiss,' Ruth says, and Laura kisses her mother's hot forehead.

'Mrs. Wilson's nice, isn't she?' Laura says.

'And Mr. Wilson,' Ruth says.

On her way out to the chemist, Laura sees Mr. and Mrs. Wilson dressed in Victorian clothes; Mrs. Wilson is all in purple, setting off her snow white hair, and Mr. Wilson looks dapper in a black velvet jacket and mauve cravat. They wave to Laura and explain they are film extras about to go out on a shoot. Laura feels quite excited; none of the others at school live in a house with film extras.

She does not mind looking after her mother: she enjoys going to the chemist and doing the shopping with Ruth's ration book. At the grocer she gets a small piece of Cheddar cheese and a tin of pilchards in tomato sauce, on points.

'Eggs are in,' the assistant says and gives Laura a large brown one.

She would like to buy her mother a bunch of flowers, but she dare not spend any extra money. She hurries back home. What a lot of different meanings *home* has come to have! She likes the Wilsons' house best of the places her mother has lived.

When she gets back in, Ruth is asleep. Her cheeks are flushed and her breath rasps. Laura boils the egg carefully for three minutes on one of the two gas rings in the recess by the window.

When Ruth wakes up, Laura gives her the pills and says with some pride, 'I've boiled an egg for you.'

'And you?' Ruth asks, 'Vot vill you have?'

There is a knock on the door. Mrs. Wilson comes in with a thermos flask of soup. She is back in ordinary clothes, but there is still some pinkish make-up on her face. She has also brought a pile of American film magazines.

'These'll while away the time,' she says and, looking at Laura, 'You managing all right, dear?'

Laura nods. It is quite a relief to know there is a grown-up about.

Ruth gets a bit better every day. Dr. Jackson tells Laura she is a good little nurse. Mrs. Wilson goes on bringing hot soup and stays to chat.

When she finds out it is Laura's birthday in a day or two, she says, 'We'll have to see what we can do about that, won't we?'

On the day, both Mr. and Mrs. Wilson come quite early. They give Laura a large tin of Libby's asparagus with half a crown taped to it.

'Happy Birthday – these are pre-war! Have a lovely day, my dear. We can't stay long; there's another shoot this morning. Elizabethan dress this time, takes me hours to get into that doublet and hose!' Mr. Wilson smiles at Laura.

'Vot a couple!' Ruth says with admiration when they have gone.

The Wilsons are different kind of English again – not like the Somerset honorary aunts or Miss Elizabeth, nor like Cockney Arthur and his parents. There is a kind of gloss about the way they speak.

Ruth says she feels well enough to go out and choose a present for Laura.

'Vot vould you like?'

'A poetry book,' Laura says and sees her mother's eyes glaze over.

'If zat's vot you really vant…'

'Let's go to Bumpus's!'

'Vair?'

Miss Elizabeth has told Laura about that famous bookshop in Oxford Street. On the bus, Laura hopes Ruth will not talk because she sounds so foreign. In fact, she hardly opens her mouth – perhaps she knows what Laura is feeling? Laura hooks her arm through her mother's by way of silent apology for her thoughts.

'Is your ear still hurting?'

'No, much better, sank you, but I was sinking about…' Ruth does not go on to say what she was thinking about. Birthday celebrations in Berlin, perhaps?

In Bumpus's Laura forgets everything except books. She loves the smell of fresh print even though the paper in the new books is not quite white and has speckles in it. But the dark blue Oxford poetry editions on India paper are there in pre-war splendour – Keats, Byron, Shelley. Laura hesitates. She takes Shelley off the shelf; it falls open at 'Ozymandias'. She knows that by heart. Yes, she'll have Shelley for her birthday.

'It's five shillings,' she says shyly, 'but I can put my half crown towards it!'

'You keep zat,' Ruth tells her. 'I pay! You looked after me so nice!'

When they get back to Muswell Hill, they open the tin of asparagus, which is quite delicious. As they get up to clear the table, Laura notices with a start that she is now taller than her mother. She takes *The Complete Works* of Shelley to bed and reads 'Ode to the West Wind'. Then, before she falls asleep, she looks at some of Mrs. Wilson's film magazines; photographs of those handsome men and beautiful girls in evening dress or bathing suits kissing each other make her feel quite woozy. It has been a good birthday – better than she expected.

She spends the rest of the holidays at Meadow House. The honorary aunts are not as cheerful as usual. Neither is Barney – he is not in the hall to welcome Laura. He lies in his basket in the kitchen and only just manages to wag his tail when he sees her.

'He's over eighteen years old,' Aunt Ann says.

'We think the time may have come...' Aunt Edwina says

'We'll take him to the vet in a day or two,' Aunt Tessa says.

'Just a whiff of gas and then it's all over; he won't know a thing,' Aunt Ann says.

'It's the kindest thing. Then we'll bury him in the garden,' Aunt Edwina says.

On the morning they are about to take Barney to the vet, Laura goes to the dining room sideboard where a box of Black Magic chocolates is kept to offer visitors. She knows Barney adores chocolates, the soft ones – he does not have many teeth left. She picks out the orange cream, the strawberry cream and the coffee cream; feels his tongue warm and wet on her hand. He goes on looking at her, hoping for more.

Ben the gardener digs a rectangular hole under one of the apple trees at the far end of the garden. Laura looks away as they put Barney's body in it; she does no want to see him dead. When the hole is covered with earth, they go indoors and Aunt Tessa gets out photographs of Barney as a puppy.

Laura has not yet told the honorary aunts about the card from Theresienstadt. She will wait until Aunt Ann asks if there is any news; she always does. But the days pass: they do a large jigsaw of the British Isles with county shaped pieces; they collect horse dung from the field next to the garden; they listen to the Brains Trust with Dr. Joad squeaking on about it all depending what you mean by whatever the subject happens to be – quite often something like the mating habits of the greater crested grebe, about which Julian Huxley is astonishingly knowledgeable and Commander Campbell reassuringly matter-of-fact.

The last day of the holidays comes, but still Aunt Ann has not enquired about family news. Perhaps they expect Laura to tell them without being asked? So after supper – the box of Black Magic has been passed round, no one seeming to notice that any chocolates are missing – Laura mentions the red card from Theresienstadt.

'It's all quite dreadful!' Aunt Ann says and strokes her head.

'Your grandfather should have been allowed to die at home in his bed!' Aunt Edwina says.

'You must remember him as you knew him!' Aunt Tessa says.

Laura feels all three of them looking at her with pity. She cannot bear that; she does not want to be pitiable.

Summer term passes pleasantly. There is tennis coaching, though Laura has to admit to herself she enjoys the idea of it better than the reality – she is not much good at getting the ball across the net, let alone making it go where she wants to. She is better at swimming, loves that sensation of total immersion, floating on her back from one end of the pool to the other; then the tingle of coolness inside and outside her body as she dries herself.

Her breasts are growing, not as big as some of the other girls', but still they're beginning to show even when she has clothes on. She wishes her hair was curly or at least wavy; her mother's is wavy and was jet black, her father's fair and straight – hers is a sort of halfway house between that, dark brown and dead straight. You can get your hair permed but that is very expensive. Will she ever get a boyfriend with boring hair like that? For the moment, boyfriends are what other people have.

They see very few boys or men, only the gardener, who is too old to be called up, and sometimes Molly's brother, who goes to a boys' school in the town. He is allowed to call for her at weekends and, when they walk out of the front gate, everyone hangs out of the window to catch a glimpse of him – once he waves up at them; afterwards the headmistress, who must also have been looking out of the window, tells Molly it is inappropriate for her brother to do that. Then there is the elderly, stooping music master who comes on Thursdays to teach them songs to the tune of Strauss waltzes. The words are silly: *Old winter wears a garment of white...* By common consent, the poor man becomes old winter wearing white combinations; no one can keep a straight face as they sing. Occasionally, there is a plumber or an electrician or a window cleaner. some of the girls giggle when they are about, but Laura hardly notices them. Except that one day it turns out that a girl in the sixth form has taken too much notice of the window cleaner and is expelled.

'They were caught doing it! In the cellar!'

Laura is not exactly sure what *doing it* amounts to. She knows it is something you are supposed not to do until you are married, because you might have a baby, but she is hazy as to what it is that people actually do. Maybe it gives you the kind of woozy feelings she had when she was looking at Mrs. Wilson's film magazines? She listens without saying much when the others talk about where babies come from.

'Out of your bottom,' one of the girls says; she has watched her cat having kittens. Surely that can't be right? But those thoughts are not really uppermost in Laura's mind.

She looks forward to Sunday evenings when Miss Elizabeth reads to the older girls while they do embroidery. Laura is embroidering a small tablecloth with ladies in crinolines in each corner; two are going to be in mauve and two in dark purple. Aunt Edwina gave her the cloth, along with skeins of embroidery silks. Laura runs her fingers over the silks and thinks of her granny, who taught her embroidery stitches; her granny who is now... She allows the cloth to fall into her lap and listens to what Miss Elizabeth is reading. It is a sad story about a man who goes blind, *The Light that Failed* by Rudyard Kipling. Laura is always disappointed when Miss Elizabeth closes the book and says, 'That's enough for today. More next Sunday, gels!'

The term comes to a fun end with a concert in the Winter Garden, Myra Hess playing Chopin. Hess's nephew goes to the same school as Molly's brother, which is why Weston is lucky enough to have a musician who normally performs at the National Gallery in London, even when there are air raids on. It never occurs to Laura that someone must have paid for her ticket; going to something at the end of the summer term is simply what happens at school.

On prize-giving morning, Laura can hardly believe it when her name is called out – she has won a prize for excellent work in English Literature! Miss Elizabeth hands her a copy of Tennyson's *Poems,* bound in green morocco leather. Laura wishes she could tell her granny and grandpa and her father about that!

Just as she is beginning to look forward to having the first part of the long summer break in Meadow House, she is called into the drawing room where Aunt Ann, looking unusually pale, is sitting between Miss Thomas and Miss Elizabeth.

'I'm afraid there's sad news,' Miss Elizabeth says.

Immediately Laura thinks: *Now my granny has died as well as my grandpa!*

But what Aunt Ann says is, 'Our dear friend Tessa passed away last week.'

'So you'll understand,' Miss Elizabeth turns to Laura, 'that it'll be better if this summer you spend the whole holidays in London with your mother.'

'I see,' Laura is dismayed and only just manages to say, 'I'm very, very sorry about Aunt Tessa!'

Then Aunt Ann says, 'And as if we have not had enough to cope with, your mother has asked to have the things we've been storing for her – those five enormous packing cases you brought from Germany!'

Aunt Ann says it as if it was wrong of them to have brought so much. Laura remembers: those crates called *lifts*, with their linen, china, glass, silver.

'Aunt Edwina sends love,' Aunt Ann says as she is leaving. Perhaps she has noticed Laura's woebegone expression?

'We'll see you in the Christmas holidays.'

Miss Elizabeth pats Laura on the shoulder as she goes out. Those little pats have great survival value.

So while the others are chattering and laughing excitedly on packing day, Laura stuffs things into her case with a heavy heart. She does not join in with them as they yell *Shout while ye journey home* at prayers and does not fully understand why she cannot go to Meadow House, even though Aunt Tessa has died. *They don't really love me*, she thinks, *they aren't really my aunts!*

As she stands by herself in the hall, much too early, waiting for the taxi to take her to the station, Miss Elizabeth comes to wish her a happy holiday.

'We'll see you back in September. It'll be noses to the grindstone then, getting ready for School Certificate. We expect you to get Matric Exempt, you know! We want to see your name up on the honours board!'

She makes Laura wish it were September now. Yes, she wants her name up in gold letters on the honours board.

§

Ruth has moved back to Golders Green and is living with a man called Heinz or Henry whom Laura has not yet met. She wonders how she is going to pass almost two months with her mother with nothing to look forward to.

When she gets to London, she takes one look at Ruth's new man Heinz/Henry and hates him. He has steely blue eyes, thin straight lips and crinkly fairish hair scraped back from his not very high forehead. He looks her up and down in a way that makes waves of anger rise inside her.

As soon as they are sitting down to a meal of Spam and reconstituted egg with bought potato salad, he says to her, 'You'll be pleased to hear your mother's found a nice little holiday job for you!' He speaks fluent English with that grating German intonation Laura cannot bear.

She looks at her mother. 'But...but... I've brought a lot of revision reading; it's school cert next year; I want to get Matric Exempt because...'

She cannot tell Ruth and Henry about the honours board on which she would like to see her name. As for mentioning her literature prize, that seems totally impossible.

'My sister,' Henry says, 'was working full time in a factory at your age. And now she's got her own business in Chicago. Clever girl!'

Laura does not want her own business in Chicago; she wants Matric exempt.

'Vell, just for a month, ze last two veeks you don't have to vork.' Ruth's voice is trembling on the verge of tears.

'What job?' Laura asks.

'A little textile vorkshop; you just do ze ironing.'

'All day?'

'I expect they'll give you a lunch break!' Henry says with a sharp laugh.

'When do I have to start?' Oh, why isn't she in Somerset? Why did Aunt Tessa have to die?

'Not til Monday. Ve have ze veekend togezzer!'

Laura says nothing more. Though she is quite hungry, she does not finish the food on her plate.

'Not good enough for you? They give you caviar at that posh school of yours?' Henry is belligerent.

Laura sees Ruth give him a pleading look. He takes out a packet of Woodbines and offers Laura one.

'Go on, one won't hurt you,' Ruth says.

Laura shakes her head.

She is to sleep on the couch in the room where they have been eating and smoking. There is a door through into another room, just big enough for a double bed. The kitchen and bathroom are across the hall; they don't have to share them. It is the largest place Ruth has lived in so far, but Laura wishes they were still in

Muswell Hill in the Wilsons' nice house. When Ruth comes to kiss her goodnight, Laura pushes her away. 'I think he's awful!' she says.

She twists and turns on the couch. At last, thinking about Barney, who liked her and who is dead now, and George the school cat who gets fat on the cook's bacon ration, she falls asleep. She is woken by panting noises from the room next door. The panting gets more and more frantic – that awful man is hurting her mother! Laura leaps out of bed and rushes through the door into their room.

'Are you all right, Mummy?' She cannot remember when she last called her mother *Mummy*.

'Yes, yes, go back to bed!'

'Shit!' Henry says.

So now Laura has a pretty clear idea of what *doing it* means: her mother with that man on top of her. She gets back into bed and holds her breath, listening for the panting to start again. How is she to get through the holidays listening out for that after ironing pieces of cloth all day?

She puts a pillow over her head.

She wakes not quite sure where she is. Sun is shining through the beige slightly torn curtains. She needs the bathroom but has forgotten where it is.

'Mummy...' she calls, but it is Henry who comes through the door.

'Had a good night's sleep, have you?'

'I've forgotten where the bathroom is,' she whispers.

'Speak up. I can't hear you!'

'I need the bathroom!' Laura yells at him.

He reminds her where it is.

She spends a good long time getting washed and dressed.

'Breakfast is served, your ladyship!' Henry shouts. He is in a buoyant mood.

The three of them sit down at the table, Ruth in a thin dressing gown, which falls open to reveal her breasts.

Laura looks away.

'Coming to the flicks with us tonight?' Henry asks.

When Laura's face does not light up, he adds, 'My treat.'

Laura's face still does not light up.

They chew their way through half burnt toast with marge and a scrape of some red jam.

'We should get Marmite again,' Laura says.

'He doesn't like Marmite.'

Henry wipes his mouth with the back of his hand and gets up. 'I'm off!'

'Vair?' Ruth asks anxiously.

'To see a man about a dog!'

'But it's Saturday!'

'Yes, all day,' Henry bends down and kisses Ruth smackingly on the mouth. Then he turns to Laura.

'Want a kiss?'

Laura does not know where to look.

He disappears.

As soon as he has gone, Ruth asks, 'Vy you don't like him?'

'Was he hurting you in the night?' Laura asks.

'Of course not. Ve go shopping now?'

The butcher gives Ruth a small piece of rump steak from under the counter. 'For your little man!'

Laura hates the way the butcher grins at her mother. 'I'm off to the library!' she says. She remembers where it is from when Ruth lived in Golders Green before.

'Vy not come back viz me? I don't sink Henry vill be back before evening.'

Laura shakes her head.

She signs up at the library and takes out one of Mazo de la Roche's *Whiteoaks Chronicles* – not exactly revision work but something she's already found in the school library. It gives her the same kind of woozy sensations as Mrs. Wilson's American film magazines. She finds a bench in Golders Hill Park and starts reading. She has no idea how long she has been sitting on the bench when someone says,

'It's our little Laura, isn't it?'

She looks up and there is Hannah Karlsberg smiling at her. She is so pleased she jumps up and kisses her. Hannah strokes her cheek. Then Klaus, with another man and woman, catches up. They invite Laura to walk with them.

'We're staying with my brother-in-law, quite near here,' Hannah says and then goes on, 'I thought you went to the country with the Quaker ladies for the summer holidays?'

For a moment Laura says nothing. She is so happy to be with Hannah, someone who really likes her. And then it all comes pouring out: not being wanted in Somerset, having to have a job ironing, her mother living with Henry.

Hannah strokes her cheek again. 'Would you like me to talk to your mother?'

'Would you really? Now? It's not far from here; I don't think Henry will be there!'

When Ruth sees Hannah on the doorstep, she changes almost instantaneously into the person she used to be in Berlin. Hannah asks if perhaps it might do if Laura worked mornings only; she is welcome to spend the afternoons with them. They are in London for most of the summer; Klaus is taking a refresher course at the London Hospital – he has to pass his exams in English.

'Vy not?' Ruth agrees. 'Ze boss at ze vorkshop von't mind, he only does it as a favour to me, anyvay.'

Laura looks at Hannah. She is bursting with gratitude.

On Monday morning Ruth takes Laura along to the textile workshop. A grey-haired man looks her up and down.

'So this is the young lady! Well, I could have taken you for her sister, not her mother,' he says, patting Ruth on the shoulder.

When Ruth has left, he says, 'You only want to work in the mornings? That's all right by me!'

Want! Laura thinks, but she says nothing as he takes her through to a large room where two women are ironing and the wireless is blaring out *Music While You Work*.

One of them says, "'Allo there, dearie, 'ere you are, 'ave this one then,' and she makes room for Laura at her ironing board while she sets up another one for herself. 'And mind, don't let the iron get too 'ot!'

'I'm only here mornings,' Laura tells them almost at once.

'Oo's a lucky girl, then,' the other woman says and then both of them sing along to the music *Mareseadoatsandozyeadoatsandlittlelambseativy...*'

Laura stands at the board in a dream, ironing piece after piece of fabric. She likes the smell of the warm ironed stuff. What will she tell the others at school about her summer holidays? She will censor this ironing episode, and Henry and those panting noises; you don't mention that kind of thing about your mother! She comes to when there is a sudden silence – the wireless is switched off.

'One o'clock, dearie,' one of the women says, 'I'm 'avin a cuppa at the ABC, want to come?'

'I'm going to have lunch with a friend,' Laura says and she feels the word *lunch* clunk heavily to the ground.

'Okydoky,' the woman says, but her face has gone stiff and she turns away.

It takes Laura twenty minutes to walk to where Hannah is staying. She passes a flower-shop with snapdragons in a bucket standing outside and spends sixpence of the shilling for bus fares Ruth gave her on a bunch for Hannah. She picks off one of the pink blossoms so she can snap it. Good word *snapdragon*.

'You shouldn't,' Hannah says when Laura gives her the flowers, but her face lights up.

After lunch, which is macaroni with a bit of grated cheese on top, they go to the park. They find a bench near the animal enclosures where a notice says *Please do not feed the animals*, but there are no animals.

'Gone for the duration,' Hannah says.

They scatter breadcrumbs for the starlings, blackbirds, a thrush and a few pigeons.

'Starlings look sort of prehistoric, don't they?' Laura says.

'Do they? Well, perhaps...' Hannah looks at her oddly.

Laura wonders if she has said something peculiar.

'Did you find the ironing very exhausting?' Hannah asks her.

'I hate ironing!'

They laugh as they walk out of the park along Golders Green Road. Hannah sighs.

'What shall I give Klaus for supper?'

Laura feels that question to be a kind of dismissal.

'I'd better go back now.' She doesn't say *home*.

'Will your mother be there?'

'I've got the key,' and then, very shyly, 'May I come again tomorrow after work?'

'Of course you may!'

'Can I bring my book of Tennyson poems? I got it as a literature prize!'

'Well done! Of course, bring it. I don't know much English poetry; you'll have to teach me!'

Laura dawdles after she has left Hannah. She passes the flower shop again but does not spend the other sixpence on a bunch for her mother.

When she gets to the house, there is a letter addressed to Ruth on the hall table. Laura recognises Aunt Ann's writing. Ruth is not back yet and Laura sits staring out of the window, looking at the front gardens opposite with their geometrical beds of standard roses, fuchsias, hydrangeas – town flowers. She misses the Meadow House garden where nothing is neat but everything seems to come up in the right place: snowdrops, daffodils, lavender, sweet scented stock, phlox, lupins, tiny pink roses in clusters, yellow poppies and, later, autumn crocuses, Michaelmas daisies, asters, small bronze chrysanthemums...

She lays the table. There is a blue and white checked tablecloth with one or two small holes in it, but she cannot find napkins. The plates in the kitchen do not match, and some are chipped. Maybe soon they will have their own things from Berlin that are being stored in Somerset?

Ruth gets in, looking tired. She lights a cigarette and takes her shoes off. Laura gives her the letter from Aunt Ann. As soon as she has read it, Ruth scrumples it up.

'Vot a bitch! Ve have to vait for our sings! Vy? It's our property!'

Laura smoothes out the scrumpled letter. It says that the cost of sending all those wooden crates would be prohibitive and probably impossible with the present transport restrictions for civilians. Best to wait til the war is over.

After a while Laura asks, 'Where would we put everything?'

'Zat's not ze question! You sink zey vant to keep our sings?'

'No, of course not!'

'Next time you see zose old vimmen, you ask again, ze sings

belong to you as vell!'

Laura knows she will do no such thing. Meadow House seems immeasurably remote but, as she turns the letter over, she notices there is a postscript: *We should be pleased to have Laura here for the last week of the summer holidays at the beginning of September.* Laura reads it out with great excitement.

'But you von't vant to go?'

'Yes, I do, very much!'

'So, you don't like it viz your muzzer?'

Laura says nothing. She does so wish she *did* like it with her mother.

'Sank you for laying ze table,' Ruth says. 'Vot did Hannah talk about? Very clever, alvays top of ze class at school, not like me, but she vasn't good at gym, I beat her zair!'

Henry comes in wearing his oily overalls. He kisses Ruth and then makes straight for the bathroom.

'I'll have my five inch bath,' he says with a grin.

Laura knows he will take more water than is allowed.

She gets paid ten shillings a week for doing the ironing. She offers the crackly brown note to Ruth; she knows her mother has to work hard for not much pay.

'You keep zis, you earned it,' Ruth says, but Henry tells her to accept it.

'Not necessary,' Ruth tells him.

There is the smoky tang of autumn in the garden when Laura gets to Meadow House. Rustling through the leaves she sees a black kitten.

'That's Tilly Kettle!' Aunt Ann says.

Laura picks the kitten up and kisses him. 'Him?' she asks.

'Yes, my lamb,' Aunt Edwina says.

'Let's see what the greengages are doing,' Aunt Ann says.

There is a ladder leaning against the tree. Aunt Ann climbs up it; she is quite old to be doing that. She drops the greengages into the trug Laura is holding with unerring aim, then climbs nimbly down. They wave to the gardener in his gaiters; he is stoking a bonfire.

'All well at home, Ben?' Aunt Ann calls.

'Yes, ma'am,' he calls back. 'We've got through the measles and Jack loved the books you sent!'

'And your chest?'

'Can't complain,' Ben says. His words come out with soft burring sounds.

Nice, Laura thinks, *different kind of English again*.

'He never does complain,' Aunt Ann says to Laura, 'but he's had quite a bad time with his TB, which is why he's not been called up. He did complain about that!'

Aunt Ann's voice seems to have got gentler since Laura last saw her at school after Aunt Tessa died. She wants to say something like *It seems strange without Aunt Tessa here,* but she is too shy.

While Aunt Ann and Aunt Edwina are having their afternoon nap, Laura explores the bookshelves in the sitting room called the long parlour. There are a good many books about the local countryside, birds and wild flowers, and a whole shelf devoted to Quaker literature, the lives of George Fox and Elizabeth Fry, the history of Barclays bank and Huntley and Palmer biscuits and Clarks shoes, all started by Quakers. But it is to the slim volumes of poetry that Laura is drawn. There is one by someone called Emily Dickinson. It falls open at a short poem beginning:

> Hope is that thing with feathers
> That perches in the soul
> And sings the tune without the words
> And never stops at all.

Laura reads it out loud to herself. It's lovely though she is not sure what the tune of her hope is.

'Are you enjoying that?' Aunt Ann asks when she comes down from her rest.

Laura nods.

'Come and help make a tart with the greengages!'

She shows Laura how to rub margarine into the flour with her fingertips and add just a drop of water, gently, that'll do. Then she kneads and rolls it out so thinly that Laura thinks it is going to break, but it does not. They halve and stone the greengages, and Laura arranges them in overlapping lines on the pastry.

'No sugar', Aunt Ann says, 'but we'll use a spoonful of the WI honey.'

She gives Laura the spoon to lick.

Presently there is a delicious smell of baking pastry with honeyed fruit.

'Go and tell Aunt Edwina tea will be in the workroom.'

Laura runs upstairs to Aunt Edwina who is at her typewriter in a tiny study with a large window overlooking the garden.

'Coming, my lamb!'

The workroom is next door to the kitchen. They sit at a wooden table, six plain wooden chairs round it. The kitten jumps on Laura's knee and purrs loudly. Ben comes in.

'Done all there is to do for today,' he says.

'You'll have a cup of tea?'

He sits down opposite Laura. Aunt Edwina cuts a large slice of the greengage tart for him.

'Is the weather going to last?' she asks.

'Tomorrow and the day after, then we'll have rain.'

'Have we got enough logs?'

'Yes, plenty to keep going through the winter.'

Laura likes the way Ben says things as if he is quite certain of them. She also has the feeling that the three adults are saying more than the words, as if the words are only a cover for all sorts of meanings, good, safe meanings, making everything seem peaceful, even though there is a war on.

Later, they listen to the nine o'clock news. There have been massive bombing raids on Hamburg.

Good news, Laura thinks, *We're beating them!* Them?

Aunt Ann and Aunt Edwina shake their heads.

'All those civilians killed,' they murmur.

On the way up to bed Laura passes what was Aunt Tessa's room. The door is open; she puts her head round it and catches a whiff of mimosa scent. She wonders what really happens to people when they die. She can imagine another kind of world, a *somewhere else* where dead people go; different but still a bit the same, otherwise you couldn't even imagine it, just somewhere nothing nasty can ever happen to you again. She closes the door of Aunt Tessa's room. She would like that smell of mimosa to stay as long as possible.

In the room where she is sleeping there is a jug of shepherd's purse on the window sill – honesty. Aunt Ann has explained why it is called that. Laura crumbles one of the transparent, parchmenty envelopes and rubs the black seeds between her fingers. As she snuggles down in bed, she thinks about her grandpa who is dead, about her granny and her father, about whom there is no news. She can see them all so clearly inside herself. She shuts her eyes and takes a deep breath. Aunt Ann and Aunt Edwina do really seem to like her; and Hannah. Laura smiles as she remembers meeting her in Golders Hill Park. Is that the kind of thing God arranges? Then it occurs to her that perhaps round little Klaus gets on top of Hannah like Henry did on top of her mother. She wishes she had not thought of that.

She wakes to pale dawn light; it is very early, no one else is about. She gets dressed and tiptoes downstairs; she lets herself out by the backdoor through the kitchen. A few mauve autumn crocuses are showing in the long damp grass. She begins to run, past the field where they collect horse dung, past the greengage tree, past the spot where Barney is buried. She runs and runs, her heart hammering hard – *I'm here, I'm here, here!*

At school, there is an unusual seriousness about everyone in Laura's year as they realise School Certificate is only two and a half terms away. Laura is not the only one who wants her name on the honours board. But to her absolute dismay she *is* the only one who does not go down with German measles. One by one, all the others come out in the rash and are transferred to the sick rooms in the end house. Every morning Laura examines herself hopefully, but there is no sign of a rash.

'I suppose Germans don't catch German measles,' they say looking at her suspiciously.

It's no good trying to explain that in German, German measles are not called that. As far as she knows there is nothing specifically German about the disease and, *of course*, Germans catch it the same as anyone else.

'Then why haven't you?' they ask.

Never in her life has Laura so wanted to become ill.

Even Miss Elizabeth, when she is giving Laura extra Latin in the library on Saturday morning, looks at her with her head on one side. 'Lucky girl, not to go down with the German measles!'

When Laura starts to tell her, as she has told everyone else, that, in German, German measles are not called that, Miss Elizabeth pats her head and starts talking about gerunds.

When Laura goes to see Hannah and she welcomes her with the words, 'Good, you haven't got German measles; it's going round the whole town!' Laura bursts into tears. Over tea and a special treat of chocolate digestive biscuits, she tells Hannah and Klaus what the others have been saying.

'Surely you're not going to let such nonsense upset you?' They laugh.

Klaus pinches her cheek rather like her grandpa used to. She cheers up.

That afternoon instead of doing German, Hannah brings out a Halma board and shows Laura how to play. Concentrating on the game makes her forget everything else.

When she gets back to school, three of the girls, including Sheila, who have had German measles, are up and about again. 'Good old Laura!' they call out to her.

So they think she's all right, after all. How quickly the scene can change!

She has got into the First Hockey XI.

'Only because I'm so fat I fill the space between the goal posts!' The other ten laugh and pat her on the back. She is not really all that enormous, only not as skinny as most of the others. She just isn't an English shape,

They play matches against other schools on the sands. Laura enjoys buckling on the huge pads, enjoys kicking the ball right across the pitch – she has got good at that – and hardly uses her stick; so that when the centre forward of the opposing team breaks her stick after a cracking shot which misses the goal, Laura does not think twice about offering her stick to the girl. Afterwards, everyone crowds round Laura.

'Jolly decent of you to hand over your stick! And we won all the same!'

The referee, who teaches at the other school, comes up to Laura and shakes her hand. Odd to be made a fuss of for what felt like nothing much at all.

Sheila's mother comes to visit and invites Laura out tea.

'You'll come and stay with Sheila for a week or two, won't you? Maybe after the exams are over in the summer and you'll both have left Mentmore? You wouldn't mind helping with the beds and breakfast, would you? Sheila always does in the holidays. It's so hard to get staff with the war on!' Sheila's mother runs a small hotel in Devon.

Of course Laura would not mind. She had no idea Sheila liked her enough to invite her to stay.

The exams are held in a large hall near the town swimming baths. They have had it dinned into them to read the questions carefully twice over and to make their answers relevant. It's no good just pouring out everything you know. Laura does her best to remember that. After the exams are over, the art mistress takes them to an exhibition of the war artist Paul Nash. Most of the paintings and drawings are from the First World War, the one Laura's grandpa and father were in – on the other side, of course. But there is one painting called 'Dead Sea' of crashed aeroplanes which has been done quite recently. Laura stares and stares at it, overwhelmed by the silent devastation. They have extra art classes. Laura wishes she could transfer the sharp images she has onto the drawing paper, but there is something that just does not happen between her head and her hand. They also have history of art lessons with reproductions of old masters on a magic lantern. Laura specially loves Botticelli 'Primavera'. It strikes her as the very opposite of that daunting 'Dead Sea'.

On the last day of her last term at Mentmore, Laura takes herself down to the boot room and sobs in a dark corner. None of the other leavers is crying; they are excited about going home, about holidays, about what they are going to do next. Laura does not know what she is going to do next. Miss Elizabeth has tried to persuade her to stay on, to take Greek as well as Latin, to try for Oxbridge. She has even written to Ruth, who has sent back a curt, not to say rude, note, saying that Laura has to realise they are refugees; going to university is out of the question and besides, a daughter belongs with her mother in these difficult times.

'Laura, Laura, where are you?' Sheila is calling to her – they are going to Devon together.

'Coming!' Laura shouts back and makes herself stop crying. She fingers a letter from Aunt Ann in her pocket, wishing her well in her new life in London, hoping there will soon be news of her father and inviting her to Meadow House once she has settled into a new routine in London. There is a postscript from Aunt Edwina: *Keep us posted of your doings, my lamb!* They have taken it for granted that she will be living in London with her mother. Laura had hoped... that thing with feathers Emily Dickinson wrote about?

She hears footsteps coming down the stairs to the boot room. It is Miss Elizabeth herself.

'Laura, there you are, come along up, my dear, Sheila is waiting for you!'

She takes Laura gently by the hand and together they go back up into the hall where the staff are waiting to shake hands with the leavers. Miss Elizabeth walks down the drive with Laura.

'You must persuade your mother to find a school in London so that you can do your Higher School Certificate. Don't forget to write and tell us how you're getting on!'

Miss Elizabeth's bright blue eyes shine through her pince-nez.

Laura gets into the waiting taxi, peers out of the window, sees George, the school cat, snuffling round some catmint. The taxi turns out of the crescent. School is left behind.

'We'll have fun!' Sheila says in the train to Newton Abbot. 'Lots of boys!'

Laura feels a touch uncomfortable at the thought of boys. Sheila is a year older than she is; she has an older brother and is used to boys.

Her mother is at the station to meet them. She hugs Sheila and begins to cry. 'Now they're both missing!'

'Oh, God!' Sheila keeps her arms round her mother.

Laura does not know what to say. She knows Sheila's father and brother are both in the army in Singapore. She looks down at her feet waiting for the moment to pass.

'Good to be home,' Sheila says when they arrive at the small hotel.

They have grilled herrings for supper; Laura has never eaten such fresh fish. They sit in the kitchen in front of the Aga, which is like the one in Meadow House, sipping rough cider called scrumpy. *Good word,* Laura thinks.

'We'll have to hope and pray for the best,' Sheila's mother says, 'missing does not always mean dead. And in the meantime, we'll have to keep smiling, it's what they'd want.'

She pours herself some more cider.

'You girls have had enough. It's heady stuff this!'

Then she asks Laura how her mother is coping.

'Any news of your family?'

Laura says her grandpa is dead and that they don't know whether her granny in Theresienstadt or her father in Berlin are still alive.

After supper, they switch on the wireless for Tommy Handley's ITMA. For half an hour they laugh and laugh. *Can I do you now, sir – what do you want, we haven't got it!*

When they are in bed, Sheila asks, 'Do you think you'll go back home to Germany after the war? It's got to end some time, hasn't it?'

Laura is taken aback. England is home now, isn't it?

'I don't know,' she says. 'Depends what happens.' She does not add that they have not got a home in Germany now.

'Hope there's good news about your father and brother,' she says.

Sheila stretches out her hand and finds Laura's. They go to sleep holding hands.

At the weekend, Sheila's mother takes them to a Thé Dansant in a large hotel in Torquay.

'You girls have got to have your fun, war or no war!'

Laura puts on a red dress her mother got cheap from a refugee friend who has set himself up in the rag trade. She enjoys the feel of the slippery rayon against her skin. Sheila has given her a pair of nylons.

'A Yank left a whole lot of them after he stayed here!'

Laura fastens the stockings on her suspender belt. She hates wearing stockings, though her legs do look transformed by the nylons.

The band is playing Glen Miller's *Take the A Train* when they get to the hotel. They sit down at one of the little tables by the dance floor and almost immediately a naval cadet comes up to Sheila to ask her to dance. Laura watches them do the quickstep; Sheila dances well; Laura pretends she does not mind that no one has asked her. Sheila's mother is chatting to the woman at the next table. When the MC announces the Conga, she gets up, takes Laura by the hand.

'Come on, we can all do this!'

Sheila has not stopped dancing, though now she is with a different naval cadet – there is a group of them smoking by the window. Somebody grabs hold of Laura's waist and off they go in a long line – *ayayayayayay conga*. She can do this. Her hair flies about; there is not much perm left in it; she is quite sorry when the music stops. The person behind her has swivelled her round to face him. He has bright blue eyes and floppy fair hair. The MC announces a polka. Laura has learnt how to do that in dancing classes at school.

'Come on, let's have a go,' the young man says. 'I'm Bob!'

'Laura,' she says. It could be, it *is*, an English name.

They go stomping round the room. Then, suddenly, the lights are dimmed, there is total silence, everyone stands stiffly to attention as the band strikes up *God Save The King*. Then there is a renewed hum and buzz of conversation as people prepare to leave.

Bob takes Laura back to her table. It turns out that Sheila's mother and her friend know him and his family. *How nice,* Laura thinks, *they all know each other.*

'My dad's home on leave!' Bob says.

Laura can see the pain in Sheila's mother's face.

'Another three days before he goes back to his squadron,' Bob tells them. 'He's a bit browned off because they haven't seen any action yet!'

Sheila's mother introduces her to her friend, saying her full name.

'That sounds foreign,' the friend says, as if she has smelt a bad smell.

Sheila's mother explains. How Laura wishes she did not have

to go through that rigmarole every time people hear her German name: refugee... mother Jewish... grandparents deported... father stayed behind...not Jewish...not a Nazi, of course...

'I see,' the friend says, still smelling the bad smell, and goes on, 'As far as I'm concerned, the only good German's a dead German!' She smiles patriotically.

Laura looks at Bob. He does not seem fazed by the revelation that her second name is a German one.

'I have to get back to the pigs,' he says – he is at the local agricultural college. 'Come to the flicks with me at the weekend? It's *For Whom the Bell Tolls*, with Ingrid Bergman.'

So it really doesn't matter about her name. Bob likes her!

Sheila has gone off with one of the naval cadets. Laura waits while Sheila's mother says goodbye to her friend.

'What a pity Sheila didn't bring a little English girl to stay,' she says without lowering her voice.

Sheila's mother hooks her arm through Laura's as they walk to the station, past a poster telling them that *Careless talk costs lives*.

It is Laura's last day in Newton Abbot, she is waiting for Bob to call for her.

'I bet he takes you into the double seats in the back row!' Sheila says. 'So you won't see much of the picture!'

'I'm looking forward to the film,' Laura says innocently. 'It's based on a novel by Ernest Hemingway. I'll get it out of the library when I get back home – I mean, back to London.'

Ruth has moved again, from Golders Green to West Hampstead. Laura has no idea where the nearest library is.

Sheila looks at her blankly. 'You've never been kissed, have you?' she asks.

Laura looks at her feet, embarrassed. Her school shoes do not really go with the tight-waisted cotton frock she is wearing.

Yes, Bob has tickets for the double seats. He puts his arm round her and his slightly stubbly cheek near hers. It feels nice, but she forgets about it when the film starts. Presently, his arm slips from her shoulder to her waist; he pulls her towards himself and kisses her. There is a whiff of hay about him. That's nice too, but Laura wishes he would wait until the film is over – it is really gripping. When his hand slips from her waist to her breast and he puts his tongue in her mouth, she closes her eyes.

The lights come on. *God Save the King* starts. They stand up.

'Did you enjoy the picture?' Sheila's mother asks when they get back.

They nod. Bob asks Laura how much longer she is staying.

'Back to London tomorrow!'

'I'll write!'

Now, *now*, Laura would like him to kiss her, but he does not. She walks with him to the end of the drive, where he has left his bicycle.

'I'll get your address from Sheila,' he says and pedals away, turning round once to wave, making the bike wobble.

'I don't like to think of you in London with those dreadful doodlebugs going off all the time!' Sheila's mother says as she is seeing Laura off at Newton Abbot station.

'Oh, I'll be all right!'

'Course you will,' Sheila says.

The train pulls out. Laura wonders how she knows she will be all right.

§

'Here ve are,' her mother says as they get to the attic flat in West Hampstead. She flings the sitting room door open with a flourish and, there, set out on a rickety table, Laura sees crystal glasses sparkling green, blue, crimson, purple, apricot. The last time she saw those they were in a glass-fronted cabinet in her grandparents' Berlin flat. So, their things *have* come from Somerset.

'Vell?' Ruth smiles at Laura. 'Now vot you say?'

Laura would like to say that they need a room to go with the glasses. She looks at the frayed curtain sliding off its rail, the sagging armchairs, the grimy walls. She sees crates upturned on top of each other to make a sort of dresser. In them are fluted china coffee cups with a pattern of black and yellow flowers and piles of damask tablecloths with matching napkins done up in blue satin ribbons. There is silver cutlery including fish knives and forks with sea creatures embossed on them. And there, too, yes, *yes*, is a little glass cage with two yellow glass birds in it.

'That's mine!'

Her granny gave her that when birthdays were real. *Two goldfinches for my little goldfinch.*

'Where's my room?' Laura asks.

The room is tiny with sloping walls. *This is my room? This is who I am?* Laura asks herself.

'You unpack,' Ruth says. 'I make supper.'

Laura puts the glass cage on the table standing against the wall. She gets out the raffia chimney sweep and stands him next to the goldfinch cage. She hangs her clothes in the wardrobe which takes up too much space, stacks her books on the table – there are too many. Maybe there is a bookshelf in the other room? Laura remembers there was a crate of books; her father made sure of that. She goes into the kitchen to ask Ruth about it.

'Oh zat, ve left it behind, zose books vould have been too much.'

Books too much? But not crystal glasses? Not fish knives and damask tablecloths? Laura looks at Ruth. *This is my mother?*

She writes to thank Sheila's mother, called a *bread-and-butter letter* – Aunt Edwina told her that. She wonders, but does not ask, if Bob has got her address.

'Ze day after tomorrow ve have ze appointment at Bloomsbury House,' Ruth says over supper.

'What's Bloomsbury House?'

'A charity for Jewish refugees.'

So that label, which had begun to fade, still clings to her.

She feels acutely uncomfortable on the way to see someone who hands out second-hand clothes. After a good deal of rummaging about, the woman fishes out a camel hair coat.

'This should fit!'

Laura tries it on – yes, it fits. She looks at herself in the full length mirror on the wall. It does not look too bad, but as she takes it off, she sees a huge pale stain, a gray mess, on the back of it.

'I can't wear this!'

'Oh well,' the woman's voice is icy, 'someone will.'

'Ve take it,' Ruth says quickly. 'Sank you.'

Laura thinks she would rather freeze to death than put that coat on ever again.

'Ze stain doesn't show so much.' Ruth says when they are out of the room.

'Not if you're blind.'

Ruth changes the subject. 'Now ve see someone about a school for you.' She had found a job for Laura in the office of the place where she had done the ironing; they would have paid for shorthand and typing courses, but after some tense discussions Ruth finally agreed that Laura should go back to school for two more years.

The woman concerned with schools suggests one on the Highgate side of Hampstead Heath. 'Wonderful headmistress, has the greatest sympathy with and understanding for Jewish refugees, a good many in the school.'

No getting away from that, Laura thinks. Is she turning into a refugee from being a refugee?

Ruth smiles and nods approvingly.

The woman makes an appointment with the headmistress's secretary.

'Then you'll be fixed up for the beginning of the autumn term,' she smiles at Laura.

Whatever the school turns out to be like, Laura feels relieved to have an autumn term in prospect.

Meeting the new headmistress, who has a kind of other-worldly look about her, goes well. She asks Laura what subjects she would like to take.

'English and French,' she says immediately. Then she hesitates, but almost against her will she adds, 'And German...' her grandfather's *Don't forget your mother tongue* echoing inside her.

She gets her School Certificate results from Miss Elizabeth. Yes, she has Matric Exempt. *Well done! You'll have to come and see your name up on the honours board,* Miss Elizabeth writes.

'I've done it, I've done it!' Laura shouts waving the letter in her mother's face.

'I'm proud of my clever daughter,' Ruth says and hugs her. 'Ve go to a Vill Hay show at ze Golders Green Hippodrome to celebrate,' she promises. Someone at the munitions factory knows

Will Hay and gives Ruth free tickets. Laura has no idea who Will Hay is. She wonders how the others at Mentmore have done, writes to Sheila, asks if Bob ever got her address, then scrumples the letter up and starts again. She writes to tell Aunt Ann and Aunt Edwina, to Klaus and Hannah – they will all be pleased.

Then she looks at the awful coat from Bloomsbury House hanging in the wardrobe and vows never to wear it; she will earn money to buy a coat of which she is not ashamed. So she spends the rest of the summer holiday back ironing pieces of fabric. When Ruth says she does not have to, Laura tells her mother she wants decent clothes. She also spends some of her earnings on whitewash for her room. There are congratulations from Hannah, enclosing a postal order for five shillings, but there is nothing from Meadow House. Laura is sad about that. Tilly Kettle will no longer be a kitten.

On the first day of the autumn term, Laura is wearing new clothes bought with her own money. Her coat from Bloomsbury House is in the dustbin. You don't have to wear uniform in the sixth form.

'You're new, aren't you? For the Lower Sixth?' a member of staff says as Laura walks into the red brick school building. She is the only new girl in the class; the other nine have all been there since they were eleven. The headmistress comes to talk to them. She tells them that being sixth formers is pretty well like being university students; they will no longer be spoon fed but be expected to use their own initiative in all sorts of ways. Then she introduces Laura to the others. Two of them have continental sounding names but, like Laura, they speak English without the least trace of a foreign accent. Another girl is English Jewish – being Jewish in London is not as strange as it was in Weston-super-Mare.

They sit at a long table, not desks, waiting for the English mistress. She turns out to be rather large with fine fair hair done up in a tight knot.

'Hallo everyone! Had a good summer? Nice to see you all. We're kicking off with Spenser; I'll tell you a bit about him, then we'll take it in turns to read. I see your edition has asterisks every now and then. Tell me when you come to them and I'll fill you in!' That does make them feel like university students.

After the mid-morning break, they have more English with a different teacher who is reading Shaw's *St. Joan* with them. Heidi, one of the other refugee girls, is given the part of St. Joan; Laura gets the part of Dunois. They enjoy the play reading. At the end of the school day Laura and Heidi catch the train from Gospel Oak to West Hampstead together.

When Laura gets back to the flat, there is a nasty smell from the kitchen. She finds stinking fish and turned milk; there is no refrigerator – not many people have one. She pours the sour milk down the sink, wraps the fish in newspaper and takes it down to the dustbins. She is hungry – it seems a long time since she had her marmite sandwiches and an apple for lunch. Nearly everyone brought sandwiches – quite a change of scene from going into lunch at Mentmore with Miss Thomas saying grace and then, if you were sitting at her table, talking French with Mademoiselle, everyone hoping someone would pass them the gravy or the salt, not being allowed to ask for it yourself.

Now she finds some stale but not inedible bread and makes tea in the brown pot. She remembers the smoky smell of Lapsang Souchong at Meadow House in cups bordered with red and purple flowers; remembers pale amber tea in glasses in silver holders that her granny put on a small white china tray. She takes the tea into her room, which is bright with the recent whitewash, gets *St. Joan* out of her schoolbag and immerses herself in Shaw's take on this quasi-mythical girl. On the whole, people who hear voices are considered mad; but Laura can hear her father's and grandparents' voices quite clearly inside herself.

Ruth comes in looking pale and tired and spends a long time in the bathroom cleaning up. Her nails are broken, the pink nail polish chipped.

'Zey give us gloves but I can't do ze vork viz gloves,' she says, rubbing cream into her hands. 'How can I give people a massage viz hands like zese!' She holds them up. 'All zat training at home vasted!'

At home: Berlin.

Laura mentions the fish.

'Vot? You srew it avay?'

'It stank!'

'Vell zen, ve can't eat it!' Ruth bursts out laughing.
They have fried potatoes and pickled beetroot out of a jar for supper.

Laura falls into the new routine: quick breakfast with her mother, train to school – she is making friends, getting quite good marks for essays – then back to the flat to do homework. Mentmore days are receding, though Sheila keeps in touch. She has not gone back to any school, is helping her mother with the hotel work and enjoying herself with Dartmouth naval cadets. There is still no definite news about her father and brother. She does not mention Bob.

Always when her mother comes home, Laura feels a little jolt of pleasure, but after the first five minutes there is nothing to talk about. She has no idea what went on in Ruth's day at the factory; Ruth has no idea what Spenser and Shaw are about. Anything she can think of saying immediately strikes Laura as pointless. She hates it when Ruth asks if she is feeling all right. Sometimes she fantasizes about having an English mother without forming any distinct image of what such a mother might look like. An English mother would probably have been brought up in the country, part of a large family. It would be fun to have English aunts and uncles and cousins. An English mother might be widowed, certainly not divorced. She does not fantasize about having an English father: she loves her real father. Sometimes she sits in her room by candlelight reading Keats or First World War poems.

The Second World War goes on around her. Doodlebugs have been superseded by the even deadlier V2s.

'Vot's ze point of going to a shelter viz zose sings,' Ruth says when the air raid warning goes. Quite often the rocket has already landed, so far always somewhere else. Every now and then she looks at Laura and says, '*Schrecklich, schrecklich!*' She picks up the raffia chimney sweep, 'You still have zis!'

There is no news from Germany. They have not had a letter from their friends in Switzerland for a long time. One morning, when she has stopped expecting it, Laura has a letter from Aunt Ann: Aunt Edwina has died; she is selling Meadow House; it is too lonely without her friends. She is moving into a Quaker retirement home where they welcome pets, so she can take Tilly Kettle, who is quite a sedate cat now. *A great comfort,* she says and *Be sure to let me know if there is news from your father.* And she adds congratulations about getting the Matric Exempt.

Laura reads the letter three times. When she shows it to Ruth, Ruth shrugs her shoulders and says, 'You write. I von't.'

Laura does not know what to say. She has never had to write a letter of condolence. When that red card from Theresienstadt signed *Widow* arrived, there was no way of replying. She sucks her pen, remembers how Aunt Edwina called her *my lamb*.

Getting on the train in West Hampstead every morning, Laura notices a boy who goes to the school next door to hers. They have not spoken, but he has smiled in her direction. Then one day he moves over to sit next to her.

'I'm Johnny,' he says.

'Laura.'

They walk the short distance to school together; every now and then his sleeve rubs against hers. Laura likes the way he strides along as if the world belongs to him. After school, there he is, standing on the platform.

'You waited for me?' Laura feels herself blushing.

He nods. 'You're new this year, aren't you?'

She tells him about the boarding school she used to go to. 'But being a day girl is much better,' she says. *Is it?*

Johnny gets off the train with her. 'I'll walk you home!'

Laura is not quite comfortable with that. Will he expect her to ask him in? She does not want him to see their dilapidated attic flat with the makeshift packing-case dresser full of things from what seems like a previous incarnation. Ruth has been selling the crystal glasses for a pound each; Laura does not know whether or not that is a good price for them.

'See you tomorrow,' is all Johnny says when they get to her house, and he smiles. That smile gets to her.

He sees her home most days. He tells her how he wants to be a journalist in Paris. Yes, he is good at French, has a French grandfather. Laura almost tells him her father is a German journalist but stops herself – it would need too much explaining.

'Paris when the Jerries have finally been turfed out… won't be long now!' Johnny says.

Laura is very glad she has not let on that she is a sort of Jerry.

One afternoon, Johnny does not say *See you tomorrow* as they get to Laura's house. He says, 'It's about time I kissed you!'

They stand in the dusk in her doorway. His face, his very beautiful face, comes closer and closer; she inclines her head towards his, too breathless to speak. He kisses her, presses his whole body against hers.

Then he says, 'You haven't done much of this, have you?'

Laura does not know where to look.

'Never mind; you will!' Johnny says and walks away.

They do not coincide on the train again.

The Lower Sixth go as a group to the Christmas dance at the boys' school next door. Laura is reluctant to go. Johnny has made her lose confidence, but he does not seem to be at the dance, and to her surprise a dark-haired boy comes up to her almost at once. They do a quickstep without talking. The boy dances rather well; Laura finds it easy to follow him. He gets her a glass of orange squash.

'I'm Jewish, you know. My parents came as refugees from Berlin,' he says before even telling her his name.

Why is that the first thing he mentions? In case she does not want to talk to him because he is Jewish? Has that happened to him?

'That's where I come from, too,' Laura says without adding she is only half Jewish. *Only?*

'That's OK then. I'm Fred,' he smiles at her.

'Laura,' she says, though on this occasion it would be all right to add her second name without embarrassment.

He invites her to his house, introduces her to his parents. They have been in England much longer than Laura and her mother and live in style with furniture they brought out from Berlin. *Why didn't we?* Laura wonders. Fred is an enthusiastic cyclist; he has a speedometer on his Rudge racing bike. When Laura confesses she cannot ride a bike, he laughs and offers to teach her. It does not take her long to learn.

He lends her one of his three bikes and they go for long rides in the countryside round London. On one occasion in the spring they go to Milton's cottage in Chalfont St. Giles; Laura has Miss Elizabeth's voice echoing inside her, reading the sonnet 'On His Blindness'. They picnic in woods and fields, the English countryside gentle round them. Sheltered by trees, they stretch out on last year's leaves and Fred tells Laura how pretty she is; this makes her want him to kiss her before he actually does. They forget about being refugees.

When she goes away for a week to stay with Sheila in Devon, Fred writes to her; Sheila is impressed. There is a muted atmosphere about the little hotel – Sheila's father and brother have both been confirmed dead. What to say? Laura hugs Sheila and her mother. Just before she leaves, Bob turns up. How nice he looks in his cords and tweed jacket! There is something mercurial about him that moves Laura deeply, something rather like the weather, one minute grey, the next silver and turquoise. Is it his Englishness? He says nothing about not having got in touch but makes her feel they are friends. When, after he has left, Sheila tells her he has a new girlfriend, it makes no difference to that feeling.

Back in London, it is too wet and windy to go for long bike rides with Fred. Instead, he gets her to come to his parents' flat when they are out. Sitting on the sofa, he fondles her in new and delightful ways. They lose track of time but then, afterwards, drinking fizzy orange straight out of the Corona bottle, they do not have a great deal to say to each other. Fred is going straight into his father's furniture business when he leaves school. When Laura says she wants to get a degree, he asks 'What for?' She does not know what to answer, but she would rather be with someone who did not ask her that. She sees less of Fred.

Laura's last year at school begins. Everyone else is getting geared up for college. She has talked to her mother about going to university, tells her she could get a grant.

'You forget ve are refugees,' is all she hears from Ruth.

'Some of the others are as well!'

'Vell, perhaps zey have fahzers viz a lot of money! Ven you leave school, you get a job! Is zat understood?'

In November the Sixth Form girls are encouraged to sign up as temporary postmen for the Christmas holidays to help deliver cards. Just before the end of term they are called for interview to the GPO in Mount Pleasant. The hall is crowded; names are called; Laura sits up expectantly, but the man calling out names does not call hers. Heidi is also still sitting there when everyone else has been called. The man comes up to them, asks who they are, passes a finger down a long list, shakes his head, looks a bit surprised, says, 'Sorry, enemy aliens not allowed!' *So that's what I've turned into,* Laura thinks. Feeling gutted, she walks out into the cold with Heidi.

Laura concentrates on her work. She may not be going to college but she wants to get the best grades she can.

The six of them doing English go to the New Theatre in St. Martin's Lane to see the Old Vic Company doing *King Lear*. They get there at six in the morning to queue for stools; they listen to the buskers – one banging spoons on his knees is always there. Then they queue again in the evening for the one and sixpenny tickets up in the gallery. Laura goes to see *King Lear* three times, not only because it is a set book but because Laurence Olivier as Lear and Alec Guinness as the Fool open up new dimensions of tragedy for her, making it both personal and universal.

She goes to see French films at the Academy and Studio One in Oxford Street to get her ear in and her accent improved for the oral exam. She does not need to practise her German accent; what she enjoys most about the German course is Rilke's poetry – the way he uses the German language surprises and delights her.

The war is coming to a frightening end. In February 1945, Dresden is destroyed by two incendiary raids in one night. In April, Belsen concentration camp is liberated; what newsreels and papers reveal sends shockwaves through the nation. *These almost-corpses are people I might have known?* Laura thinks. On May 8th, European victory is celebrated. Ruth and Laura listen to the King's broadcast:

War battered but never for one moment daunted or dismayed... Our cause was the cause not of the nation only, not of this Empire and Commonwealth only, but of every land where freedom is cherished and law and liberty go hand in hand.

They hear Churchill:

My dear friends, this is your hour!... I say that in the long years to come not only will the people of this island but of the world, where the bird of freedom chirps in human hearts, look back to what we have done... Now we have emerged from one deadly struggle – a terrible foe has been cast on the ground and awaits our judgment and our mercy.

But in July Churchill is defeated by Clement Attlee in the General Election. There has not been a Labour Government since 1931. Laura is not quite sure of the significance of all this; could we have won the war without Churchill? But she does understand that men who have fought side by side will no longer put up with touching their caps and being called *My good man* by some toff in brogues.

There is still no news of her father or her granny or any of the other relations who left Berlin in one way or another. Bernard, one of Ruth's young cousins, was sent out to Bangkok to make his way with Unilever; every now and then she mentions him hopefully.

As soon as the exams are over, Laura goes for job interviews with publishing firms; she feels comfortable in the world of books and print. At the first interview, it turns out they wanted someone older. At the second, the woman interviewing fiddles with the cross round her neck and tells her that, though in many ways she seems the right sort of girl for the job, they could not possibly employ someone with a German surname like hers; what would the liftman say, who's just lost a leg in the war? At the third interview, the man who sees her treats her at once as if she were a fellow member of staff and does not comment on her foreign-sounding name. He explains that theirs is a strict union house and that she will automatically belong to the clerical union. He adds regretfully that, if he allowed her to write so much as a caption for a photograph, he would be in deep trouble with *his* union. Laura takes the job, puts herself down for shorthand and typing classes and looks forward to a youth-hostelling holiday before she begins life as an office girl.

'You sink ve vill hear from your fahzer now?' Ruth asks as she sees Laura off on her bike.

It is not comfortable to have a mother who says *your fahzer* like that, as if he had no connection with her.

'And granny?' Laura looks at her mother.

Ruth looks away.

Laura meets Heidi who has got into Bedford College to do English. Heidi has come with her brother, who has brought a friend. While they cycle across the countryside towards Stratford-on-Avon, the Japanese capitulate. Atom bombs have been dropped on Hiroshima and Nagasaki. The horrifying photographs of bomb victims in the papers dampen the spirit of relief and jubilation.

In Stratford they go to see *The Tempest*. Once the curtain has gone up, Laura forgets everything, until Prospero breaks his magic staff. She is sitting next to Heidi's brother's friend. He has been scribbling in a notebook, only looking up occasionally through horn-rimmed spectacles to take in what is happening on the stage. While they are clapping, Laura asks him what he has been writing. Alec holds the notebook open and she sees he has been sketching the characters on the stage. On the way back to the youth hostel he tells her he has got into Camberwell School of Art.

'And what about you?' he asks.

'Publisher's office in Long Acre,' she mumbles.

'That's near the opera house, isn't it?'

'Right opposite!'

'We'll go,' he promises. He does not seem put off by the fact that she is not going to college.

She gets back to West Hampstead in good spirits, but the moment she looks at Ruth's face, everything she was going to tell her mother about the holiday dries up inside her.

'Sit down, dahlink... ve have to talk... I have to tell you...' but Ruth gets no further. She sobs and sobs. Laura holds her hand.

'Zis voman came vile you vere avay, told me everysink, how in ze end...'

How in the end Laura's granny was in one of the last batches – *batches?* – who were gassed in Auschwitz.

'Zis voman, much younger, could still vork, zat's how she survived... said zat... zat after grandpa died granny vent out of her mind... how she looked after her like a daughter... but... but... *I* am ze daughter!'

Laura goes on holding her mother's hand. People's grannies die all the time, don't they; it's what you expect grannies to do... only... only... not... not... How can she talk about *The Tempest*, about Prospero and his magic staff? In spite of the awful news, Laura somehow feels her lovely granny safe inside her. Nothing can stop her from being her granny's little goldfinch.

There is a letter from Aunt Ann. Ruth gives it to Laura.

'Perhaps she has heard from your fahzer?'

But Aunt Ann is only writing to ask if *they* have had any news. She goes on to say that she has settled quite comfortably into the retirement home, and so has Tilly Kettle. Tilly Kettle! Laura can feel his fur soft and warm under her hands. She starts to cry and will not let Ruth put an arm round her. She runs into her room.

Before she has got round to replying to Aunt Ann, there is a letter, readdressed many times, from their Swiss friends. Inside the envelope, there is another envelope with a letter from one of her father's colleagues. *How sad I am,* it says in German, *to have to tell you that your father perished in a bomb attack over Berlin on...* Laura reads no further, drops the letter on the floor.

'Vot you doing?' Ruth picks it up, reads it, puts a hand on Laura's shoulder. Laura pulls away.

'I don't understand you!' Ruth says.

Nothing to understand, Laura thinks. Like her granny and grandpa, her father is safe inside her, but she cannot explain that to her mother.

§

The publisher who appointed Laura introduces her to his colleagues. One of them raises his eyebrows when he hears her name. 'Sounds suspiciously German,' he says and walks off.

Suspiciously? Isn't the war over?

Everyone else shakes her warmly by the hand. One of the secretaries shows her how to do filing, takes her out to lunch and asks if she is doing shorthand and typing classes. Laura goes to them reluctantly. They type to music on typewriters with covered keyboards; everyone giggles; they make a lot of mistakes.

She decides not to bother with touch typing; she is managing reasonably well on the large Remington on her desk in the office. Shorthand is more interesting – she passes the first test easily. Not long after she has had the news about her father, her boss asks if she can manage to take a letter in shorthand. She can, but she has to start the typing three times because she does not want to use the rubber, which will make holes in the austerity-quality paper. When she finally takes the letter to be signed, her boss says, 'Well done!' and pats her on the knee. Laura almost tells him about her father but just then his phone rings, so she goes away.

Ruth has stopped working at the munitions factory and has found a job as a masseuse with a beautician in the West End; an actor called Rufus whom she met at the Golders Green Hippodrome has recommended her. Having done war work has made it easy for her to get the work permit.

Laura is usually first back in the flat, lights the smelly oil stove in her room, warms up some baked beans and eats them straight out of the tin. The raffia chimney sweep stands on her table; the broom has slipped out of his right hand, but he still has his ladder. She picks him up, shuts her eyes and feels her father's hand warm in hers as he gives her it on the Anhalter Bahnhof. Six years ago! She has an image of him in his short black overcoat with the velvet collar.

She writes to Aunt Ann in her retirement home, as well as to Hannah and Klaus who have moved to Yorkshire where Klaus has got a post as consultant anaesthetist – he passed all his exams in English – and before Ruth comes home, she goes to bed, looking forward to meeting Alec after work. Unlike Bob, he has kept in touch and they are going to see *La Bohème* in Covent Garden.

At breakfast, Ruth tells her that Rufus, the man who helped get her the job with the beautician, is coming to visit that evening.

'So you vill meet him!' Her voice carries instructions to be civil.

'I'll be out,' Laura says.

Ruth also shows her a letter from Henry, who has settled in Chicago near his sister. He has a new girlfriend but promises to help Ruth over if she wants to come, for old times sake.

'I knew he vould,' Ruth says.

Laura says nothing.

At the end of the office day, Laura walks out into the dusk; it is lovely to have the streets brightly lit after years of bumbling about with torches in the blackout. Rationing goes on; there are queues for bread and potatoes, and once she found herself in a queue which turned out to be for birdseed! Just as she was about to walk away, the woman behind her begged her to buy some – her canaries could do with a bit of extra!

Alec is waiting for her. He holds her hand as they cross the road to the opera house. Their seats are in the front row of the gallery, where there is adequate legroom. Puccini's music moves Laura to tears; perhaps she will tell Alec about her father. Afterwards, on the way to the underground, Alec tells her about life classes at Camberwell; about landscape drawing with Victor Pasmore; about learning to throw pots on the wheel; about a girl called Milly who is very good at that; about a fancy dress ball coming up just before Christmas – 1890s, Toulouse-Lautrec, that kind of thing; would she like to come? Of course! She has never been to a fancy dress ball. She does not let on that she is not quite sure who or what Toulouse-Lautrec is. She will find out. She does not mention her father.

'Margot Fonteyn's dancing in *Sleeping Beauty* tomorrow; I'll get up early to queue for tickets. And there's this amazing Van Gogh exhibition at the Tate – let's go Saturday morning!'

Laura is excited – opera, ballet, art, a fancy dress ball! Yes, yes, the war *is* over! As she unlocks the front door, she remembers that Ruth's friend Rufus might be there. The light is on in the front room but there is no one talking, instead there is the sound of sobbing. Laura opens the door gently to see Ruth curled up on the couch, head buried in a satin cushion, shoulders heaving. She turns a blotchy face towards Laura.

'It's all over,' she says crumpling a handkerchief in her hand.

Laura sees a bunch of yellow roses lying on the table. She picks them up – they need putting in water.

'Leave zem alone, srow zem avay!'

Laura drops the roses.

'*La Bohème* was lovely,' she says sheepishly. 'And ballet tomorrow night!'

Ruth sits up. Laura notices grey hair reappearing at her temples where the dye is fading. The black has an uncomfortable sheen of bronze about it.

'Tomorrow? You go out again tomorrow? If you...' Ruth sobs, 'go out tomorrow you vill find... I vill put my head in ze gas oven... if it's not enough for you to have your fahzer dead, your grandparents... zen you vill have a dead muzzer as vell!'

Laura cannot believe what she is hearing. Ruth looks across at the wilting roses.

'He came for five minutes to tell me zair is someone else, ze bastard!'

'You mean Rufus?' Laura asks stupidly. She is very tired.

'Don't ever say his name again!'

'Goodnight then!'

'Give your muzzer a kiss!'

Reluctantly Laura kisses her mother.

At breakfast Ruth says, 'So I see you here for supper. Vot vould you like to eat?'

'But...'

Ruth's chin trembles. 'If you vant to see me again alive you vill be here!'

Miserably, Laura goes to work. Miserably she meets Alec.

'I can't come out tonight, my mother isn't... isn't well.'

'Oh, it won't be hard to sell your ticket,' Alec says. 'See you at the Tate Saturday morning then?'

Laura wishes he sounded more disappointed. How lightly he walks away from her. Doesn't he mind at all? She knows that not showing you mind things is very English. She will try not to show it when *she* minds; but perhaps Alec *really* doesn't mind? How can you tell?

When she gets home, Ruth is standing in front of the bathroom mirror patting her face with a large pink powder puff; then she takes out a lipstick and paints her mouth crimson. She looks at Laura surprised.

'Back early? I sought you vere going out?'

'But...' Laura's heart is hammering hard.

'I go out in ten minutes,' Ruth says.

'With Rufus?' Laura asks bewildered.

'Don't be silly, of course not!'
The phone rings, Ruth rushes to answer it.
'Eddie, hallo, dahlink. I'm ready…'
Laura goes into her room, sits on her bed with clenched fists. She can hardly breathe; she has never been so angry in all her life. She looks at the raffia chimney sweep, at the little glass bird cage on her table. Gradually she calms down. In the morning, she eats her cornflakes in her room by herself.

She meets Alec on Saturday outside the Tate Gallery. The queue stretches right round the building; this is the first major exhibition since the war. After about two hours, they get in. Alec is almost trembling with excitement as they walk round – all he can say is, 'Look, look, look!' Laura looks. There are the sunflowers, the chair, the cornfield, the stars in the dark blue sky; there are the self portraits. Not picture postcards, the real thing! Alec is poring over glass cases with drawings.
'I'll have to come again!' he says, his grey eyes shining.
They stroll along Millbank, walk past the Houses of Parliament and down Whitehall into Trafalgar Square. Alec buys them hot meat pies and mugs of tea at a street stall. Laura is beginning to be a Londoner.
She gets ready for the 1890s fancy dress ball. She has made a pale blue high-necked taffeta blouse with a remnant she got without coupons. She goes looking for a long black skirt; there is no time to make that as well – she has to pass another shorthand exam. So she swallows her pride and anger and asks Ruth, to whom she has been speaking as little as possible, if maybe her friend in the rag trade could…
'Of course, dahlink.' And a few days later Ruth produces a long black skirt for Laura, which does not look cheap.
'Thank you,' Laura mumbles.
'Do I get a kiss?'
No, Ruth does not get a kiss.
There is a crowd round the bar when Laura gets to Camberwell Art School. She cannot see Alec, but Heidi and her brother are there. He looks comic with a burnt cork moustache under his nose. Alec appears.

'Hallo, all!'

Laura is a bit hurt she is just one of the all.

'Here's Milly,' Alec says.

A young woman swathed in black velvet, her fair hair swept high on her head, steps out of the crowd. Laura looks at her face, *not such a very nice face,* she thinks. Perhaps faces don't matter so much if you're a wonderful shape?

Alec dances with Laura, but he keeps looking at other girls. 'There's a party at Milly's afterwards,' he tells her.

Laura, Heidi and her brother pile in to the back of Milly's old banger. Alec sits in the front next to her.

'A bit young, aren't they?' Laura hears Milly say as they go down some steps into her basement flat. How old is *she?* And Alec? Quite soon Milly's flat is jammed with couples on each other's knees, kissing in corners, shedding skirts, trousers. Laura cannot see Milly or Alec.

Heidi comes over to her. 'Shall we go?'

'You'll have to come to an IVC dance; they're really good,' Heidi says on their way home.

'IVC?'

'Intervarsity Vacation Club!'

'But I'm not a student!'

'Doesn't matter at all,' Heidi assures her.

The IVC dances are in Chelsea Town Hall along the King's Road. Laura sits waiting for someone to ask her to dance; she has almost forgotten why she is there.

'Will you have this dance with me?'

There is this young man with a long nose in his thin face looking at her, a mauve scarf flapping round his neck. He does not dance very well, but Laura likes the way he grips her firmly round the waist. Then he buys her a shandy at the bar. He is called Francis, has a degree in botany and works in a lab. 'But what I really do is write poetry,' he says.

Laura warms to him.

Suddenly he says, 'There's Tom!' in a voice loud enough to make everyone near them turn round, except this Tom, whoever he may be.

'Tom and I were at college together; he did zoology, but what he's brilliant at is philosophy. Couldn't do a degree in it because of the war, all philosophy departments closed down for the duration.' Francis speaks of this Tom with great admiration; Laura is not quite sure what being brilliant at philosophy involves.

Francis sees her to the bus stop along the King's Road and asks her to meet him in a coffee bar along Old Compton Street the following Saturday. 'Excellent coffee there!' he says. Laura dare not tell him she does not like coffee. Well, from now on, she *will* like coffee.

'What time shall we meet?'

'Let's say five past one. Up to one is Thomas time – we do the Bond Street galleries on Saturdays.' The bus comes; Francis gives her a shy peck on the cheek.

'You've just missed him,' Francis says when she arrives in Old Compton Street at five past one as requested. Laura is not sure whether he is sorry or relieved.

'We went to see the John Tunnards at the Beaux Arts,' he tells her. Laura tries to look as if she knows what he is talking about. She asks him what he is reading and he holds up a battered Everyman edition of Marlowe's *Dr. Faustus*. 'It's coming on at the New Theatre, not often done. Want to go?' He puts the book down and gets her a coffee. Then they walk across to Better Books in Charing Cross Road. Francis picks up a volume of Henry Treece poems called *The Black Season* and buys it. 'New Apocalypse, great stuff!' He talks about Henry Treece as if he were Keats or Shelley. Laura admits that she has not read much contemporary poetry; her anthologies end with the First World War.

They amble along Charing Cross Road hand in hand. 'Now, I want to know everything about you!' Francis says. Laura loves the way his mouth turns down rather than up when he smiles. She tells him about her grandparents and her father, and the barest minimum about her mother. He stops in the middle of the road.

'My God, that's monstrous! One has only heard, read about it, hardly believed...' he squeezes her hand hard. 'I'd never, never have known you weren't born and bred British; you haven't the least trace of an accent!' Laura likes Francis better and better.

'You have your mother!' he goes on.

'Yes,' Laura says.

By the time they have got to Green Park, Francis is telling her that he is about to start printing a little magazine on an ancient printing press he has recently bought. 'It's going to be called *Reflections!* Tom's contributed a piece of luminous prose for the first number.' Then he asks if she would like to help with the setting up. Yes, she would love to help. Arm in arm, stars bright above them, they cross the park. Gently, Francis draws her to himself and kisses her.

She goes to see him in his basement flat in Highbury. The printing press takes up a large friendly space in the sitting room. 'Over a hundred years old,' Francis says with pride. He shows her how to hold the composing stick and gives her a poem to set up. She begins to find her way round the type font; the letters make a satisfying click as they fall into place. 'Taken to it like a duck to water,' Francis says presently. Laura barely looks up from what she is doing. He gets up to ink the platen; they pull a proof of the short poem she has just set up – there are quite a lot of literals. She extracts the wrong letters, puts them carefully back into their right compartments in the font, finds the correct ones. They pull another proof – only a couple of commas out of place now.

This is how Laura spends her Saturdays, growing into what begins to feel like her real self. When they have finished printing, Francis gives her coffee in a pint-sized mug and those squashed fly Garibaldi biscuits they had during air raids in the cellar at Mentmore. He talks about Marlowe's *Faustus* and about the magical novels of Charles Williams, of whom Laura has not heard. He lends her *The Place of the Lion,* which grips her while she is reading it, but leaves nothing much in its wake.

One Saturday, instead of making coffee when they have finished setting up and printing, Francis takes her into his bedroom, undresses her, spends time gazing at her while her heart beats wildly. Now… now… now… Laura loses her virginity.

'Stay the night?' Francis asks.

'My mother…' Laura says, thinking *wouldn't care*, but she would like Francis to think that she has a mother who *does* care. She wonders if somehow Ruth will be able to tell she is no longer a virgin. He sees her to the station, looks and looks at her, says

'My girl', is reluctant to let go of her hand as his mauve silk scarf flaps in the wind. *Do I truly love him?* Laura asks herself on the way home. *Was it wonderful?*

Unusually, Ruth is in when she gets back to West Hampstead. 'Come, here, come here, I vant to show you somesing!' Her eyes are shining. *This is what she must have looked like when she was young, before I happened to her,* Laura thinks. Ruth pats the place next to her on the sofa. 'Sit viz me a minute, dahlink!' She waves an envelope with exotic stamps at Laura, pulls a typed letter on blue air mail paper out of it. 'It's from Bangkok – he's alive – he's coming on leave to see us!' Laura, the feel of Francis's skin still on hers, looks bewildered.

'But who?'

'Bernard, our cousin Bernard!'

Slowly it dawns on Laura who this letter, which excites her mother so, is from. Bernard is her grandpa's nephew, closest to her in age in the family, though his being seventeen when she was only eight put a vast distance between them. He was sent out to Bangkok apprenticed to Unilever. Laura remembers how at the farewell supper for him what the old people talked about was whether the boy should wear Bermuda shorts on the voyage out, preening themselves on the fact that they knew what such things were. Light-hearted talk to mask the fact that they might never see him again. She also remembers her outrage when Bernard took the last helping of green ice cream that she had her eye on.

So, someone in the family has survived. This cousin is going to show up in flesh and blood.

'He vill be here in two veeks,' Ruth says.

'He can't possibly stay here,' Laura says at once. What will Bernard, last seen surrounded by Berlin opulence, think of the way they live? When he sees the fluted coffee cups with the black and yellow flowers in that packing case dresser? Even though it is now covered with sheets dyed pale brown.

'He is staying viz a colleague, don't vorry!'

Laura goes to bed elated. She has a real live cousin. And she has a lover.

Bernard arrives with an enormous bunch of white lilies, the kind of bunches that were the thing in Berlin. Laura sees the glow of affection on his face, on Ruth's face, sees the family likeness – they have the same shiny brown eyes, the same downward turning mouths. Laura has forgotten for the moment that she, too, has those. Bernard blushes a little when he turns to her and shakes her warmly by the hand. She hopes he will not say something like *You've turned into a proper young lady.* No, he is better than that: he says, 'I can hardly believe I'm talking to both of you!' He tells them that his mother was deported the day he had all the papers for her to join him in Bangkok. Ruth tells him about her parents; Laura tells him about her father. Bernard bends over, kisses them on both cheeks. Perhaps this is what it might feel like to have a brother?

Ruth has put a yellow and white damask cloth on the table with matching napkins. There is apple strudel on a glass stand. 'Almost like Berlin!' she says. Laura sees Bernard wince.

He calls in every day. Ruth looks years younger. When Laura has to have a tooth out with gas, Bernard picks her up from the dentist and takes her arm as they walk out into the rain. 'My God, this weather,' he says, hailing a taxi.

'I'd like to take you both out to the theatre before my leave's up,' he says, 'though I shall need a bit of guidance.' He looks at Laura.

'You take my daughter, dahlink,' Ruth says, blinking her eyes at Bernard, 'I von't come.'

'Just as you like.' He sounds quite pleased.

Laura suggests Shaw's *St. Joan*. 'I read the part of Dunois at school,' she tells him. 'And a friend of mine was St. Joan, she was brilliant!' Bernard looks at her blankly.

'And we'll find somewhere to eat afterwards,' he says.

'I only know coffee places and British Restaurants and Lyons Cornerhouses!'

'You can leave the restaurant to me. How about Saturday?'

'Can't manage Saturdays,' Laura says, without mentioning Francis. She will ask Francis what he thinks of Shaw; probably not enough magic about him. Quite soon they are going to see *Dr. Faustus* and probably the mysterious Tom is coming with them.

209

Bernard has got tickets. He brings more flowers when he picks her up – huge yellow chrysanthemums. He gives them Siamese silk stoles. Laura can see he would like her to put hers on; she has never worn anything so luxurious. Ruth has thrown hers over her shoulders and is prancing about the room with it.

Bernard wants to get a taxi again, but Laura won't let him. 'It's quicker on the underground.'

'You do this a lot?'

'Every day; it's just part of life!'

They have seats in the front row of the dress circle and, when the curtain goes up, Laura is immediately enthralled, though she can tell from the way Bernard is flicking the pages of his programme that he is not enjoying the play much. During the interval, while they are sipping gin and tonics, he asks her to explain one or two things. 'Don't get much time for reading!' Laura cannot imagine a life without time for reading.

He has booked a table in a French restaurant in Old Compton Street. When Laura tells him it is less than ten minutes walk from where they are, he is surprised how well she knows her way about. 'I go to a coffee bar the other end of Old Compton Street,' is as close as she gets to telling her cousin about Francis.

It begins to rain. 'We should have got a taxi!' Bernard says as they get to the door of the restaurant.

They walk in through a velvet curtain. A man with slicked back hair bends over Laura's hand and kisses it. Are her nails quite clean? Another man helps them off with their coats. Laura is glad she is wearing the Siamese silk stole. They are shown to their table: their chairs are pulled back; menus in leather covers are brought. When she looks at hers, Laura knows she is out of her depth.

'You choose,' she says to Bernard.

'Well, it's either boeuf bourguignon or coq au vin,'

'You choose,' she says again – she has never eaten either.

Bernard orders the beef. Then he disappears behind the wine list.

'Something red, don't you think? How about Nuits St. Georges?'

Laura is flattered that he thinks she knows what that might be like. She does not want to say *you choose* again, so she just nods. She would like to get the ordering over so they can discuss the play, but the wine waiter has arrived with the bottle. Bernard scrutinises the label; the waiter pulls the cork and pours a drop into Bernard's glass. Bernard sniffs it, swills it round in his mouth.

'This is corked! Bring another bottle!'

'Sir!' The waiter disappears.

Laura is ready to sink through the floor. Bernard tucks the napkin under his chin and waits for the new bottle. This one passes the test; he does not thank the waiter, so Laura does. She no longer feels like talking about the play. Bernard does live in a different world! He asks about her job.

'It's not wonderful, I'm not allowed to do editorial work, only clerical, because of the unions.'

'Oh, unions!' Bernard says acidly.

'But I'm going to find somewhere they'll let me do a bit of writing.'

'Like your father,' Bernard says and puts his hand on hers.

There are not many people now who would know that.

'My leave's almost up,' he says.

'But you like *your* job?'

'On the whole. Not always easy being a manager, but I'm up for promotion again – assistant director next, though they prefer...' He stops to wipe his mouth and does not finish the sentence.

'They prefer?' Laura asks.

'I was hoping...' Bernard's voice trails away again.

The waiter brings the bill; Bernard pulls a thick wad of notes out of his wallet and puts some in the leather folder.

It is still raining when they get outside, so this time Laura does not stop him from getting a taxi. 'I was hoping,' he begins again and puts his arm through hers as they settle back in the taxi, 'I was hoping to take a wife back with me. Is there any chance you would...' Again he leaves the sentence unfinished. He picks it up again with, 'It's not a bad life out there, better than...' Laura knows he was going to say *better than this awful place you live in now, better than going to some office on the underground every morning.* She does not blame him for thinking that, but blames him for not realising he has ruined that sense of familial affection so lacking in her life. She moves away from him in the taxi.

Back up in the flat, she sees Ruth look at him questioningly. Then her mother knew he was going to… Was that why she didn't come with them? Laura stands there forlorn while Ruth and Bernard chat.

'Ven vill ve see you again?' Ruth asks as he is leaving.

'Next year, with a bit of luck!'

Laura runs downstairs after him.

'You know, I do love you, you're my cousin, you're what's left of the family, that's how I love you!' She puts her arms round him and hugs him.

'I know. I'm sorry,' he says and leaves quickly. Laura can see he is very upset.

The days feel empty without him.

'You know, ven he vas a boy…' Ruth says.

'Yes? When he was a boy?'

'He vore green knickerbockers. Harris tveed, and ve said k-nickerbockers,' she adds, sounding the k. They laugh. Laura waits for Ruth to go on; she can sense her remembering things she is not saying.

'Such a nice boy! How happy you vould have been viz him!'

'I'm happy with my boyfriend Francis!'

Laura goes to her room.

§

She starts a letter to Hannah to tell her about this cousin who turned up out of the blue but does not mention that he wanted to take her back to Bangkok. She also tells Hannah about Francis and his printing press and that perhaps, later, he might allow her to contribute a piece. She has been keeping a notebook. And she has registered for evening classes in Latin so that she can go ahead to do an Arts degree. The letter flows freely; it is so much easier to say things to Hannah than to her mother. And yet, since Bernard's visit, things have been easier between them. They lead their separate lives; there does not seem to be a man in Ruth's life, though occasionally someone called Benny occurs in the conversation.

Laura does not press for details; she has a man of her own now and has a feeling her mother respects her for that – much more than for any academic ambitions.

Making love with Francis grows in intensity. He cannot wait to take her clothes off, to gaze before touching. Laura is amazed at the response he kindles in her, the almost unbearable sweetness. So she is a little affronted when, fully dressed again and ready to begin printing, Francis looks at her balefully and asks, 'What happens to us?' almost as if he wishes nothing had happened.

'You know what happens,' Laura says sharply. Perhaps it is not really love?

One Saturday Laura arrives early at the Old Compton Street café. She sees Francis talking to a broad-faced young man who is gesticulating with large hands.

'Hallo, you're early!' Francis says and Laura feels reprimanded. 'Tom, this is Laura, Laura – Tom,' Francis looks anxiously from one to the other.

I will not say *I'm sorry to be early* Laura thinks as she hears herself say, 'I am sorry to be early!'

'Tom's just about to go.' Francis looks at his friend, who shows no sign of leaving.

'You're coming to the Marlowe with us?' Tom asks Laura. He has good grey eyes.

'Of course she is, next Friday!' Francis says.

Laura would have liked to reply herself. Tom gets up, swinging a shabby music case.

'His great thoughts in that', Francis says.

Tom smiles at Laura. He has jaggedy teeth.

They go to see *Dr. Faustus*. Robert Eddison is a magnificently malign Mephistopheles to Cedric Hardwicke's tortured Faustus.

'*Tonight I'll conjure, though I die for it!*' Tom whispers sepulchrally as they walk out of the theatre into the damp night. Francis stops stock still in the middle of Charing Cross Road and shouts '*Christ cannot save thy soul, there's none but I have interest in the same!*' His mauve silk scarf flies out behind him in the wind. People turn round and stare. 'Yes, Harry Andrews was awfully good as Lucifer, wasn't he?' Laura says to cover her embarrassment. The two boys on either side of her grab her arms. 'We'll walk home,' they say and cross into Tottenham Court Road. They live quite close to each other.

'But...' Laura begins, then stops. Here and now, between these two young Englishmen there are no *buts;* she is released from otherness, is fully alive in the present – *that* is the magic.

It begins to rain. Tom, not Francis, opens his umbrella and holds it over her. By the time they get to Warren Street, the magic is beginning to wear thin.

'I'll get myself home from here,' Laura says.

'You're coming home with me, my girl,' Francis tells her.

'Printing tomorrow,' Laura says and turns quickly into the station without looking at either of them.

On the escalator down she feels a new and intoxicating sense of freedom. She belongs to no one but herself.

It is past midnight by the time she gets back to West Hampstead, still feeling elated. The light is out in her mother's room but she hears murmured voices. It takes her a long time to fall asleep. Idiotically, she is thinking *Why wasn't it Francis who held an umbrella over me?* She seems still to be thinking that when she hears Ruth's voice. 'Vakee, vakee!' Laura opens her eyes to see her mother offering her a cup of tea.

'Drink zis, zen come and have breakfast viz us!'

'Us?'

When she opens the sitting room door, she sees there, facing her, a man with a drooping moustache, stark naked.

'Zis is Benny!'

'Come in, come in; don't be shy,' Benny says from under his moustache.

Why isn't *he* shy?

Back in her room, Laura makes a decision: she will move out. What kind of mother dishes up naked men for breakfast? This mother! Buoyed up by the new found sense of belonging only to herself, she tells Francis what she has decided without mentioning what triggered the decision.

'Great,' he says, 'find somewhere round here!' But he does not suggest she move in with him.

Tom arrives to help with the printing. 'Speed things up a bit,' he says and asks Laura if she got home all right.

Laura is not quite sure whether Francis is pleased – he begins to hum loudly. She makes more mistakes than usual with the setting up; she cannot get rid of the image of Benny's veined torso and her mother's sickly smile. They pull a proof, correct it and put the press to bed under its striped blanket. When Francis has given them coffee, he announces that he will be away for a conference the following weekend.

'Come to a concert with me?' Tom asks Laura.

'Yes, good idea, keep her out of mischief,' Francis says. He never goes to concerts, blithely admitting that he is tone deaf. Laura would like to make her own decisions.

'What's the concert?' she asks.

'Beethoven quartets. Rasoumovsky 59 Nos 1 and 2; the Loewenguth playing at the YM in Great Russell Street.' Tom's eyes are shining, but it conveys very little to Laura. She has only ever been to proms at the Albert Hall.

'I'm not sure,' she says, not because she would not like to hear Beethoven quartets but because... The reasons fizzle out unformulated. As Francis is seeing Tom out, she hears him ask 'How's that mature lady you've been seeing?'

'Oh her,' is all that Tom says.

'You know I love you, my dear,' Francis whispers as they are lying on his bed in the dark.

'I love you, too.' But even as she is saying it, Laura is not absolutely sure. How can you ever be absolutely sure? It is so long since she felt absolutely sure anyone loved her – like her granny and grandpa, like her father.

On the day, Laura decides there is no reason why she should not go to the chamber concert. She has not seen Tom again and on the way it occurs to her that she might not be able to get a ticket. Well, if not, not – *che sera sera*, that line from the Marlowe has stuck.

She does get a ticket, looks round for Tom but does not see him. The lights dim; the musicians settle down round a standard lamp. As they begin to play, Laura is taken out of herself into a dimension where thought is replaced by a sense of wholeness which stays with her even when the music has stopped and the

Loewenguth quartet are bowing to rapturous applause. The lights go up. She feels a ping on her head, puts her hand up to find a pellet of paper. *Look up,* it tells her. She does and there is Tom waving from the balcony.

'See you later,' he mouths at her.

The quartet begin to play again. No music has ever stirred Laura like this. There is a moment of rapt silence between the last note and the applause, which goes on and on. At last, people move slowly towards the exit. Laura moves with them. Tom is standing outside, his dark hair tousled in the wind. *Please don't say anything,* Laura prays. He says nothing, takes her hand in his large paddy one; they walk along in silence.

'Let's eat,' Tom says when they get to Shearn's vegetarian restaurant in Tottenham Court Road. Laura has been there once or twice with Francis: they don't go often – it is too expensive. When they are sitting down inside, the only reference Tom makes to the concert is 'I thought you'd come!'

On a mild March Saturday morning she finds a room less than ten minutes walk from where Francis lives, not much further from Tom, though she has not visited him. The landlady in her flowery pinny, who is not over-friendly, takes Laura up two flights of stairs into a fair-sized room with a sash window overlooking tree tops. The furniture is adequate: there is a small sink in one corner and a gas ring. The landlady pulls a flap from the top of the gas fire.

'Another ring 'ere, and I'll replace these,' she points to three broken elements in the gas fire. 'And 'ere's the meter; takes bobs and tanners; bathroom one floor down. Rent's 17/6d a week, payable in advance. And no gentlemen callers after nine pm!'

Laura can afford that: she earns £4 5/- a week now, working for a small publisher in Soho who syndicates magazines for factory workers. She is writing all the pieces except the sports page. The American editor Hank sees to that and sometimes he edits what Laura has written, cutting words like *quotidian* and *nevertheless* which, according to him, would put factory workers off. Apart from him, there is only the director Mrs. L., which is all she ever calls herself; she has a head of shiny red curls and green fingernails. Neither she nor Hank blinked an eyelid when Laura said her

German name, Mrs. L even spelt it correctly. Of course, Laura knows that what she writes at work is hardly *writing* compared with what goes into the little magazine she has been helping to produce. She arranges to move in the following Saturday, pays and leaves her name. The landlady looks her up and down, says,
'That's never an English name!'
'No,' Laura says and walks away.

The raffia chimney sweep and the little goldfinch glass cage are on the windowsill; a pink and white damask tablecloth that Ruth has given her is spread on the table. With the bit of herself that still thinks the label *mother* ought to mean what the word leads one to expect, Laura wishes Ruth had come to see her into her new room. But then, if Ruth were that kind of mother, she would not be in this room. Laura is annoyed with herself when she feels tears rising. She will *not* cry: she is exactly where she wants to be.

She puts her hand on a blue envelope which is lying on the pink tablecloth. It is a letter from Hannah; the crinkly white £5 note that came with it is in her wallet. Laura makes a cup of tea with an egg-shaped metal tea infuser that leaks leaves into the cup; perhaps she will spend Hannah's fiver on a teapot. She reads the letter again. Hannah has invited her to spend a weekend in Yorkshire; Klaus has been made consultant anaesthetist at the local hospital.

I'll go, Laura thinks, *it'll give me a breathing space*. What does she need a breathing space for? She has just moved into a room of her own, is enjoying her job, so... What she needs the breathing space for is to ask herself whether she is getting too fond of Tom. He has asked her to another concert; she has said no, not because she did not want to accept but because she is Francis's girlfriend. The three of them have spent several evenings stapling red card covers on two hundred copies of *Reflections* and trimmed them with Francis's guillotine. To celebrate they went to see *Le Jour se lève* with Jean Gabin at the Hampstead Everyman Cinema. Laura felt just as comfortable with Tom's arm against hers as with Francis's. She loves the tweed jacket with its flecks of many colours that Tom wears; she wishes Francis would not always, always wind that mauve silk scarf round his neck. But if you love someone, then what they wear is not important, is it? Besides, the times she has with Francis when neither of them is wearing anything are wonderful. Are they? Aren't they? What would such times be like with Tom? If she finds out, will she become like her mother – this man today, another tomorrow?

Ruth still has not been to see her, but she rings on Saturday mornings. Laura hates it when the landlady yells up 'That foreign lady on the phone for you again!' Ruth tells her she is thinking of going to Berlin to visit old friends who have survived the war. 'Half Jewish, like you,' her mother says and Laura somehow feels disowned by that remark. 'I go ven ze Russian blockade is over. I sink ze Americans are vonderful viz this airlift, don't you?' Laura has been too taken up with her own life to take much notice of the news – what's happening in Berlin no longer has anything to do with her now that her father and her grandparents are dead. 'You heppy in your own room, my big daughter?' Ruth changes the subject. 'Yes, thank you, you'll have to come and see it, won't you!'

Laura puts the receiver down.

She goes to Yorkshire. Hannah and Klaus live in a Victorian grey stone house at the top of a steep drive. Laura gives Hannah a blue and white vase she saw in Heals; she spent that fiver on it, remembering how her granny told her always to give presents you would like to keep yourself. 'For me?' Hannah gives Laura a hug. They have tea, not coffee, for breakfast. 'You see? we've become quite English,' Klaus says, helping himself to porridge. 'By the way, has my wife told you her news?' Laura is moved by the way he says *my wife* with such pride. It must make you feel safe to be called that.

'I passed my driving test, second try,' Hannah says.

'Not that, dearie, your work!'

'Oh yes, I'm teaching German at the Grammar School here – only part-time,' she adds modestly. Klaus gets up, pats Laura on the head, pecks Hannah on the cheek and takes himself off to his hospital.

'Shall we go to the Brontë Parsonage in Haworth, it's quite near?' Hannah asks.

On the drive there, Laura wishes Hannah would stop talking

about *Jane Eyre* and poor Mr. Rochester because she has almost driven through red lights and keeps stalling up hills. 'I need more practice,' Hannah admits when they get to Haworth.

No wonder the Brontës wrote what they did, Laura thinks, looking at the heavy moss-covered tombstones in the churchyard. When they have finished walking round the house, Hannah buys a copy of *Jane Eyre* with the parsonage stamp in it for Laura. As she is paying, the woman at the till says 'It's so nice to have visitors from abroad coming again! Where are you from?' Rather peeved, Hannah says, 'Actually, I'm quite local – I live just outside Keighley!' The woman gives her the change without further comment.

Driving back, Hannah says, 'I don't intend to retail my life story every time I go into a shop! Though I don't suppose we'll ever count as really English, British passport or not!'

I will, Laura thinks stubbornly. She is determined not to wear the refugee label for the rest of her life.

Later, relaxing in front of the sitting room fire, Klaus uncorks a bottle of Burgundy.

'Got a case of this from someone whose stomach we repaired!' They clink glasses.

'Lechayim, here's to Eretz Israel!'

Israel declared independence a few months earlier, though that news did not touch Laura any more than the advent of the Berlin airlift. The arrival of West Indians on the *Windrush* has made a greater impression; she feels for them when she sees notices in the windows of bed-and-breakfast places saying *No Blacks*. They remind her of the *Juden Unerwünscht* signs plastered all over Berlin.

'I can't wait to go and see my cousin who's settled in Tel Aviv,' Hannah says.

'As soon as I can get away, dearie!'

'You wouldn't go and live there?' Laura asks anxiously.

'Well, you never know…' Hannah says.

'We belong here now!' Klaus says, to Laura's great relief.

She opens up and tells them about her job, writing those pieces about films and beauty products and London parks; about the little magazine she has been helping to print, about Francis and

Tom and how she loves going about with them.

'And who do you like best?' Hannah asks.

'Oh Francis, of course!'

But she talks about Tom.

'He's getting himself as second degree, in philosophy – it's what he's always wanted to do. Didn't do well in zoology because he hated dissecting those rabbits and things; he's just teaching at a crammers for the moment.'

'And what does your Francis do?'

Laura is a touch uncomfortable with that *your*.

'He works in a lab doing experiments with chlorophyll or something – and he writes poems!'

She tells them about going to do Latin in evening classes so she can go on to do an English degree.

'Could you manage all that with a full time job?'

'Yes!'

'How old are you now?'

'Nineteen!'

'The whole of life before you, lucky girl! And as for boyfriends, don't rush into anything, there's plenty of time!'

'Only I don't want to...' she does not finish the sentence, she was going to say *become like my mother*.

Not long after Laura has got back from Yorkshire, Ruth finally comes to see her in Highbury.

'I vant to tell you somesing, my independent daughter,' and she leans forward to stroke Laura's cheek.

'Yes?'

'Vell, now you've made a life for yourself, I have decided to move to America!'

'Really?' Laura asks in a daze.

'You remember Henry?'

Laura wishes she did not.

'Vell, he alvays promised to get me over to Chicago.'

'But...' Laura knows Henry has long been with another woman.

'Ve're still good friends,' Ruth adds quickly.

'And Benny?'

Ruth looks at the floor. 'I have to admit, zat vas a mistake!'
'I thought you were thinking of going to Berlin?'
'Yes, I vanted to go, but zis is more important – a new life for me!'
Ruth pulls out a bundle from her carrier bag. Wrapped in a red-bordered drying up cloth are the silver-plated fish knives and forks from Berlin.
'I sought you vould like zese!'
What is Laura going to do with a dozen fish knives and forks?
'Ze ozzer sings I take viz me,' Ruth tells her.
'You think you'll like Chicago enough to live there?'
'Vy not?'
Laura does not go to see her mother off, because on that day she has an interview at Birkbeck College. It goes well. Provided she gets her Latin Intermediate, she will be welcome in the English department. Good. She goes back home, yes *home*, to Highbury. She has the day off work. Mrs. L and Hank are encouraging about her proposed degree course; besides, they are winding up the business – not enough factories have opted for those syndicated magazines. They have told Laura to find a new job and will go on paying her until she has. Hank tells her to dip her hand into the petty cash on Fridays. 'No one's looking!' How different from that trade union house in Long Acre! Better or worse? Mrs. L and Hank have given her the chance to try her hand at a bit of journalism; the other job offered security, but for the moment Laura can afford to flout security.

She fingers a letter in her pocket which arrived in the morning post. It is from Tom. There is a photograph of him and a note telling her he has fallen in love with her. When can they meet? Something inside Laura falls into place. Yes, she will see Tom; she will not let Francis make love to her again. But she has to see Francis that very evening: his mother has come up from the country specially to meet her; they are going to Christopher Fry's *Ring Round the Moon*.

'What a tremendous help you've been with the magazine,' Francis's mother says. She has pink country cheeks and grey eyes that radiate good will.

'Oh yes, and Tom as well,' Laura says, feeling terrible.

'Nice boy.' But there is something iffy about the way Francis's mother says that.

'You must come and stay with us,' she goes on, 'Francis will show you his favourite walks through our woods!'

No, she will not do that.

Laura cannot wait for the play to begin, but when it does she cannot concentrate. How to begin to tell Francis that… that… He takes her hand; she lets it lie inert in his.

She has sleepless nights, answers one or two advertisements for jobs, but not Tom's letter. There is a picture postcard of Chicago from Ruth. On Saturday she does not go to see Francis as usual though he is expecting her. Quite late in the evening, he calls round.

'Is all well, my dear?' he asks, and Laura can tell he knows that it is not.

'I thought your mother was still with you,' Laura lies. She hates doing that.

Francis gives her a copy of Hermann Hesse's *Siddhartha*, which has just come out in English. She could, of course, have read it in German. She backs away when he tries to kiss her, then stretches out her hand when she sees the pain in his eyes. Perhaps she does still love him?

'I'm going to have to concentrate on my Latin,' she says. 'You have Tom to help you with the printing.'

'I see.' Francis's whole body sags; his head droops. 'Then I'll leave you to your Latin,' he says so softly she can barely hear it. She has not yet written to Tom.

She gets one of the jobs she applied for, a bit of a dogsbody appointment with a publisher in Piccadilly, where she will be working for two people. The first is an ex-RAF pilot with a grey handlebar moustache who tells her he does not know the first thing about publishing and will expect to learn a great deal from her.

'For instance, what the hell do they mean by format, do you think?' he asks, looking at some papers on his desk.

'Shape and size of things?' Laura says diffidently.

'Good old girl!' He gets up and shakes Laura's hand.

The second person is a rather fierce-looking not-quite-young woman who says she wants to put Shakespeare on the map. She peers at Laura. 'I was really hoping for a blonde ferret, but I suppose you'll do!'

Laura is introduced to the director, who tells her he himself might occasionally call on her. 'When there's a crisis,' he says, laughing. Laura says *Yes* to everything. The salary is £4 10/- a week – five bob more than she has been earning. No one has asked about the provenance of her surname.

Pleased with herself, Laura takes the short cut through Swallow Street across Regent Street into Brewer Street, where she buys herself a quarter of humbugs to celebrate; sweets have come off points, though everything else is still rationed. Back in the office, Mrs. L and Hank wish her luck and give her a month's holiday pay. Hank tells her that two guys have been on the phone wanting to talk to her, urgently.

She does not return the phone calls and takes a week's break between jobs. She wanders up and down Charing Cross Road, in and out of the Old Compton Street café. She spends time looking at what is on the round table in Better Books: Kafka's *The Trial* has just come out in English – Francis has talked about that. There is Orwell's *Animal Farm* and Aldous Huxley's *Brave New World* – Tom has mentioned those. How she misses them on either side of her, talking to and across her. She buys all three books with some of her holiday pay. On her way out, she sees copies of *Reflections* on the rack with the other magazines: *Horizon, Partisan Review, Outposts, Twentieth Century*. She buys a copy of *Reflections*, although she has three copies of it at home, and re-reads Francis's introduction with its insistence on the importance of fantasy, fable and journals and Tom's piece of prose poetry, which is like an abstract painting of an autumn morning. She tries, and fails, to read these pieces as if she did not know the people who wrote them. The only shadowy way that she exists in the magazine is an acknowledgment of help from friends with the printing.

She takes herself back into the café with her new books. There is iron foot Jack; there is the young man who wears purple silk socks and carries a twee little shopping basket; there is the bag lady, her skirt held up by a large safety pin, fluting away in her Chelsea voice, *My deah, I was the belle of Paris...* No Francis; no Tom. Back at home in Highbury, there is post: a note from Francis, claiming he cannot live without her. Tom, writing from Yorkshire where he is taking a break with his mother, claims that he cannot live without her. *And without whom can't I live?* Laura asks herself, without allowing an answer to surface. She begins a letter to Francis. She will not be able to get out of hurting him. *He'll get over it*, she tells herself; *I mustn't overestimate my own importance.* She scrumples the letter up and begins a letter to Tom. Yes, she looks forward to meeting him... flings the sheet of paper across the room; makes a cup of tea, swallows it too hot.

There are three more letters: a printed notice informing Old Mentmore Girls that, following the death of the elder Miss Thomas, the school is to close. Miss Elizabeth has scribbled a note saying she is staying on in the middle house in the Crescent and would be very pleased to see Laura, if ever she felt inclined to visit. Laura feels much more inclined still to be sitting in one of Miss Elizabeth's English classes.

There is a letter from Hannah, who writes as affectionately as ever – soon Laura must come again; they are about to adopt a nine year old boy, having given up hope of having children of their own, and are getting a puppy for him. Laura wishes she were nine years old again and someone would buy her a puppy; but when she was nine... She picks up the raffia chimney sweep.

There is a bulky envelope from America, the writing on it in bright blue ink unchanged since those Saturday morning letters at school on which she relied to make her feel like the others; now a pair of nylons falls out of the envelope. Ruth writes that things are not going well: she has had a gallstone attack; Henry's woman is a bitch; as soon as she has scraped the fare together, she will be back in London. The letter veers off into maudlin endearments. There is a PS saying that if the worst comes to the worst, if she cannot find the money, it might be necessary to leave the china, glass, linen, silver behind in exchange for the fare back to London. *Those things are mine as well*, Laura thinks with some bitterness. Then she remembers the fuss her grandpa used to make when the maid broke a Meissen china cup or, God help her, a Dresden figurine – she got the sack immediately. In the end, her granny had to pretend it was *she* who had broken whatever it was. Laura stops caring about the things her mother might leave behind in Chicago.

She decides it is not good enough to write to Francis. She must go to see him. She will tell him how much their times together have meant to her. Now.

'I knew you'd come, I knew...' he says when he sees her. No, he does not know. Laura gets him to come out for a walk; she will not go inside.

'I think Tom and I...' she begins.

'Have you slept with him?'

'No!'

'I don't believe you!'

This is not how it was meant to go. He has not given her chance to say what she intended. So instead she says,

'I can't help that!'

He grabs her by the shoulders.

'And you and me? Has all that meant nothing?'

The mauve scarf blows against his face, muffling his words. Laura pulls away from him.

'Of course it has meant something, meant a great deal but...' But, looking at his face distorted with anger, she cannot bring herself to go on.

'He's incapable of love, you'll find out!' he yells.

Laura turns away from Francis. His words penetrate her back like shrapnel. *Dear God,* she prays when she is back in her room, *show me... show me...* Laura does not know how to put into words what she needs to be shown. It is a long time since she has said or thought any kind of prayer, in English, German or Hebrew. She remembers wanting to go to church when she was at school, not because she believed in God or Jesus but because she wanted to be like the others; she remembers how, after the air raid on Weston when Molly called her a Jerry, she murmured the *Shma Yisroel* her granny had taught her. She did believe in God then, but now she is not at all sure if there is anyone to pray to – God is just another word, isn't it? But even as she thinks this, she knows it is not quite true, that perhaps God and Truth mean the same thing and that she is far from knowing *what* that is, only that, in some mysterious way, it *is*.

The moment she sees Tom standing on her doorstep, Laura feels a great burden drop from her.

Inside, they sit opposite each other, breathless with love. She strokes the lapel of his many coloured coat. 'Well!' he says and again 'Well!' and 'Here we are then!'

And. They are making love. Laura does not know where her body ends and his begins; it does not matter who is who in this ecstasy of oneness.

They fall into tranquil sleep. In the morning, Tom sings 'La Donna e mobile' joyfully in the bathroom.

'Miss Laura, Miss Laura,' the landlady screeches, 'I want ter see yer, come down ere this minnit!'

Laura puts her hand over her mouth. She had forgotten all about the embargo on gentlemen callers.

'Is that a man I can 'ear singing in the bathroom?'

'That's funny,' Laura says. 'I thought I heard it too!'

The landlady tilts her head to one side. 'Thank Gawd for that then. There's nothing wrong with me 'earing!'

Laura runs back up two steps at a time. Tom can't stop laughing when she tells him. 'Good sport, your landlady! We'll have to find somewhere to live together, won't we!' *Together!* Lovely word! Tom goes on, 'I went to see Francis before I came to you. He's taking it badly; says the bottom's fallen out of his life, doesn't know if the ground's going to be there when he puts his foot down, and it's all my fault. Shame it had to happen like this. We've been friends since our first year in college. Well, eventually he'll get over it!'

Laura does not tell Tom what Francis said about him.

They have breakfast; coffee has never smelt so good. 'What a great tablecloth!' Tom says, passing his hand over the pink and white patterns on it. Laura explains its provenance and goes on to talk about her mother in Chicago, about her grandparents and her father and how they died. Tom reaches across the table and holds her hand.

'Just goes to prove, if it still needed proving, what fools people are who believe in any kind of God!'

Laura is startled into drinking her coffee too hot.

After quite a long silence, she says, 'I'm not sure... You don't think perhaps, in a way...'

'Certainly not!' Tom interrupts her before she can finish the sentence. 'I knew it was all mumbo jumbo by the time I was fourteen, told the priests at school as much...'

'You went to a Catholic school?'

Tom nods. 'They told me to shut up and get on with my work, which I did. The biology master was a layman; he became my friend, helped me get into college.'

'What about your parents?'

'My Irish dad had to promise to bring up any children Catholic when he married Mam. She didn't care one way or the other, but she wasn't too pleased when Father This and Father That kept calling round after Dad died to see she was doing things right.'

'But how can you be quite so certain there isn't a God?'

'Easy – I'm a naïve realist!'

Laura is not quite sure what that means, but when she looks at Tom she *is* quite sure she loves him. And it occurs to her that God *does* have something to do with that.

They finish their breakfast. 'Come to see where I live?' Tom asks. On the wall of his quite small book-lined room, there is a photograph of a very beautiful woman.

'My grandmother,' Tom says, grinning.

'Really?'

'Don't be daft, that's Virginia Woolf!'

Laura goes red with embarrassment. They read *A Room of One's Own* at school, but she has not read any of the novels.

'Committed suicide a few years ago, kept on going mad,' Tom speaks dryly. He pulls a volume off the shelf. '*The Waves* – marvellous. No one else can do what she does!'

He opens the book and begins to read aloud. The luminous prose flows between them.

§

Ruth has come back to London from Chicago; Tom and Laura go to see her. She has moved to a different street in West Hampstead.

On the way to see her, Laura can't help feeling a small frisson of elation triggered by the phrase *going to see my mother who has come back from America*. Beneath the elation, there is apprehension: what will Tom think of Ruth?

'Laura's so pleased to have you back!' Tom says to her when they arrive.

His saying that helps Laura to make it so. She looks round the room.

'You look for our sings? I had to leave everysing in Chicago, vouldn't have got back ozzervise! And I vouldn't have got zis room if Bernard hadn't sent me somesing! But now I manage, still have friends here! Not Benny, don't vorry!'

Good of Bernard to help Ruth. Laura thinks of him with affection and hopes he finds a wife; then they could perhaps go on being cousins.

Ruth gives Laura two pairs of nylons.

'Quite a character your mother, isn't she!' Tom says later.

Laura is relieved that is how Tom puts it. 'Her accent's ghastly, isn't it!'

'Just wait til you meet mine! *Eee, our Laura, cum raht in, you must be starved.* She has her own accent, has me Mam!'

All that is left to show Tom is a Northerner are his short a's.

They think about finding somewhere to live together, somewhere in a different part of London where they will not run into Francis. Tom suggests putting an ad in *The New Statesman*. 'How about *Young married couple seeks...*'

'No, no!' Laura interrupts him. 'Young *unmarried* couple...' She will not pretend to be his wife before she is. When she thinks about marriage, she sees her granny and grandpa at the large dining table in Berlin. Her granny passes the most delicious morsel on her plate to him; he passes it back. Whatever it is goes back and forth from plate to plate until it is not delicious any longer. Then they smile at each other in complete accord.

Tom and Laura are inundated with replies to their advertisement and settle on a large room in Kilburn with windows overlooking a long narrow garden with lime trees. They have their own bathroom! Bliss! When they move in, there is a jug of asters on their table; the couple who own the house give them a cup of tea and chocolate biscuits, and then they are left agreeably to themselves.

Tom has found a job teaching at a boys' grammar school. 'The headmaster asked if I was married. I said *almost!*'

Laura tries her hand at cooking; she buys rock salmon so they can use the fish knives. Tom just pushes it about on his plate. He doesn't notice the fish knives and forks with the sea creatures embossed on them.

'You know rock salmon's dogfish, don't you? he says. 'And I've been dissecting it all day with the boys!'

No, she did not know.

He leans across the table and kisses her.

'I'm not marrying you for your culinary skills!'

'For my brains, of course!'

They laugh and laugh.

They go to spend Christmas with Tom's Mam in Middlesbrough. Ruth has gone to Berlin.

Laura leans against the antimacassar on the head rest of the plush Pullman train seat. The pink light of the little cornucopia lamp shines on *The New Statesman,* which she is not reading. The table is laid for lunch. Tom orders sherries.

'You won't be getting sherry at my Mam's,' he tells her; 'more like iron brew or dandelion and burdock!'

Laura watches the waiters as they balance heavy metal trays on the palm of one hand, undulating with the movement of the train. Not a drop of anything gets spilt.

A coalman's cart is standing outside the small terrace house when they arrive; the horse has its head inside the front window – Tom's Mam is feeding it apples. The moment she sees Tom and Laura, she opens the front door and the horse takes its head out of the front room.

'Cum raht in, ee, you must be starved!'

They step inside. Tom got the sound of her exactly right. There, on a gate-leg table, is a bottle of sherry. Tom looks startled when he sees it; Laura grins at him. Tom's Mam follows their glances. 'Oh aye, Uncle Alfred brought that yesterday; thought you'd cum; wants us to go round there Boxing Day.' Tom's eyes turn bright turquoise as he looks at his mother, but they don't touch. Laura sees she has the same broad paddy hands as her son.

Tom carries their things upstairs into a backroom with a window overlooking a coal shed and outside lavatory in the backyard.

'Dad used to lock me in there when I'd done something wrong,' he says.

'Like what?' Laura asks appalled.

'Don't remember!'

But Laura can see he does.

Tom's Mam comes in. 'Tek her things next door, ee, our Laura, you won't mahnd sharing mah bed, will you?'

Share a bed with a total stranger? 'Doesn't she know we're living together?' she asks Tom while his Mam is busy in the back kitchen.

'Of course, but what would the neighbours think if we slept in the same room, not married?'

'How would they know?'

'How wouldn't they!'

The doubled bed Laura is sharing with Tom's Mam is wide enough for them not to have to touch. Laura tries not to take more than her fair share of the blankets. The thin paisley eiderdown slips to the bottom of the bed.

They have roast beef and Yorkshire pudding for Christmas dinner. Tom's Mam brings in steaming platefuls for them but, not sitting down, disappears into the back kitchen. Laura gets up to ask her to sit with them. 'Ah'll have mahn after, our Laura!' But Laura insists, and at last the three of them are sitting at the table together.

Tom has put out shiny red crackers. 'Never saw these for the duration, did we!' They join hands to pull them and put on their paper crowns. Tom's Mam tells Laura about the time he was so hungry when he came home from school that he put furniture polish on his bread instead of dripping. 'Raht gormless, our Tom, always has bin,' she says, beaming at him.

On Boxing Day, Uncle Alfred comes to pick them up in his Austin 7. He is a baker and has made a fortune during the war with some synthetic cream he dreamt up that tasted almost like the real thing. His wife, Auntie Pearl, Tom's Mam's prettier sister, never helped in the shop, too ladylike for that – too ladylike, as well, to have children.

When they arrive at the bungalow, Auntie Pearl offers Laura a limp hand to shake. 'Very pleased to meet you, Ah'm sure,' she says; Laura is not convinced. Tom's Mam sits uneasily on an armchair with petit point roses embroidered on it. They have tea in ivy-bordered bone china cups. There are small squares of Christmas cake arranged in a pyramid on a green leaf plate. Laura admires that. 'Ee, Ah've got one just lahk it, never use it; you're welcome to it, luv, if you fancy it!' Tom's Mam says.

Uncle Alfred looks at them with a conspiratorial smile. 'How was your cake then?' he asks.

'Delicious,' Laura says. It was.

'Last year's, weren't it!' Uncle Alfred is triumphant.

The next day they go to see Tom's school friend Alex, who lives in a leafy suburb. His father is a retired headmaster who tested and passed Tom for his eleven plus. There is a large family party going on in their house, in which the furniture has seen better days and the carpets are faded. Alex's mother, in a high-necked white blouse, reminds Laura of the great aunts who used to gather at her granny's coffee parties.

'I hear you're from Germany,' Alex's father says to her. 'Well, the war's over, thank God!' *As if I were an enemy he's forgiven?* Laura wonders.

When they play charades and she is swathed in a heavy green and gold brocade curtain from the dressing-up box, Laura, as Queen Boadicea, stops agonising about what people might or might not be thinking about her – she is enjoying herself in this lively family gathering. But when the charades are over and they are sipping mulled wine, Laura hears someone on the other side of the room say 'Jewish? I don't believe it! Ghastly bunch of money grubbers, Jews! I don't blame Hitler for persecuting them! But she seems such a nice girl!' Oddly enough, that remark does not disturb Laura too much. She feels safe with Tom about; there will always be prejudiced people – she does not have to know them, nor they her.

Alex sees her and Tom to the bus stop. 'I could wring my

cousin's neck. What a moronic remark! I'm really sorry!' He pats Laura on the shoulder. 'Oh, it doesn't matter,' she says and means it. The bus comes. Alex waves, 'Invite me to the wedding, won't you,' he shouts.

They say goodbye to Tom's Mam. She has wrapped up her green leaf plate and gives it to Laura.

'You'll come and see us in London, Mam,' Tom says, his eyes lighting up again.

'Ah will an' all, and mebbe Ah'll get to meet your Mam, our Laura?'

'But where will she stay?' Laura asks Tom on the way back to Kings Cross, not in a Pullman train this time.

'We'll find a b & b near us.'

'Whatever will our mothers talk about if they meet?' Laura can't imagine. Or perhaps she is imagining it too vividly?

'About us, I expect! By the way, Mam said that you've got an old head on young shoulders!'

'Is that good?'

For a moment Tom does not answer, then he says quietly, 'Everything about you is good!'

All doubt falls from Laura. She is as sure of Tom's love for her as she was of her grandparents' and her father's. She knows that without them behind her she could not have come through. She does not dwell too graphically on their terrible deaths: if time is circular, and perhaps it is, then their moments of full life are equally valid. She remembers her father pulling her on her sledge along Unter den Linden to the Christmas market in Berlin. She remembers her grandpa letting her peer down his microscope and her granny counting the linen, putting aside sheets and towels for when her little goldfinch gets married.

Happy together, Laura and Tom are asleep in their double bed. When they wake up, it will be their wedding day.

They wake up. Laura gets into her new blue dress with the row of tiny buttons all down the front and a wasp waist. She does not have a wasp waist, but this dress pretends she does. She makes sure the hat with the blue feather sits at exactly the right angle on her head. Tom is wearing his father's three piece suit; she has never seen him in a waistcoat, it makes him look so... so... so like a man about to be married? Side by side, they stand in front of the mirror.

'I can't believe it's really happening!' Laura says.
'Believing doesn't come into it, it just *is!*' Tom tells her.
He takes her hand in his.

§ § §

EPILOGUE: 1990

Now Laura is the widow. She has lived her life in England married an Englishman; her daughters are English. English has become her first language. Is Laura English? The past is always present.

Every now and then in the trancelike state between sleeping and waking, fantasy patterns of unreal rescue scenarios unreel themselves: somehow to get her granny's name off the Auschwitz list – yes, it can be done; she will do it. But who is she? a little girl or a woman about the same age as that granny who was gassed?

Cut.

Perhaps Hugo appears at the eleventh hour – after all, he is not Jewish; he can snatch her granny from the gas chamber. But by the time her granny is being gassed, Hugo has been killed in the bombing of Berlin.

Cut.

Laura, the little girl in her new red velvet dress that she wore for the farewell supper, flies, yes, flies, into the concentration camp and finds her granny, takes her by the hand and they fly, yes fly, out, like in a Chagall painting. Nothing is impossible. You only have to find a way.

Cut.

Dreams, dreams, Laura thinks and tears stream down her face.

She is taking her daughters to the village in Thüringen where her father was born. At least that is possible.

All these years later, Laura suddenly writes there. Her cousin Rose, daughter of her Uncle Joachim whom she never met, still lives in that Thüringen village...

The train stops at the little country station. A deep sense of unreality overcomes Laura – or is it a deep sense of reality? How can you tell the difference? She steps across the threshold of the house in which her father was born, remembering how much he wanted to take her there. Germany has recently been reunited, and something is being reunited in Laura, who is having to find her way back into what seems like a previous incarnation.

She opens her mouth; the German gushes out like water from a rusty tap.

'At last, after all these years!' her cousin Rose says. They do not quite know what to say next.

Rose's sons say, 'Your German's pretty good!'

'She's one of us,' Rose's husband says.

Laura blushes. 'Us': that small word has never truly settled on her. When she was growing up in England, German was the language of the enemy. Her husband did not speak it; she has not taught her daughters to speak it.

'I can just remember your father,' Rose tells Laura. 'The summerhouse where he used to stay is still in our field. Shall I take you there?'

One of Rose's sons undoes the ancient padlock on the door. Rose and Laura step inside. Laura takes a deep breath, tries to feel her father's presence. The young people stay outside. They are cousins too, cousins a degree further removed, who do not speak each others' language. They have all heard over and over again how Hugo, the Communist anti-Nazi journalist, got killed in a bomb attack over Berlin. As far as these young East Germans are concerned (they are still 'Ossies', the others 'Wessies'), 'Communist' is such an ordinary word. Until very recently, everyone they knew was a Communist, was not allowed to be anything else. They were not even allowed to put a cross on the obituary notice when their old aunt, Hugo's sister, died. They wonder what this odd-man-out who married a Jewish girl was like. They have never met any Jews.

They look at the three young English women, Laura's daughters. The girls look at the young men. They smile; they want to like each other. By the end of a week, they have picked up phrases of each others' languages. They enjoy themselves. Laura's girls envy Rose's boys their rootedness – they still pick cherries from the same tree as their grandparents did. These boys do not have to travel to another country to find out who they are. How to connect?

235

Laura takes her daughters on from Thüringen to Bonn. Lola, one of Bella's twins, is celebrating her seventieth birthday. The other twin, Frieda, is dead. The family connection here is tenuous. Laura's girls are hazy as to exactly who it is they are about to meet. Like them, everyone is Jewish to some extent, half, a quarter, an eighth – who cares? They find their places at the long table next to Lola's grandchildren, who have learnt English at school. They can talk to each other.

Luise sits on one side of Lola, Stephanie on the other. Yes. Luise got her sister to England once the war was over. Although they are all three settled in England, Laura has had very little contact with these cousins. They and her mother, whose first cousins they were, never got on. Laura can understand that; she found her mother difficult too, though the girls loved their granny, who kept her hair dyed jet black until she was well over seventy – then, as it were, she turned white overnight. The girls cried and cried at her funeral. Laura could not.

Laura looks with curiosity and affection, mingled with a certain envy, at this German family to whom she is remotely related. They seem so intact. Laura has never known a family intact.

Stephanie, still wearing her cross, looks at Laura and thinks: we have the same dark eyes, the family eyes. She still has Magda's photograph on her dressing table. Magda had those eyes too.

Now Stephanie closes her eyes. She is feeling her age. Lola digs an elbow into Stephanie's ribs.

'Don't go to sleep at my birthday party,' she says.

Stephanie does not open her eyes. She remembers how Lola would not walk on the same side of the street as her, because she looked so Jewish. Everyone laughs. Stephanie decides to join in the laughter. Why not?

Laura hears one of her daughters say to Lola's grandson, 'Come and see us in London!'

'I'd love to,' he says, 'and you must come to Germany again!'

'We will!'

After all, there is nothing to prevent it.

CPSIA information can be obtained at www.ICGtesting.com
Printed in the USA
LVOW06s0444231215

467605LV00019B/947/P